PRIDE WARS

PRIDE WARS

THE SPINNER PRINCE

BY MATT LANEY

HOUGHTON MIFFLIN HARCOURT

BOSTON   NEW YORK

hmhco.com

The text was set in Berling LT Std.
Series logo design by Sammy Yuen
Map art © 2018 by Jeff Mathison

Library of Congress Cataloging-in-Publication Data
Names: Laney, Matt, author.
Title: The Spinner prince / by Matt Laney.
Description: Boston ; New York : Houghton Mifflin Harcourt, [2018] |
Series: The Pride wars ; book 1 | Summary: "In the distant future, when a new species rules the
earth, thirteen-year-old Prince Leo struggles to hide a dangerous and forbidden power he cannot
control while trying to unlock the mysteries of his origins."—Provided by publisher.
Identifiers: LCCN 2017001207 | ISBN 9781328707260
Subjects: | CYAC: Science fiction. | Princes—Fiction. | Identity—Fiction. | Ability—Fiction.
Classification: LCC PZ7.1.L342 Spi 2018 | DDC [Fic]—dc23
LC record available at https://lccn.loc.gov/2017001207

Manufactured in the United States of America
DOC 10 9 8 7 6 5 4 3 2 1
4500695793

For my children and
in loving memory of my father, David A. Laney

CHARACTER LIST

LEO   thirteen-year-old prince of Singara.

KAYDAN   one of the four generals in the Royal Army; Leo's trainer and mentor.

ANJALI   a young soldier with a special interest in Leo.

RAJA KAHN   Leo's grandfather and ruler of Singara.

TAMIR   Leo's power-hungry older cousin.

SARIAH   a captain in the Royal Army.

MAVRAK, BIKU, AND JIMO   soldiers under Sariah's command.

THE KEEPER   the keeper of slaycons used in the hunt.

GALIL   the Royal Scientist and close friend of the Kahn.

STORM   the slaycon Leo must kill in his hunt.

DAVIYAH   the Eleventh Shakyah who appears as the Great Firewing.

SHANTI   a wise shepherd.

MANDAR   a captain in the Royal Army; loyal to Tamir.

HOLU, JATARI, AND NORA   soldiers under
    Mandar's command.

DAGAN   one of the four generals in the Royal Army.

JAKAL   the chief instructor at the Royal Academy of
    War Science.

ZOYA   one of Leo's quadron-mates and fellow cadets.

STICK   Zoya's brother and one of Leo's quadron-mates
    and fellow cadets.

ALPHA   the Royal Academy master.

WAJID   the Maguar prisoner held captive at the Royal
    Academy of War Science for twenty-five years.

AMARA   Tamir's daughter and a second-year cadet at
    the Royal Academy of War Science.

PRIDE WARS

CHAPTER 1

There is a power in the universe greater than all others.
Whoever serves that power masters the world.
— *Sayings of the Ancients*

I AM LEO, PRINCE OF SINGARA, and I am about
to die.

Time of death: tomorrow afternoon.

Cause of death: slaycon bite. It's not a pleasant way
to go.

At the moment things don't look much better. A
Singa soldier is swinging a long blade at me so hard and
fast, you'd think I just stomped on his tail and retched a
hairball into his food.

The blade slices the air and I duck.

A thrust and I dodge.

A hack and I jump.

I'm bouncing around the training hall like a
spooked rabbit.

The soldier is my trainer, General Kaydan. Like
most adult Singas, he has powerful legs and broad shoulders. Muscles coil around his arms and back. An auburn
mane flows over his head and neck.

Singas are the crown of creation. We evolved from the great cats of ages and eons ago. Unlike our four-legged ancestors, we stand upright on two legs. We kept their tail, retractable claws, agility, strength, and keen senses, but we have fingers and thumbs, language, and superior intelligence. We value strength, tradition, and science.

Mostly science. We have a science for everything:

The Science of Nature.

The Science of Building.

The Science of Numbers.

The Science of Medicine.

The Science of Law.

The Science of Weaponry.

The Science of War. That's why a training hall is also called a battle laboratory.

Here in this laboratory, Kaydan wears no armor, just a pair of antelope-skin leggings. He brandishes the blade as if it's a natural extension of his arm.

Here it comes again.

I tuck my tail and tumble across the floor while the blade whistles overhead.

The point of this training session, and the count-less ones before it, is to prepare me to hunt and kill a slaycon.

What's a slaycon?

Take your most horrible day and wrap it in your nastiest nightmare. Put it on four legs, then cover it with scaly skin and mangy black hair. Add razor-sharp claws, a three-and-a-half-meter tail, and top it off with a bad temper, and you would end up with something very much like a slaycon.

And let's not forget its venomous bite.

If slaycon teeth break through your hide, the saliva will paralyze you in a matter of seconds. Then the slaycon will eat you whole, like a snake gulping down a mouse.

It takes skill and courage to slay a slaycon, and not everyone succeeds, which is the point. On the first full moon after our thirteenth birthday, all Singas must prove themselves by slaughtering one of these brutes.

Even a prince like me.

I'm not exactly a textbook specimen of the Singa race. Most younglings at thirteen are nearly full grown and ready for the rigors of battle. I'm small for my age. My mane has not yet bloomed. My fur is a shade darker than the golden pelts of my kindred. My voice scratches out a cublike yowl, rather than the skull-rattling roar of my peers.

Few believe I will survive the hunt tomorrow.

Nevertheless, at daybreak I will go to the city square and choose a slaycon from the Keeper. The beast and I will be transported to an enclosed section of the Border Zone at the very edge of our domain. If I defeat the slaycon by sundown, I will go on to the Academy and train to become a soldier in the Royal Army.

If I fail, I will be slaycon food. Our law of "survival of the strongest" leaves no room for the weak or cowardly.

Yeeeow! The broad side of Kaydan's blade whacks me on the shoulder and again on my thigh.

"Stay alert, Leo! Focus!"

Kaydan is one of our finest warriors. He fought with my grandfather, our supreme leader, in the Great War. Twenty-five years later, he still has a lot of fight in him. Training a scrawny youngling for the hunt is beneath a general, but Grandfather will have only the best for his grandson and heir to the throne. Most Singas are trained for their hunt by a parent or by a professional trainer if one can be afforded. I wish I could take Kaydan into the Border Zone and watch him slice the slaycon up with a few flicks of his blade.

Kaydan growls and comes at me again. This time my blade blocks his, marked by the high-pitched shriek of metal smacking metal. Instead of making a counterattack, I spring back, beyond his reach.

"You know the length of my reach," Kaydan affirms. "The question is, how will you get inside my reach and make your move? That is the Science of War."

Reach is the combined distance of a warrior's arm and blade. Multiply that by strength and speed, and you have the product of their deadly force. I have speed on my side, but not much else.

Even time is against me.

The light is fading, signaling the end of the day and of this final training session. Soon I will head to the feeding hall, where soldiers are already piling their plates with meat from silver serving trays.

The thought of food makes my stomach rumble. I hope Kaydan didn't hear that.

"Hungry, are you?" He positions himself between me and the door. "You may eat when you score a blow against me."

Kaydan twirls his blade as if it's only a broom handle. His tail sways over the floor. I know he wants me to survive the hunt tomorrow, but no slaycon waits to be attacked. And while I'm on the subject, slaycons don't use weapons to extend their reach. They have their teeth, their claws, and a battering ram of a tail. To simulate a true slaycon encounter, Kaydan should be on all fours, leaping and snarling with jaws snapping, claws flying.

But if Kaydan wants to change the pace, I can play along.

I drop my blade and arc around him to the door. Kaydan regards me curiously, as if studying a specimen under a magnifying glass.

"Where do you think you're going?" he asks.

"Dinner."

In a blink, Kaydan resumes a combat stance, his

weapon carving a path toward the back of my head. But I'm already in motion, stepping behind and between his legs.

I sweep his weight-bearing leg into the air, which is a bit like kicking a tree, but it's enough to knock him off balance. I thrust my shoulder into his waist. My left hand secures his blade.

Kaydan crashes to the floor. I pounce on top of him, surprised to see my claws pressing into his neck.

He's knocked out cold. I'd think him dead if not for the pulse beneath my hand.

Kaydan groans. His eyelids flutter, and I prepare to be brushed away like a piece of lint. He remains still, except for the smile breaking across his muzzle.

"Excellent defensive attack, Leo. I'd say your slay-con has good reason to worry."

I'd say I got lucky catching him off-guard.

"We're through, then, Master Kaydan?"

I regret the words as soon as I speak them. We are through, but our relationship as teacher and student is also ending. We've spent an hour a day, every day, for the past year preparing for tomorrow. For the first time I notice the aroma of his sweat mingling with my own.

"Almost." The warrior sits up, rubbing the back of his head. "First, recite the Ten Theorems of the Slaycon Hunt."

I kneel and dip my head to show respect. "The Ten Theorems of the Slaycon Hunt are:

"One, do not be afraid. Slaycons can scent fear and it excites them.

"Two, therefore it is best to stay downwind of a slaycon. Their noses are keener than their eyes and ears.

"Three, slaycon skin is difficult to pierce. Only a strong blow into the softer underside can inflict a fatal wound.

"Four, a slaycon bite leaves the hunter paralyzed and defenseless. Hunters should mind well slaycons' jaws and teeth; however, after closing their jaws for a bite, slaycons cannot open them again for several seconds, giving the hunter a brief advantage.

"Five, a slaycon can leap several meters in one pounce, but it cannot bite while airborne. If a slaycon jumps, the hunter should dive beneath and strike upward.

"Six, always keep one eye on its tail.

"Seven, slaycons cannot climb trees. If hunters need to take refuge, they should climb! But only unnoticed. The last thing a hunter wants is a slaycon circling the base of the tree. If that happens, the battle is over, because as the hunter descends the slaycon will surely bite.

"Eight, slaycons do not like water. Crossing a stream is the best way to slow them down.

"Nine, the slaycon must be killed by sundown.

"Ten, think. A hunter's best weapon is the superior Singa brain."

Kaydan kneels and bends low to the floor, the way soldiers do before my grandfather in ceremonies.

"I fought in the Great War alongside your grandfather, the Singa-Kahn, may he live forever. I have trained hundreds of fine soldiers, captains, commanders, and legionnaires. Even so, preparing you for your hunt has been the greatest honor of my life, Lord Prince."

That's Kaydan's way of saying he's taught me everything he can about the Science of Slaycon Hunting. By tomorrow afternoon, we'll know if it was enough.

CHAPTER 2

Do not run from those who walk the path with you; each
one has been sent as a guide from beyond.
— *Sayings of the Ancients*

THE FEEDING HALL IS EMPTY. Without the
bustling throng of feasting soldiers, the high-
ceilinged room makes me feel smaller than ever. Like
every part of the castle, the floor tiles, paneled walls,
even the tables and benches create an array of geometric
shapes, perfectly measured out in multiples of twos and
fours.

I fill my plate with every last scrap I can scavenge
from the serving trays and find a table near the edge of
the hall. From the corner of my eye I catch Anjali, a
young soldier wearing her blades and light armor. She
glides over to my table.

"Big day tomorrow," she says.

I turn away and feed, but Anjali doesn't give up.
She eases herself onto the opposite bench. Her green
eyes, flecked with gold, sparkle with light from the can-
delabra above.

"What's your strategy? What weapons will you take?"

Even if I felt like talking, this is the last thing I want to chat about.

Three years ago, Anjali killed her slaycon in record time: less than twenty minutes. It was the military's first clue that Anjali had talent for soldiering. Right after graduating from the Academy, she was called up to serve in the castle—a high honor, rarely given to one so young.

Even Kaydan, who is not known for compliments, says Anjali's mind is as sharp as her blades. She could become a legionnaire or a general one day. He says Anjali notices and remembers everything, which is exactly why I avoid her.

The less she observes about me the better.

I take my plate and swing one leg over the bench. Meanwhile, Anjali casts about for something to say that will keep me rooted to my seat.

"I have something to tell you," she blurts out, "something important."

I pause, on the off chance it actually is.

She speaks softly. "There's a diseased Singa in the castle."

I freeze. "What do you mean?"

"I mean the castle has . . . *a Spinner!*"

The last word is barely a breath, but it hits my ears like a pickax.

Spinners are cursed with a dangerous disease officially known as the fiction affliction or story sickness, which causes them to spew fiction without warning. Because we value facts above all else, fiction is considered poisonous to the mind, more toxic than a slaycon's bite. Singa cubs are taught a saying as soon as they can talk: "Fiction is a dereliction of a scientific prediction." The only thing worse than encountering a Spinner is being one yourself.

I plop down, glancing left and right, making sure we are still alone. "A Spinner? How can you tell?"

"Easy." Anjali grins, displaying rows of pointed teeth. "He barely says a word, keeps to himself, and runs off suddenly to private places: a closet, the dirt room, an empty hall, behind some curtains, as if he's going to be sick."

"That doesn't prove anything," I say, relieved she doesn't have actual evidence.

Now it's Anjali's turn to glance about the hall and sniff the air to make sure we are totally alone. "Can you keep a secret?"

It's a little late to be asking that.

"My older brother was a Spinner," Anjali continues. "I never witnessed the sickness overtake him, but I recognized the signs. I know a Spinner when I see one."

Anjali's eyes bore into me and I want to dash out of the room. Unfortunately, I'm bolted to my bench by curiosity about her brother. Spinners are rare, and I've never heard anyone talk so openly about them.

"Go on," I say.

"One day, when I was still a cub, I found my parents weeping in their den. They said my brother had been found out by his captain."

Anjali's voice wobbles. "They took his tongue, sent him to live among the exiles. We never got to say goodbye. My family hasn't mentioned his name since. It's as though he never existed. It's worse than death. At least we talk about the dead." Her face hardens. "It's wrong what we do to Spinners." She lowers her eyes. "That's why I can't bring myself to report the Spinner in the castle."

This puts Anjali dangerously close to breaking the law. All Singas are obliged to report suspected Spinners immediately. If the disease is proven, Spinners get banished and live among the exiles on the other side of the Great Mountain, right after having their tongues cut out of their heads and nailed to a post in the city. I've had many nightmares of my tongue pinned to that post, twitching like a dying fish.

"So you want me to report the Spinner in the castle for you, is that it?"

Anjali wrinkles her nose in frustration. "No!" She leans in. "I don't want to get rid of him. I want to learn about the fiction affliction so I can know more about my brother . . . and I thought maybe the Spinner in the castle could help."

My throat goes dry. "Sounds risky, Anjali. And from what I know, Spinners don't control the disease. It flares up whenever it wants, not when the Spinner wants, which I suspect would be never."

"So a Spinner's brain is like a bookshelf, and every now and then a book falls off and dumps out fiction?"

"That's not all. Things happen when the sickness strikes. Things that are not easy to explain."

"I'm not afraid," Anjali declares.

Without warning, the affliction awakens, as it always does: a rush of wind between my ears, and my stomach turning with nausea as a lump of fiction tumbles down from my brain. It lands on my tongue and begins to expand. Soon my mouth will be so full, I will have to let it out. I instinctively clamp a hand around my muzzle.

Anjali brightens. "I knew it!"

I wince at having given myself away so easily. The fiction pushes against my teeth and gums, desperate to be free. I have to get out of here. I have to find a private place to release this load of sickness. And whatever else comes with it.

"It's happening, isn't it?" Anjali exclaims.

I jump up and bound away from the table.

"Wait!" she cries.

Anjali leaps over the table, tackles and holds me to the floor. The wind is knocked out of me, along with the fiction welling up in my mouth. Instantly, the disease takes over my vocal cords, tongue, and lips, and I am powerless to stop it.

Once there was a merchant who found a nest of young firewing birds abandoned by their parents.

The words spin into a vision. It's nothing unusual for me, but Anjali startles as the very scene emerges: the merchant discovering a firewing nest packed with downy, rust-colored chicks on a lonely mountain cliff. The scene is clear as day and bursting with life, growing larger with every phrase. Anjali paws at the vision, her hand passing through it as though it were smoke.

"Aha!" the merchant said.

Anjali yelps when the merchant's voice flows from my mouth.

"When firewing birds are fully grown, they are the largest, most magnificent birds of prey on earth and

their flame-colored feathers are treasures! I will catch these hatchlings, fatten them up, and sell them at the market for a good price."

He flung a net over the nest and trapped the little firewings. He carried them home and put them in a cage. All day, every day, the trapped birds cried and wailed. Whenever the merchant tossed meat inside the cage, the firewings gobbled it down. All the birds ate the merchant's food except one, and that bird became thinner and thinner while the others grew fatter and fatter.

The vision expands until we are surrounded and inside the world of this story. The characters and scene swirl about, unaware of our presence. The growing firewings have shed their fluffy, downy feathers for brilliant, blood-red plumage edged with gold.

The day arrived when the merchant would bring the firewings to market. He inspected his birds and noticed that one was much smaller and thinner than the rest. The merchant opened the cage and grabbed the scrawny firewing.

"You are little more than feathers and bones!" the merchant exclaimed.

As soon as he said it, the littlest firewing wriggled from his hand and flew to a nearby branch.

The other firewings cried out for their brother to save them. So the freed firewing followed the merchant as he carried the birds to market, flying unnoticed from tree to tree.

As the merchant set the cage of birds on a table and attracted a customer, the free bird waited for his chance. At last it came. When the merchant opened the door of the cage to get a bird for his customer, the freed firewing swooped down and pecked at the merchant's eyeballs. The merchant smacked him to the ground, where he lay stunned and nearly broken in two. Seeing their opportunity to escape, the other firewings dashed from the cage in a flurry of wings and a burst of joyful screeches.

The vision fades, and we are back in the feeding hall. In fact, we never left.

"So you *are* a Spinner!" Anjali marvels, scanning the room for any remaining images. "Incredible."

Her eyes drift back to me and she gasps, fixated on something just over my head. I feel claws digging into the fur between my ears. Glancing up, I find a young firewing bird perched there: the bird from the story.

No matter how many times this happens, I never get used to it. A character or creature is always left behind when the disease hits me. These beings are faded, ghostly, and freakish.

The phantom firewing stretches flamelike wings, screeches, and flaps into the open air of the feeding hall. He circles the room and soars through the doors.

Anjali follows his every move.

I watch her, astonished.

These stranded beings are not new for me, but this is the first time anyone else has seen one. Then again, this is the first time I've been caught in the act. Maybe hearing the words and seeing the creatures that follow are linked.

"You saw that?" I sputter.

Anjali tries to speak and fails.

A chill sweeps over me. Anjali not only knows what I am—she's also seen what happens when the sickness strikes. If I die tomorrow, the problem will be solved. If I survive the hunt, my troubles will be far from over.

CHAPTER 3

Beware the one who hugs you with a dagger in hand.
— *Sayings of the Ancients*

NIGHT COMES SWIFTLY in Singara. The castle, carved into the Great Mountain and looming high over the city, faces east. As the sun dips behind the mountain, Singara is plunged into shadow before the final curtain of darkness falls.

Only half of the castle is built out from the face of the mountain. The other half is carved into the mountain rock.

I haven't slept all day, and after my training session with Kaydan and the episode with Anjali, I can barely keep my tail off the floor. Singas don't get all their daily sleep at one time like some creatures. We bed down for a few hours several times a day. I could retire to my own den, but the comforts of Grandfather's lair tug at me like a magnet.

I bound up the leaping platforms that spiral the walls of the central hallway. These platforms lead to the entryways of the castle's ten floors. I spring and flip to the eighth level, which holds the Kahn's chambers.

The darkness and density of guards thicken as I draw closer to Grandfather's lair. Singa vision is well suited to the dark. We have a special coating at the back of our eyes that captures and magnifies any available light. Our night vision reduces everything to shades of black, white, and gray, but the world is no less visible. The light of the sun, or from a fire, brings color back into view.

I focus on each pair of glowing eyes among the guards, who look my way. Anyone else would be halted and questioned, but I have been coming to this part of the castle nearly every day of my life. They know the light pattern of my eyes, in addition to my shape and scent. And I know theirs.

The outer hall of the royal den, known as the Hall of Kahns, is furnished with lavishly carved chairs and benches. Paintings of the Singa-Kahns of old, my ancestors, line the walls. Beneath these portraits are smaller pictures of the invention each Kahn presented to Singara: tools and laboratory instruments, paper and writing implements, a carriage, a riding saddle, windows, eyeglasses, a telescope, a clock, a printing press, a water wheel–powered sawmill, and more. The Singa-Kahn is expected to be a great scientist as well as a great warrior.

The hall ends with a tapestry, marking the entrance

to the Kahn's lair. It hangs like a curtain from one wall to the other. Embroidered in gold, greens, and deep reds, the tapestry illustrates the Great War against our enemies, the Maguar, twenty-five years ago. After the war, Grandfather ordered the construction of the Great Wall and the Border Zone Fence. It was a magnificent victory, but still we train, still we watch their lands from towers along the wall. Should the Maguar ever breach the wall, they would find themselves trapped in the fenced-in Border Zones.

The Maguar are related to the Singa. We share the same biological family of *Leos*, the Maguar being the dumber and less evolved of the two. That makes my name, Leo, the most unimaginative and generic name possible. It's like naming a goat Goat or calling a deer Deer. I hate it.

The embroidery shows the Maguar as similar to the Singa but their pelts are marked with dark stripes. As the larger of our two races, the Maguar have longer arms and therefore greater reach. That's why our blades are so essential.

I'm thankful to have seen this much. Most Singas will never lay eyes on this tapestry. Only elders like Grandfather and Kaydan who fought in the Great War know what the enemy are really like. We younger ones have to be satisfied with the bits of information elders share about the Maguar's ferocity, savagery, and superstitions.

Before passing through the slit in the middle of the tapestry, I hear two familiar voices locked in debate. I can make out only snatches of the conversation. I lean closer until the fur on my cheek interlaces with the threads of the tapestry.

"He is not ready! You are sending him to his death!"

It's Tamir, Grandfather's nephew and my elder cousin. Tamir is a high-ranking commander. According to many Singas, Tamir should become the Singa-Kahn after Grandfather, not me. Tall and powerfully built, he certainly looks the part.

I, on the other hand, don't.

And there is the problem of my parents.

My mother died giving birth to me. My father's identity died with her, but the shame of the secret lives on with me. No Singa-Kahn has ever had such a disgraceful entrance into life.

Nevertheless, I am the grandson of the Kahn and direct heir to the throne through my mother, his daughter. As the Kahn's nephew, Tamir's claim to the throne is weaker.

Grandfather snarls. "It is the first full moon after his thirteenth birthday, and the law states he is ready. We are a pride of laws, Tamir, do not forget that."

"Does the law say we should throw an undersize Singa before the jaws of a hungry slaycon? Even with a long blade his reach is less than two meters! And how many times has he gone beyond the castle gate in his life? Four times? Five? What does he know of the world, let alone of hunting a slaycon?"

"He knows more than most Singas his age, Tamir."

"Because he has studied with tutors, inside the palace, and not in the science centers of Singara, like other younglings? You want to protect him, but instead you have deprived him of the opportunity to develop strength and courage. Consider the evidence. Don't let your feelings cloud good judgment."

"Don't lecture me on judgment!" the Kahn shouts. "He may not be strong, but he is clever!"

"He is too small!"

"He is my only heir! All my sons are dead at the claws of the Maguar. My youngest child, his mother, is dead!" His voice falters. "He is all I have. He will face a slaycon tomorrow, train at the Academy, and become a soldier in accordance with the law. And one day he will sit upon the throne!"

Grandfather coughs and wheezes, the force of the argument bearing down on his aged body. I hear the creak of wood as he settles into his reading chair.

"Forgive me, Uncle." Tamir adopts a more respectful tone. "I care only for the prince and for the throne I am sworn to protect, even at the cost of my life."

"I know what you care for most, nephew."

"All I ask is that you give Lord Leo a year to gain in size and skill. A slaycon will be no match for him then. I will take over his training if you wish."

"He has a trainer whom I trust. You are dismissed, Tamir."

Tamir likes to have the last word, even with the Kahn, so I wait for his next comment. Instead, I hear footsteps marching toward the tapestry.

The hair on my pelt sticks out like a porcupine. In a few heartbeats Tamir will be tripping over me, irritated. Far more so when he finds out I have been eavesdropping.

No time to run and hide. Besides, my scent is all over the place.

I pounce back to the center of the hall and stride toward the tapestry as though I am just making my entrance. The tapestry shakes, and a brooding Tamir, wearing his light armor and draped in a cloak made from Maguar pelts, emerges, his tail lashing.

"Lord Prince," he says with a halfhearted bow. "Up so late on such an important night? Don't you know a slaycon can sniff out a tired Singa twice as easily as a well-rested one?"

Tamir rarely expects an answer from me, but tonight he lifts his chin, inviting a response. The words bubble up and spill out of my mouth before I can stop them.

"My trainer says an overconfident beast is the easiest kind to kill."

Tamir scowls as though I said something about him. He surges past, nearly knocking me to the floor.

I wiggle through the tapestry and exhale with relief. This chamber's painted ceiling, fur rugs, and warm fire are a safe haven for me, removed from the many watchful eyes of the castle. There is a broad bed, an ample oak desk, shelves lined with thick, leather-bound books, an observation balcony with telescopes pointing into the open sky, and tables covered with all sorts of scientific instruments.

And there, in the center of the room, is my grandfather, Raja, the Singa-Kahn, slumped to the side of the chair. His once-golden fur has taken on a silvery sheen. His movements are often stiff and slow. Sometimes he stares into space for long stretches and mumbles to himself.

"Grandfather?"

The Kahn lifts his regal head. For a moment he seems not to recognize me.

"Leo?" He stretches out his hands. "Come here, dear one."

I rush forward and fall into his arms. My cheek rests on his mane.

"Your heart is racing!" he says. "Well, who could blame you? Tomorrow is . . ." Grandfather's voice trails off, as though he'd rather not think about it.

"I saw Tamir leaving your den. Is everything all right?"

Grandfather grunts. "Nothing will be right for

Tamir if he isn't the Singa-Kahn. Do not underestimate him, Leo. His desire for power is beyond even his ability to control." It's Grandfather's most frequent warning about my cousin.

"That's why tomorrow is so important. Success means you will be confirmed as my heir and claim the throne when I am gone. And I am getting old . . . in case you haven't noticed."

"I haven't."

"Ha!" Grandfather chuckles. "Consider the evidence, Leo. Always consider the evidence. As Kahn you must learn to put aside your own feelings and think clearly about the facts before you. Your brain must always be your sharpest weapon."

Grandfather rubs the thick layer of skin at the back of my neck and purrs a little tune.

Music! A rare treat.

Our law limits music to formal ceremonies. Music is played with caution due to its power to stir the imagination and spark fiction.

This doesn't concern Grandfather now as he cradles me by the soft glow of firelight. The notes coming from his chest are unlike anything I've ever heard. They have the ring of something ancient and otherworldly. I try to fasten the tune to my memory, but my mind is a kaleidoscope of sounds, smells, and images as I slide into sleep.

"These are the plain facts, dear one," the Kahn intones. "I don't have much time left. The sun is setting on the Age of Raja Kahn. Tomorrow, if you succeed, you will be my undisputed heir. You must succeed, Leo. The future of the Pride depends on it."

CHAPTER 4

You make yourself by the choices you make.
— Sayings of the Ancients

A FOREST GLADE ECHOES with birdsong. Warm breezes caress my fur.

Then I see her: a Singa, stately, graceful, appearing as a marble sculpture on the far side of the dell.

Mother!

I bound forward, running with unnatural speed, like an arrow sprung from the bow. The statuelike figure gets closer but doesn't react to my approach. When she is but ten meters away, my feet become heavy, until I am a statue myself, frozen in midstride. An inky-black darkness rolls in, blotting out everything—the sun, the sky, the trees, and finally . . .

Mother! I scream into the night. Tears fall as tiny pebbles down stony cheeks. An odor invades my nostrils, accompanied by the footfalls of a snarling creature: a slaycon. Soon the beast is close enough to feel its hot breath puffing at my leg.

Go ahead, bite me! I'm already paralyzed. Let's see if your teeth can cut through stone!

Thunder explodes, not from the sky above but from the earth below. The ground gives way. The slaycon and I fall through the air, as if pitched from the peak of the Great Mountain. The ground rushes to meet me. Instead of my body smacking the earth, I hear the flap of wings. Giant talons wrap around me as I'm held in the tender grip of a massive firewing. Light cascades from its broad feathers like living flames. The great bird circles lower and lower until I am back in the forest glade, the slaycon dead at my side.

I sit up, grateful to be alive. My heart lurches as eight figures tower over me, silhouetted against the bright sky. Their scent is unknown. One of them thrusts a spear at my head. "What are you doing here, infidel?"

. . .

Then a different voice beckons: faint but familiar.

"Lord Prince?"

The dream forest fades. The figures melt into shadows.

"Excuse me . . . Leo."

The wheels in the waking side of my brain begin to turn. I breathe in the smells of Grandfather's lair.

"It is now the ninth hour and you are due in the city square to select your slaycon."

I wince.

The speaker is a blur, but I recognize the voice. Not

her again. I rub my eyes and behold Anjali, wearing her armor and blades.

Does she sleep with that stuff on?

Does she sleep?

I lean on one elbow and find myself in the Kahn's bed, a canvas tarp stretched between four posts, covered with antelope- and deerhide blankets and silk pillows.

I arch my back, stretch, and yawn. "Who sent you here?"

"His Majesty . . . your grandfather."

I swing my feet over the side of the bed and wiggle my toes. If it is the ninth hour, only one hour remains to choose a slaycon and begin the long trek to the Border Zones.

"Thank you," I say. "You may go."

Anjali doesn't budge. Her brow is furrowed like a plowed field, as if she's working on a tough problem from the Science of Numbers. There's something she wants to say, and I don't want to know what it is.

"The young firewing . . ." she begins.

My heart drops. I'm not doing this. Not now.

"What you said, the things we saw," she gushes. "I can't stop thinking about them."

"Try to forget about it, Anjali."

"Does it happen every time? Things appearing? Creatures getting left behind?"

I flick my tail as a silent affirmation.

"Can *you* forget them?"

I take her point. The truth is I've gotten good at forgetting. It's the only way to keep from going completely insane. She's lucky it was only a firewing. The fiction might have featured a draycon. Draycons make slaycons look like mosquitos. There's no use explaining any of this to Anjali.

"You'd better go," Anjali advises. "Captain Sariah and her quadron are waiting for you at the castle gate."

As I brush by her, Anjali grabs my arm. What now?

"Do you have one of these already?" She opens her hand to reveal a green pellet, like a large cocoon.

"What's that?" I ask.

"It will mask your scent. Swallow this and the slaycon won't smell you at all. There's no better way to sneak up on them. Don't take it until after you've entered the Border Zone. The effect only lasts a few hours."

I consider the pellet resting in the gray skin of her palm.

"It's nothing to be ashamed of, Leo. Lots of younglings use these in the hunt."

"Did you?"

"Well . . . no."

"Then why should I?"

I take the green bundle, just to end the pleading look on her face. Like everyone else, she knows the odds of survival are stacked against me.

"Strength and truth, Leo," she says in farewell.

"Strength and truth," I repeat, and pocket the pellet.

Returning to my den, I change into fresh leather leggings and strap on my chest plate, which is fashioned into outstretched wings, the symbol of the Kahns. It was forged for me from the last bits of metal found in the Great Mountain. Most of our metal was used in the construction of the Border Zone Fence, and there is almost nothing left for new tools, weapons, or armor. The chest plate's polished metal is a striking contrast to my golden-brown fur and way too flashy for a slaycon hunt. Still, Grandfather wants me to wear it whenever I'm in public, which isn't often.

A large raven is perched on my balcony, black wings tucked, watching me. I ease onto the balcony and he flaps away in fright.

The sun hangs low in a hazy sky, spreading yellow rays over our realm. From this perch I can see well beyond the city, past the meat farms dotted with livestock, to the forest. Above the tree line, watchtowers poke up from the Great Wall, keeping a steadfast eye on the Maguar's land.

I look down into the city, expecting to find the usual smattering of Singas moving about cobblestone streets between homes, taverns, shops, and courtyards.

Today the main road extending from the castle gate to the city square is packed with Singas. Thousands of them. Soldiers struggle to keep the mob in order.

Of course slaycon hunts happen frequently, but rarely does the fate of the throne hang in the balance. All of Singara has come to look upon their next Kahn or to behold the prince for the first and very last time.

I may have stopped breathing, because my next breath is a deep and hungry one. I can't let all these Singas down. I can't let Grandfather down.

Anjali's scent-masking pellet is still nestled in the pocket of my discarded leggings. Could that leafy thing be my salvation? I step back into my den and rummage through the leggings like a thief searching for a jewel and transfer the pellet to the pocket of my new leggings.

I strap on a utility belt and a water bottle hanging beside my bed. If nothing else, the belt makes me look rugged and ready for action.

I bound down the leaping platforms to the central hall on the main floor. The central hall is a tribute to the castle's builders, with its marble columns, golden wall patterns, and carved doors leading to the feeding hall, throne room, armory, battle laboratories, and storage rooms. A crack, large enough to slip your fingers into, runs down the middle of the hall floor. The crack was created by an earthquake during the Great War just before the battle turned in our favor.

I hop back and forth over the crack, zigzagging to the castle's main doors. I'm so focused on my footwork, I crash into a guard.

"Excuse me, Lord," the soldier says, as though he

has caused the collision. He scoops something off the floor. "Did you drop this?"

It's the green pellet Anjali gave me.

I stuff the pellet in my pocket. "Thank you," I mumble, and slink past him.

Sariah's quadron waits in the courtyard. A quadron is a group of four warriors, one being the captain; it makes up the basic unit of our military force.

Four quadrons make a company.

Four companies make a brigade.

Four brigades make a battalion.

Four battalions make a legion.

Quadrons train to fight as a single body and defend one another to the death. It is a fearsome and wondrous thing to behold an experienced quadron in action, fending off attackers from every corner, wordlessly responding to one another's movements as though their minds were fused together.

In addition to pieces of armor attached to their legs, arms, shoulders, and chest, soldiers carry several blades: a short blade attached to the upper back along with a circular aero-blade, a long blade worn at the hip, and a dagger or two strapped to the upper leg. The rank of each soldier is shown by the armor color on the upper arms. Captains, like Sariah, wear blue.

Sariah's quadron have dark red cloaks about their shoulders, hoods pulled low over their brows. By their height and bearing I identify them as Biku, Mavrak, and

Jimo. Captain Sariah looks grim. That's not unusual, but she appears especially thoughtful this morning.

"My prince," she begins, "no doubt you have seen the rather sizable gathering of Singas beyond the gate all the way to the city square. We have a brigade of soldiers out there, and you can trust my quadron to do whatever is necessary to deliver you safely to the square."

Sariah observes my trembling whiskers. "Mobs are fickle, Leo, lacking in reason. On top of that, Tamir has many followers who believe he should be the Singa-Kahn after your grandfather. Some beyond this gate will praise you, and others may do just the opposite. I advise you to ignore them both and stay true to your course."

If that was supposed to make me feel better, it didn't.

I edge closer to the gate, and the quadron takes up positions around me, Jimo in the lead, Mavrak and Biku at each side, and Sariah at the back. Jimo's nose is less than a meter from the gate.

"Open!" Sariah shouts up to the gate master. Gears click and chains rattle as the doors groan to life and separate. A shaft of sunlight pushes through the gap.

Sariah rests a hand on my shoulder, and I hear a blade sliding out of its scabbard. For a heartbeat, I'm terrified she will stab me from behind. Is she among those who believe Tamir deserves the throne?

Sariah's purr in my ear puts that fear to rest.

"Don't worry, dear one. Take a breath. Try to relax. We will have you in front of the Keeper in no time."

Great.

Being stuck in a Border Zone with one hungry monster is bad. Dealing with the oddball Slaycon Keeper and choosing from several of her caged monsters in the city square is not much of an improvement.

Or so I hear.

Since Grandfather keeps me in the shelter of the castle, I never actually witnessed the ritual of slaycon selection. I'll have to rely on Kaydan's instructions.

When the opening is wide enough for the five of us, Sariah gestures to the gatekeeper, and the doors grind to a halt. I'm suddenly possessed by the urge to spin on my heel, run back into the castle, and bury myself in bed. But that would be as good as surrendering the throne to Tamir and accepting a life of banishment among the outcasts beyond the Great Mountain.

"Forward," Sariah commands.

We step into the brightness of day on the other side of the gate. My legs feel like lead posts, making it hard to keep pace with the quadron. Besides that, thousands of eyes are fixed on me. It's going to be a long walk to the city square with all of those stares boring into my pelt. Behind us, the doors roll shut, sealing off any hope of retreat.

"Steady," Sariah whispers.

As if on cue, a surge of energy enlivens the crowd. There are shouts of praise that morph into cheers, rising into an explosion of voices. Bodies flood the road. Some are weeping and bowing; others scowl and shake their fists at me.

We've been outside the gate for less than a minute and already things are unraveling.

In a swirl of metal and cape, Jimo leaps into a combat stance, bares his blades, and roars so loudly, I want to cover my ears. Mavrak and Biku respond in kind.

The mob freezes.

Behind me, Sariah lifts her voice. "Good citizens of Singara! Loyal subjects of Raja Kahn, who brings peace and prosperity to the Pride! We mean you no harm and we trust you harbor no ill will toward the prince. Like all Singas on the first full moon after their thirteenth birthday, he will go to the city square to select a slaycon from the Keeper. Like all young Singas he will hunt the creature in one of the Border Zones against the Great Wall. Like any other young Singa he will emerge victorious or not at all. Or be sent into exile. The laws of nature will decide. You survived the hunt and served in the Royal Army in your time. Do permit this youngling to prove himself worthy of the same honor."

Sariah studies the crowd, heightening the sense of drama.

She's good at this.

"Because if you do not, my quadron will carve a path right through you until we reach our destination."

The image is gruesome, but Sariah speaks as if she were merely predicting a change in the weather. The sea of bodies withdraws, and the road empties out. The three soldiers stand down but do not sheathe their blades.

"Forward," says Sariah.

And we are off again.

We pass the block of military housing outside the castle and Sariah says, "We're going to pick up the pace, Leo. Be ready.

"Stride!" she barks, and the quadron accelerates, moving as gracefully and swiftly as a waterbird glides across the surface of a lake. I'm sprinting to keep up, feet slapping the cobblestones in contrast to the hushed footfalls of my protectors.

Occasionally, I feel Sariah's breath on my neck or a hand urging me onward. The crowd on either side of the road becomes a blur of color and sound.

Too soon we arrive at the edge of the city square, a one-hundred-meter space marked off by a low wall. At the center of the square is a towering statue of Sayzar, the first Singa-Kahn, only a cub when he claimed the throne over two hundred years ago. It was Sayzar Kahn who proclaimed the slaycon hunt as the law for all young Singas, so it is fitting to begin here. In those days, the ritual hunt took place in a vast pit at the edge of our realm. The creation of the Border Zone Fence along the Great Wall provided a series of larger, more natural arenas for the hunt. Today Sayzar's pit is used as a garbage dump.

The crowd pours in and around the square. Expectant faces peer out of windows and from every balcony in view. Even the rooftops are packed.

At the far end of the square, the Slaycon Keeper surveys the crowd with delight. Next to her is my trainer, Kaydan, and beside him is Galil, the Pride's chief scientist. To their left are four carts, each supporting a huge boxlike object, three meters high and five long, covered by a canvas tarp. The boxes are slaycon cages. The Keeper has brought these four from the hundreds of slaycons under her care. To their right is a table full of tools and weapons. I will choose from among those, too.

Sariah and her quadron fall back, leaving me to step into the square alone, a step that will put the whole bloody event into motion. As if guided by someone else, my feet pass over the threshold of the square, and I cross the stretch of empty space to the Slaycon Keeper, hoping she will be quick about this.

Not likely.

The Keeper's eagerness sickens me, so I focus on Kaydan and Galil. Kaydan's expression is as hard as the armor strapped to his shoulders, arms, and legs. Galil is dressed in a white robe. His plump face is set with eyes that twinkle.

When I am only a few paces away, the Slaycon Keeper bows and bellows more to the crowd than to me. "Good morning, Prince Leo, grandson of His Majesty, Raja Kahn, who brings peace and prosperity to the Pride! Today is the first full moon after your thirteenth birthday, the day of your hunt. By sundown you will prove your place among the Pride or . . . you will not! You have several choices before you. The first is the most important: Will you hunt or will you choose exile?"

Some younglings, only a few, to be sure, choose exile right away rather than face a day locked in a Border Zone with a famished monster.

I don't blame them.

If I weren't the heir to the throne, I would be very tempted to choose a life among the outcasts, on the other side of the Great Mountain.

Thousands of ears strain to hear my reply. I struggle to get the word out, knowing how bad this looks. I close my eyes and think of Grandfather.

"Hunt," I whisper.

"I'm sorry, I didn't quite hear that, Lord Leo," the Keeper yells to the crowd, cupping a hand to her ear.

"I will hunt," I repeat, louder.

"He will hunt!" the Keeper shouts, and the crowd roars its approval.

The Keeper turns to Galil and asks the traditional question of the Royal Scientist: "Is this young Singa fit to hunt? Is he ready to kill or be killed?"

Another formality, another piece of ceremony, but there is a reason to question my readiness. Galil, for his part, answers without hesitation.

"He is."

"Excellent!" says the Keeper. "Let us proceed! There are four slaycons before you, Lord Leo," she says, motioning to the covered carts. "They have all been denied food for half a moon."

In other words, these monsters are dying to eat.

"All but one are experienced hunters," the Keeper continues, giving me a wink.

Meaning all save one have a well-developed taste for Singa flesh.

"The one you choose will be transported to a Border Zone, where you will engage it in claw-to-claw combat!"

Everyone knows this already. She's just lathering herself up with the sound of her own voice. Every word steals time from the hunt.

"You will have until sundown to make a kill, cut off the slaycon's tail, and present it to your family, your grandfather, that is, and—"

"Stop wasting time!" I shout, startling even myself. Out of the corner of my eye I see Kaydan's mouth spread into a smile.

The Keeper is stunned. "Very well, my lord, very well!"

With a flourish, the Keeper pulls a rope, causing

the coverings to fall away from all four carts at once. Now it is obvious that the boxes are sturdy metal cages, each holding a slaycon. The beasts screech and hiss and roar at the sight of so many Singas. The crowd recoils as the Keeper draws closer to her monsters.

"There, there now, my darlings," she coos, as though the beasts were cuddly pets and not dreadful demons. To my astonishment, the Keeper reaches into a cage and pats the snout of the beast within. The slaycon whimpers and sways its tail.

"You see, Lord Leo, they are gentle creatures if you know how to approach them. Aren't you, my pretty pets?" The Keeper beckons with her tail. "Come. Make your choice!"

The Keeper drops back and I approach the first cage. Its stench overwhelms me. When I am a meter from the cage, the beast leaps as though it could break through. I pounce back. The old metal bars arrest the slaycon but do little to dull its enthusiasm. The creature presses itself against the cage, thrusts out a foreleg, and swipes furiously.

"Oooooh, he likes you!" says the Keeper, and laughter ripples around the square. "That one is called Storm, and you can see why. He has defeated more Singas than any of my other slaycons."

Someone in the crowd begins to sob, perhaps remembering a son or daughter fallen to the brute.

I move to the next cage. This slaycon is smaller. It

watches me, head tilted, a forked tongue flicking from its mouth. When I am close enough to touch the cage, the slaycon sinks into a crouch, its haunches pulsing with anticipation. I growl at the creature, but the slaycon just sits there, inspecting me.

"This one I call the Professor!" the Keeper cries. "She likes to study the movements of her prey, waiting for just the right moment to strike."

I circle the cage. Without a sound, the slaycon shifts, matching me step for step. The glint in her eyes creeps me out.

I turn away to examine the next slaycon.

The third monster is fat and lies on one side as if glued to the floor by its own bulk. Yellow teeth, broken claws, and a maze of cracks running through its hide suggest this is an aged and tired beast. The Keeper gives words to my thoughts.

"That one looks too old to participate in the hunt, doesn't he, Lord Prince?" She waves to the crowd as if to pull them closer. "Perhaps every one of you believes this old, overweight challenger would be an easy kill. Perhaps you think the creature should be put out of his misery, but you would be wrong. This one is named Quicksilver!"

The name floats like a leaf on a quiet pond before being dunked by a sudden wave of laughter. The Keeper grins. She's enjoying herself way too much.

"Would you like to know why he is named

Quicksilver?" Without waiting for an answer, she produces a rabbit from a burlap bag sitting unnoticed on the ground. The rabbit kicks and struggles to get free. "Observe!"

She hurls the rabbit over my head into the cage. With blinding speed, Quicksilver launches up, snatches the rabbit from the air, and swallows it whole in less than a heartbeat's time. Now on all fours, the slaycon is massive and fearsome. It considers the crowd hungrily for a moment, then yawns, slumps down, and burps.

No one is laughing now.

"Do not worry, Master Leo!" the Keeper says merrily. "That one could eat a herd of deer and still have room for dessert. Have you made your choice?"

"There is still the fourth," I remind her.

"Right you are! Right you are!" the Keeper crows. No matter what I say, she finds a way to work it into her routine. "I think you will be very interested in this one, sir!" She strides alongside me like a slimy seller. "She is young and small and not as terrible as the rest, doesn't even have all of her adult teeth yet. Her history is a sad one, I'm afraid. Her mother was killed by a young hunter two years ago, and now she is an orphan."

The Keeper bends low, whispers, "She's a lot like you." Then she hollers to the crowd, "This one I call Baby. If chosen by the prince, it will be her first hunt!"

This slaycon shouldn't be here, even if she was handpicked to improve the odds. Baby crouches in the back corner of the cage, head low, eyes bouncing from me to the Keeper to the crowd. I suppose the Keeper is trying to do me a favor, but the sight of the frightened little creature makes me nauseous.

"Prince Leo, son of Raja Kahn . . ." The Keeper stops in midsentence, catching her error. It's an unfortunate blunder. Everyone knows the Singa-Kahn is my grandfather and not my father. A few Singas, sheltered and hidden in the horde of bodies, take the opportunity to comment on my family background.

"He is the son of nobody!" someone jeers.

"A royal bastard!" calls another.

These insults are not only offensive to me, but a sign of our divided domain. I look back, hoping to find Sariah's quadron springing into action to search out the name callers, but they too are lost in the crowd. To my relief, the Keeper ignores these taunts and carries on, more anxious to continue her performance than to preserve my dignity.

This time, I'm all for it.

"Leo, *grandson* of Raja Kahn, make your choice!"

"Choose! Choose! Choose! Choose!" chants the sea of spectators.

I consider my options one last time. Baby is a wobbly little thing. If any slaycon is deserving of death, it isn't her.

That leaves Storm, the Professor, and Quicksilver.

"Choose! Choose! Choose! Choose!" thrums what might be the whole Pride of Singara by now.

The choice comes easily. I move to a slaycon cage while the beast within sizes me up, a wild fire raging in his eyes.

"Choose! Choose! Choose!"

I raise my arm and point. The chanting stops. Disbelief washes over the crowd.

The Keeper is equally undone, head shaking. "No, Your Majesty. No." Clearly this was not the choice she anticipated.

"I choose Storm!" I say to remove all doubt.

The Keeper is truly off her game now, and it's clear I will have to keep things moving. The sun has climbed higher in the sky, a glaring reminder that time is running out.

"Take the slaycon to the Border Zone. I will select my gear now."

I don't look at Kaydan or Galil as I pass. If their faces show anything close to the shock on the Keeper's face, my one seed of hope will be crushed.

I make for the table covered with weapons and tools: blades of various sizes, bows and quivers of arrows, spears, shields, armor, helmets, ropes, hooks. I am permitted three choices from this table and no more. The armor is too big for me, and most of the blades are too heavy and cumbersome. The bow might prove useful, but I don't have the strength to pull an arrow back far enough to penetrate a slaycon's hide.

I select a dagger and a crudely made slingshot. The dagger won't extend my reach by much, but it won't slow me down. The slingshot will increase my reach and, with a good shot, might slow Storm down.

And the third item? Where is it? The one thing that could change the equation of battle between me and the slaycon. The one thing that could prove more useful and deadly than any blade or arrow. Yes, there, on the ground behind the table: the sack that held the rabbit only moments ago. If it works the way I hope, it will work on any slaycon, so why not put the biggest Singa slayer permanently out of business and protect future hunters from this brute? If my experiment fails, at least no one will remember the bastard grandson of Raja Kahn as a coward.

I attach the blade in its scabbard to my belt along with the slingshot, tuck the bag into the back of my leggings, and spring across the square, feeling the blade and slingshot slap against my legs.

"Fascinating choices, Leo," Sariah says as I arrive at the other side.

"Just get me out of here, Sariah."

"Right away, Lord."

"Is Grandfather still in the city?"

"The Kahn is on his way to Border Zone Eight,

next to the zone appointed for your hunt. He will stay there to await the outcome."

Sariah guides me to the royal carriage waiting outside the square. The carriage is hitched to a team of two karkadanns, large four-legged creatures who move with surprising speed, given their bulk. Bearing the royal sign of the Singa-Kahn, they snort and stomp the ground with heavy hooves, anxious to power away from the mob.

We exit the square. The crowd parts and permits the royal carriage to pass. Karkadanns have that effect. Few are foolish enough to get in their way. I lean against the plush interior of the vehicle, grateful to be alone.

It's a ninety-minute journey to the Border Zone. Sariah drives the team of karkadanns, and her quadron rides two in the back and one next to her in front. The karkadanns spirit us all out of the city, through swaths of countryside, past quarries, mines, and farmland, until we reach a military outpost. These little forts are stationed along every road leading from the city to the border region. The karkadanns are given water and grain while Sariah's quadron chats with the warriors stationed here.

I stay in the carriage to avoid questions from these soldiers. Watchtowers rise up over the tree line from the Great Wall. From this short distance they are tall and imposing, not at all like the sticks they appear to be from the castle.

When the karkadanns have had their fill, Sariah guides the carriage back to the road leading to the forest, the last piece of land between the outposts and the border region.

The familiar feeling begins. My brain tingles, my heartbeat quickens, a rushing wind fills my ears as my stomach turns—a wad of fiction is about to drop into my mouth and swell up like a balloon. This time, alone as I am in the carriage, I'm free to let the words and the vision come without fear. I lean back, open my mouth, and the sickness streams out.

Once there was a great hunter with a trusted servant who had a habit of saying "How fortunate!" at every opportunity. In times of blessing or sorrow, the servant would say, "How fortunate!"

The characters and the scene burst into view, filling the interior of the carriage: the hunter in his grand house, preparing for a day of hunting, and his servant offering the standard comment. It's all here, a three-sixty waking dream according to the words of my possessed mouth.

The hunter and his servant went hunting together. As they pursued a deer, the hunter's left foot got stuck between two rocks and was badly injured, so badly his foot had to be removed.

After the hunter's foot was taken away, the servant inspected the bloody stump and said, "How fortunate!"

The hunter was furious. "How can you say that? There is nothing fortunate about losing a foot! You are a useless and heartless servant! Get out of my sight!"

The servant, of course, responded, "How fortunate!" He left the employ of the hunter and found a new job as a teacher in town.

Some months later, the hunter went hunting again, assisted by a wooden peg attached to the bottom of his left leg. On this occasion he wandered too far from his own land and was captured by the enemy. The enemies stripped the hunter in order to roast and eat him at their ritual feast.

Naturally, the hunter was terrified, especially when the enemy chief came forward brandishing a blade. The chief inspected the hunter from head to foot, marveling at his fine teeth, his well-fed body, his smooth and silky hide. But when he discovered the hunter's false leg, he said, "He is missing part of his leg and therefore he is unworthy to be served at our feast."

Instead of using his blade to cut the hunter's throat, the chief sliced the ropes that bound the *hunter and released him. As the hunter hobbled away, he found himself saying, "How fortunate! How very, very fortunate!"*

Returning to his grand house, the hunter sent for his old servant. He recounted the whole terrifying ordeal and said, "You were correct. It was fortunate that I lost my foot. Because I was missing one foot, my life was spared! It was very fortunate indeed! I was a fool to dismiss you." Then the hunter said, "Yet there is still one thing I don't understand. Why did you say 'How fortunate!' when I sent you away?"

The servant answered, "For those who seek Alayah, who is the greatest good of all, good fortune can come from anything if you are patient enough to find it."

"And has that good fortune been revealed to you?" the hunter asked.

"Yes! Had you not dismissed me, I would have been hunting with you the day you were seized. And since I have both of my feet, I would have been roasted and eaten right after you were set free."

"You are correct, my friend! That was fortunate! Please accept my apology and return to my side and serve me for the rest of my days."

The servant returned to the hunter's home and never stopped saying "How fortunate!" and the hunter never tired of hearing it.

The story ends, as does the vision, fading like steam. I close my eyes and waggle my tongue, making sure it's under my command once more.

Trees pass by the carriage windows. The air is cool, laced with the scents of moss, leaves, and pine.

It's true what Tamir said last night. I've been this far out of the city only a handful of times. Nothing in this forest is familiar.

I recall the servant's words: "For those who seek Alayah, who is the greatest good of all, good fortune can come from anything if you are patient enough to find it."

Patience has never been a strength for Singas. We like to reach scientific conclusions based on the evidence in front of us. If I end up in the belly of a slaycon, that will be more than enough evidence to prove that this fiction, however charming, is nonsense.

I open my eyes and yelp.

The hunter from the story lounges opposite me. He is a Singa, dressed in light armor and fine green robes trimmed with gold. The bottom of his left leg is supported by a wooden peg.

He is in the halfway state: ghostly, phantasmal. I can almost look through him to the velvet seat of the carriage.

Over time, I've learned to ignore, chase, or dash away from these apparitions. Since we're both sitting inside the royal carriage, running is not an option. Ignoring him won't be too easy either.

"You're not real," I say, more to myself than to him.

The hunter laughs. "Not real? I'm as real as they come!" He slaps his chest and stomps his peg leg on the carriage floor. The thump on the floor is muted, proving he's not fully here, not as solid as I am.

"We're going hunting, yes?" he asks.

"Not we. *Me.* Go away."

"Why would you send me away? You are the one who brought me into this world. I am here to help you in any way I can!"

"The only thing you are going to help me do is lose my tongue!"

The hunter frowns and shakes his head. "Oh, dear prince. Haven't you figured out how this works? The story brings us here and we are yours to command!"

I glance at his wooden leg. "No offense to you and your . . . injury. But I don't think you could keep up with me."

The hunter sighs. "Ah! You think I am not fit to hunt. You think I will slow you down, yes? Every battle is an equation of reach multiplied by strength and speed. Survival of the strongest and all that?" he adds with mock seriousness.

"You are not even solid," I argue, leaning forward and pushing my hand directly into his torso without much effort. "You are only an apparition, a phantom. How much help can you be?"

The hunter watches with amusement as my hand

enters and exits his chest. "That is easily remedied, Lord. You have the power. Just say my name and I will be solid and visible to one and all! I can be of great service to you."

"I'm sure you are a fine hunter, but I'm supposed to do this on my own. Please just return to wherever it was you came from."

"I can't do that. I can disappear for a time, but only you can send me back."

That's what they all say. They all want me to "send them back" in exchange for helping me.

"I don't know what that means."

The hunter winks at me. "You don't have to know —you only have to be *willing*, yes?"

I fold my arms and frown.

"Then I guess I'll be stuck here, with all the others. You will remember my name, won't you? If you need help, speak my name." He draws forward, and I flatten myself against the carriage wall. "My name is . . . Oreyon." His breath is sweet and flowery, like a spring breeze. "Will you remember?"

I nod, just to end this encounter as quickly as possible.

"How fortunate."

And he is gone.

CHAPTER 5

To defeat your enemy, you must first defeat yourself.
— *Sayings of the Ancients*

THE CARRIAGE JERKS TO A STOP.

We're here.

Border Zone Seven.

Sariah opens the carriage door. "We made good time, Lord. You have at least six hours of daylight to make your kill."

The sun is overhead, that brief moment at midday when there are no shadows.

The Border Zone Fence, stretching for many kilometers from the sheer cliffs at the seacoast to the Great Mountain, is a series of iron poles, eight meters high. The top of each pole is sharpened and curved inward like a claw. A metal net hangs on the inside of the poles.

Nothing gets in. Or out. Unless you have a key like the one dangling from Sariah's belt. Each two-kilometer section of the Border Zone has a small locked gate, just big enough for a Singa to duck under or for a slaycon to slither through.

The Great Wall and Border Zone Fence prove Grandfather's genius. It was he who led the victory against the Maguar. It was he who designed the Great Wall and the inner ring of Border Zones to ensure they would never again invade our lands. Even though I'm about to be locked into one of these cages with a hungry monster, I'm proud of Grandfather and the many years of peace he brought to Singara.

The fence came at a tremendous cost. It drained the metal from the mines of the mountain, which is Tamir's main criticism of the Kahn. Tamir believes the fence should be dismantled and the metal repurposed for advancements in the Science of Weaponry.

"The slaycon is already here," Sariah says, fitting a key into the lock.

It's true.

Storm's scent is abundant. I estimate he went through the gate less than half an hour ago.

The lock clicks and the bolt retreats, allowing the gate to swing open on its hinges.

"Remember your training, Leo," Sariah counsels. "These beasts are clever, but your greatest weapon—" She concludes by tapping the side of her forehead. "I will wait for you here."

I gape at the landscape beyond the fence. I'm struck by how beautiful it is.

And how lonely.

"Do not forget the tail," Sariah adds.

I glance behind me. How could I forget my tail?

"Not *your* tail, Majesty. The tail of the slaycon. You must cut it off and carry it out as evidence of your kill. No *living* slaycon will easily give up its tail."

"Thanks," I mutter.

"And if it pleases Your Highness, you might unsheathe your blade before entering."

With a hand that trembles as much from embarrassment as dread, I pull my dagger from its scabbard. The metal, old and worn, still flashes in the sun. Although the blade is nearly the length of my arm, it looks like a dinner knife compared to the weapons strapped to Sariah.

I swallow and dip through the door into Border Zone Seven.

The gate clangs and locks behind me. No doubt an experienced slaycon like Storm knows the sound and what it means: dinnertime.

I wonder if Storm is watching me from an unseen roost, camouflaged by shrubs or nestled in a cleft of rock. Or maybe he's exploring the open terrain, marking his territory with squirts of hot yellow pee. Slaycons probably enjoy the hunt as a chance to escape the confines of the Keeper's cages and have a good meal out after playing with their food.

All is silent except the buzz of insects and the creak of branches stirred by the afternoon wind. Wildflowers bend and sway. The clouds are plumes of white against a cobalt sky.

I push deeper into the zone, stretching out my senses and steering clear of anything Storm might use as a hiding place. My claws extend and retract from my fingertips, pulsing with my waves of anxiety.

In a clearing, I spot a dark mass, half covered by tall grass. A mist of flies hovers above it. The wind shifts, and I catch the stench of decaying flesh. I close in, sweeping the flies away. A few more steps and the scent's source is revealed: a rotting, tail-less slaycon corpse, slain by a young hunter. I could stay here and be safe from Storm if I wanted to. There's little chance he would come to investigate this place. I can barely stand it myself.

Pushing on, I delve into the woods. Three ravens erupt from the branches of the outermost tree, calling and screeching like a bunch of excited cubs.

Something spooked them.

I part my jaws to taste the air, eyes scanning the area, ears swiveling about.

No slaycon except for that decaying mess behind me. Wherever the living monster is, he isn't here.

After an hour or so of wandering, my ears prick at the hum of moving water. My nose agrees. A river or a stream is up ahead. The promise of water prompts a memory from my training.

Slaycons do not like water. Slaycon hunt theorem

number eight. We Singas are not too fond of water either.

Nevertheless, I run. The canopy of tree cover thickens, plunging my surroundings into shadow as the temperature dips to something like nightfall. Then I see the river, carving its way through the forest floor. My pace quickens, feet thumping full tilt, announcing my whereabouts to every creature within a hundred meters.

The riverbank is lined with boulders draped with green moss. Light filters through the trees in long golden bands. The river's water is swift, and at least five meters from bank to bank.

And there, on the opposite bank, is the slaycon.

My blood runs as cold as the river.

How did he get over there?

Storm's tongue laps water into his mouth, eyes pinned to his prey. He saw me long before I saw him.

One point for the monster.

I have the advantage of the river between us, but Storm is downwind, which means he can smell my fear wafting over the water.

Storm goes on drinking, untroubled by my arrival.

I untie the water bottle from my belt and dunk it into the river. When it's full, I harvest smooth stones from the riverbed and drop them into the bag. Storm never takes his eyes away from me.

When I have collected about twenty stones, I remove two from the bag and fit one into the leather pouch of the slingshot. With a single motion, I raise my arm, pull, aim, and fire. The bands snap. The stone whistles through the air just over Storm's head, shattering on a boulder behind him.

Storm turns toward the noise.

Exactly what I was hoping for.

I've already tucked a second stone into the shot pouch and fire again. This time the stone sails across the water and pounds the brute in the snout.

A hit but also a miss.

I was aiming for his eye. A half-blind slaycon would make my day much easier.

Storm recoils and whimpers with the impact. He shakes his head, snarls, and charges straight into the river.

This isn't supposed to happen.

Storm is up to his stomach now, holding his tail and head high to stay balanced in the current. Water batters his side and swirls around his shoulders.

I fit another stone in the sling.

Before I can pull back and aim, Storm vanishes under the surface and does not return. The river rolls on as if he was never there.

Seconds pass.

No bubbles appear.

No churning of water from a desperate beast.

Nothing.

Hope blossoms in my chest.

Could it really be this easy?

Could I kill a slaycon simply by luring him into the river and letting him drown?

Will that even count?

How will I fish him out to prove he is dead?

These questions are eclipsed by a new and less comforting thought: What if this beast can actually swim? What if he's underwater, paddling his way to my side of the river?

I return the slingshot to the bag, grab my dagger, and point it at the river. Nothing moves or changes beyond the bits of twigs and leaves riding the current. If Storm surfaces in front of me, I will have the upper hand. While he heaves his bulk onto the shore, I will unleash a fury of blows with my blade.

My battle plans are interrupted by a splash and a grunt. Downriver, Storm's dark head bobs up and down, struggling to keep his snout above water. He crashes into a rock, bouncing him toward the shore.

My side of the shore.

Storm scrambles up the riverbank and collapses on the ground, exhausted. Silent as a shadow, I creep from tree to tree until Storm is only five meters away. Surely he knows I'm here and understands the danger. By the look of it, he's too worn out from his underwater adventure to do anything about it.

The distance between us shrinks to three meters.

Then two.

Storm's coarse hair is speckled with drops of water, glistening in the sun as though he's covered in diamonds. His tail lies on the ground like a fallen tree. His belly is white, hairless, and exposed. Except for his sides rising and falling with breath, he is as lifeless as the corpse I saw earlier. Soon he will be one.

I swallow, preparing to pounce and bury my blade in his gut.

One step, then another. I'm so close now, I can see the wrinkles on Storm's stomach and the bones of his rib cage. I recall my lessons with Galil on the Science of Nature, specifically the design of animals, and envision where his heart beats beneath layers of skin and muscle. If I angle my blade right, I can puncture it with just one stab. Steady now.

Storm's haunches tremble. His tail blurs and I'm knocked off my feet. The blade flies from my hand. I hit the ground and roll away while Storm springs to his feet, fully recovered and preparing to strike again.

The plunge in the river was a trick, a trap to lure me to him. How many young Singas has he defeated exactly like this?

Storm positions himself over my blade, twisting side to side, chopping the air with the long reach of his tail. I leap and bend and dodge, appreciating all those hours in the training hall with Kaydan.

I need to get Storm away from my weapon. The next time Storm's tail swings, I run as if I've been shot from a catapult, bounding down the riverbank. My ears angle back to confirm Storm's pursuit. His claws scrape earth and rocks as he springs from boulder to ground to tree stump. The forest to my left and the river to my right form a tunnel of green and bluish gray. Storm's hot breath pulses on my tail. He's closing in for a bite.

I tuck my tail. A shadow covers me. Storm's scent is overpowering, as if he's right on top of—

I drop and watch Storm sail overhead. This would be the perfect moment to strike upward if I had my weapon. Storm wastes no time regrouping for another attack. His haunches quiver and I know what's coming. That blasted tree trunk of a tail is about to—

Whump!

The tail lands centimeters from my head and lifts again for another strike.

I whirl and bolt back the way I came, heading straight for my blade.

Storm gives chase, and this time he's lagging behind, breathing hard. His dunk in the river must have cost him, after all.

I return to the spot of our first tussle; my weapon blazes daylight at me like a beacon. I dive, grab the hilt, roll, and leap, expecting to find Storm bearing down on me.

Yet Storm is nowhere in view.

I strain my ears, combing the forest for the pop of a twig or the crackle of a leaf crushed underfoot. The scene is eerily quiet except for the warble of the river. The breeze carries no scent, save the aromas of earth and water.

How could a slaycon just vanish?

What's his game?

My feet fall back, moving upstream. Storm must be somewhere nearby, collecting his strength, waiting. Or he's running away from the river to draw me into new terrain, into a different trap.

"*Show yourself!*" I shout to the trees, a thousand unseen critters, and one slaycon.

"*Aren't you hungry?*"

A bird calls, and its mate responds with a similar-sounding trill.

"*I'm right here!*"

I'm still backing up, stepping gingerly over rocks, through the mud.

"*You stupid, smelly hairball!!!*"

The next step lands my right foot in a narrow gap between two rocks. I yowl and tumble backwards, but my foot holds fast. My view is limited, and the fur around my lower leg and ankle feels ripped. I pull and heave and yank, which does nothing but deepen the gash and release a stream of blood into the darkness below.

I picture my severed leg discovered in this very spot after Storm has devoured the rest of me. I imagine the news coming to Grandfather and spreading around Singara that the prince failed to make a kill because of a stuck foot. They would say it was meant to be, the expected outcome of nature stacked against me.

Tamir, of course, would not mourn my death.

The thought of that traitor and the searing pain of my leg makes me wail: *"Aaaaggghhhh!"*

A muted roar sounds in the distance, echoing my cry.

Storm.

He sounds off again. Louder this time, which means he's putting more air behind it or, more likely, he's getting closer.

I clutch my blade and dig at the base of the rock pinning my leg. When the rock is loose enough, I pull, and the mud releases my bloody leg with a belch.

Scraps of skin and fur dangle from my leg. When I try to extend it or move my foot, a lightning bolt of pain shoots through.

At least I'm free.

There's no way I can outrun Storm now. Standing and fighting won't be easy. Can he smell my blood? My fear?

I could really use some help, but I'm all alone out here.

A name forms on my trembling lips, the name of the hunter. Or . . . Ori . . . What was it?

"Oreyon!"

Though I summoned him, the appearance of Oreyon startles me. He sits at my right hand, his fine cloak draped on the muddy riverbank. He is no longer a phantom, a quasi-physical apparition. He is real. Vivid. Solid. Completely in this world.

"What took you so long!" he bellows. "Do you have any idea how aggravating it is to be invisible, floating around you all afternoon and powerless to do anything to help? It's enough to drive us all insane!"

"I've got a problem here."

"What? That?" He examines my bloodied leg. "That is fortunate!"

"What do you mean?"

"You can use your injury to lure the beast close to you. Slaycons can be lazy when they think the kill is certain. Let him draw near. And then use his confidence against him!"

"Will that work?"

"It is your best course, young prince. Unless you would like me to butcher the beast for you, which I would gladly do. It will only take a moment." He grabs my blade and draws himself up.

I tug on his arm. "No, I can do this."

Oreyon returns the blade to me, smiling.

"I understand," I say. "You can go now."

The hunter sighs. "There is much you do not yet understand, Lord. But I will go, as you command."

He does. And I am alone again.

I remove the bag from my belt and dump out the contents. The stones tumble to the ground. The slingshot gets tucked into my belt. My foot goes back in the hole, which is much more spacious without the rock. I toss my blade three meters away, between me and where Storm is likely to approach from.

I scream again and clasp my leg as if my foot were still stuck. I moan and whimper, playing the part of trapped prey.

Storm slides into view, emerging from an outcrop of rocks, and slithers forward. He pauses over my blade, gives it a good sniff, and presses it into the ground with his front foot.

I yank at my leg and claw the ground, trying to appear desperate. Despite my lack of experience in pretending, Storm seems convinced enough. He saunters closer, nostrils drawing in the aromas of my blood and fear. His eyes sparkle with glee. When Storm is only a meter away, his jaws part, revealing knifelike teeth dripping with venomous saliva.

Almost there.

Storm is so close, I can see the grime lining his gums and hear the rumble in his throat. His scent covers me like a moldy blanket.

He twitches, preparing to strike.

I grab the bag and pounce, limbs splayed out, ignoring the burst of pain in my injured leg. Storm's jaws snap, but he's too late. I now have four or five precious seconds before he can open his mouth again. Leapfrogging over his snout to his neck, I loop the bag over his head, yanking it all the way up to the ears, and pull the drawstring. Satisfied the bag is secure, I hop down. My injury screams with the impact. Storm writhes and shakes his head, but the bag holds. I reach for my dagger as Storm's tail sweeps the ground and flings my legs out from under me.

I should have anticipated that.

I land in a heap and scamper on all fours like a panicky insect to my blade. I spin, dirty weapon in hand. Storm has gone off the attack, dragging his head along the ground in a failing attempt to remove the bag, whining like a wounded pup.

It worked! He's confused. Struggling. Defenseless. Easy to kill.

I glide forward, noting the multiple targets available to me: the throat, under the forearm, the white of his belly. My body sizzles. For the first time my blade isn't a burden, but an extension of my arm. With it, I will rip away this killer's life.

Is this how it feels to be a warrior? Ready and eager to take life? Confident of the outcome?

Storm rolls onto his side. He rakes his head across the ground, but the bag clings to him like a determined parasite.

Even better. Now the whole of his underside is facing me, a wide-open invitation to finish this with a single thrust into his black heart. Storm's clawing at the bag becomes weak and labored.

Goodbye, murderer.

Had that thought never entered my mind, the hunt would have ended right there. I would have stabbed him as easily as puncturing a sack of grain. I would have secured my place among the Pride and cemented my path to the throne.

Yet with Storm twisting on the ground, looking helpless and defenseless, I am moved with compassion against all logic and reason. Besides, making a kill like this would turn me into a murderer. Not that Storm would hesitate to do the same.

But isn't that the point?

Isn't that what separates me from him . . . or from the Maguar?

I guide the tip of my blade to Storm's exposed throat and sneak it under the bag's drawstring. With a jerk the string is cut, and the bag loosens. Feeling the change, Storm pushes it off with his forelegs. In a heartbeat, he's back on his feet, dazed and feverish.

Without a second thought for the Singa who just spared his life, Storm charges, preparing to bite. I dodge, and my blade lands behind his head, lopping off an ear as I roll to the ground.

Not exactly a death blow. Or a graceful finish.

Storm howls, spins, and leaps. I dive under him and land a decent slice to his underside and another to his right back foot. Blood squirts onto my face and torso.

Score two for me.

I scurry back while Storm teeters about on his injured foot, snarling and hissing.

My own ankle is throbbing, but it's a sight better than his. I suspect Storm will be dead in a matter of minutes from the gash I've given him. I hobble away and climb a tree before Storm can take stock of my whereabouts.

Turns out he's still paying attention.

Storm's nose traces my scent to the base of the tree, where he collapses on his side, head angled upward. From my perch, it's clear his belly wound is not as deep as I hoped.

He's down but clearly not done.

I was foolish to jump into the first available tree. Now Storm will wait me out. Meanwhile, the sun is sinking. There are maybe two hours of daylight left.

I wiggle onto a sturdy-looking limb and Storm crawls, matching me centimeter for centimeter. I slide back to the trunk to review my options. I have my blade and my slingshot, but no rocks. And no bag. Not that the bag-over-the-head trick will work twice.

And I have . . . the pellet Anjali gave me!

I had forgotten. I was supposed to swallow it as soon as I entered the Border Zone to mask my scent. Now it will do me about as much good as eating the bark off this tree.

Maybe it isn't completely useless.

Holding the pellet and slingshot in my right hand,

I loop my left arm around the branch. Heart pounding against my rib cage for the umpteenth time today, I slide off the branch. My legs and tail dangle for a terrifying moment.

Storm perks up, his tail brushing the ground. As I shimmy my way down, he tries to jump, but his damaged foot will not cooperate.

Storm balances on his good rear leg, stretching up the trunk with his forelegs. When I'm about a meter from his snout, I tighten my leg grip on the tree and fit the pellet into the slingshot. It's an awkward position for a shot, but I can't be picky.

The pellet won't do any damage. I only want to stimulate his jaws to snap shut. That will give me five precious seconds to jump down and finish him off before he can open his mouth for another bite.

Slaycon hunt theorem number four.

Problem is, his mouth is already closed, bared teeth guarding the entrance. I will have to tempt his appetite. I wiggle lower and allow my bloody right foot to dangle, still hugging the trunk between my knees. A drop of my blood falls.

Storm's eager mouth opens.

Just what I wanted.

I take aim and release the shot pouch. The pellet vanishes into the tunnel of Storm's throat. However, Storm is too focused on my foot to notice or care.

His mouth does not close.

Instead he reaches higher, mouth agape, pushing himself up on his tail. His jaws snap, and I feel teeth puncturing my right leg.

No!

Triumphant, Storm lowers himself to the ground and waits.

The new pain doesn't last long. A tingling sensation climbs the length of my leg until it goes completely slack, hanging like a piece of meat. I grip the tree with my claws, but I know it is only a matter of time.

I've lost. It's over.

In seconds, my waist is numb, and all feeling retreats from my other leg and torso. My arms become limp, and thoughts become foggy. My claws are all that's left, and soon they too give way under the spell of the slaycon's venom.

Then I'm falling.

Falling.

Falling.

I can't move, or see, or scream.

CHAPTER 6

The Light enters by our wounds
and shines through them as well.
— *Sayings of the Ancients*

AT FIRST there is darkness.

Stillness.

Nothingness.

And yet I can sense the darkness and stillness and nothingness, so there must be something of *me* left. Otherwise, how would I be aware of them?

But I can't feel anything. I'm floating in something like a giant inkwell under a pitch-black canopy. Am I inside Storm's stomach, waiting to be digested? In that case I'm very grateful for the venom's power.

Maybe this is a dream. A trick of the mind to protect me from the horror of what's happening to my body.

Those would be the logical options, given the way the hunt ended just moments ago. Yet neither one feels right.

So where am I?

The answer comes in a burst of dazzling white light,

brighter than a hundred suns. But it does not burn. The darkness is banished.

The light cradles me. I may have been held in its embrace for a few seconds, an hour, or a lifetime. The light is both now and forever.

The light pulses and swirls, caressing me with long, feathery fingers. Each movement and gesture is accompanied by sounds more rich and delicious than anything I've ever heard. I would call it music, but it's nothing like that dreary stuff we have in Singara. And I don't just hear the sounds. I feel them coursing through me like blood. Instead of being distant like the sun, I sense that this light and music are just under the surface of every leaf and rock and creature, hiding within every visible thing.

The light recedes and gathers into a star glittering in a sapphire sky. I hear the lap of waves and find myself lying in golden sand on an endless beach. I rise, noting the weightlessness of my body, as though I could float up and soar away.

I wouldn't be the only one.

The sky is flooded with countless winged creatures arcing and playing in the soft, salty air. Most I can't even describe, let alone name.

The desire to join them is overwhelming, but my feet stay rooted to the beach, as if they are stuck in mortar instead of sand.

Compared with the scene above, I feel banished, imprisoned.

"Please!" I beg the light. "Let me join them!"

There is a flash to my right and a being appears, the strangest and most wondrous yet. His shape shifts, ebbing and flowing between a two-legged creature and a giant firewing bird of the same height and stature. His words echo with many voices, speaking together.

"You can't join us, Eliyah. Not yet."

He is so bright, I can't make out his face. "Who are you?"

"I am Daviyah. I was the Eleventh Shakyah in your world until I passed from that life in the battle you call the Great War. Now I fly on the wings of the Great Firewing along with all the Shakyahs before me."

"Why did you call me Eliyah?"

"It is your true name."

"Am I . . . dead?"

My companion extends a wing-arm over the sand between us. The sand billows like a curtain stirred by the wind, and I see my body at the base of the tree.

I look very dead.

If my body is there, what part of me is here? We Singas don't believe anything goes on after death. When you die, that's it. You're done.

Yet this beach, Daviyah, all the winged creatures, and the light suggest we are wrong about that. Very wrong.

"What you call death is only a door. You have crossed the threshold of that door, but you cannot stay."

"What is this place?"

"This is the Haven, the home of Alayah, the source of all life, the beginning and the end of all stories."

"Why can't I stay?" Who would ever want to leave here?

"Your story is just beginning and you have much to learn, Eliyah. Tomorrow, you will meet the wisest Singa in your realm. And before the setting of the next sun, you will meet Wajid, my former servant. That will put everything in motion. You must find out who you are. You must learn to trust Alayah."

The light in the sky glows larger, getting nearer. *"It is time to return. Your story, Alayah's story, must continue."*

I'm not sure what that means, but the idea of leaving this place and returning to my world, where I am a diseased Spinner and in danger all the time, is not a happy thought.

"Will I see you again?" I ask. The light is drawing closer, and I sense my conversation with Daviyah is coming to an end. "If I speak your name, will you appear . . . like the others?"

The light enfolds me, embracing and caressing. My companion is blotted out by the brightness. The beach and the sky and the horde of winged creatures disappear as well.

"You don't need to," Daviyah counsels. *"I am always with you."*

. . .

My eyelids are like bricks; my limbs feel like wooden beams. Instead of the roll of waves on that beach, I hear the rush of river water and the wind stirring up leaves.

I'm back. Back in my body, lying beside the river in the Border Zone.

My eyes fly open. Where is Storm?

I rotate my head and find the beast lying next to me, his head centimeters from mine. Fear pumps life into my limbs. I roll away, ready for Storm to pop up and subdue me with another bite.

He doesn't move.

Not even his sides rise and fall with breath.

I push up to my hands and knees and crawl to investigate Storm's body. With each jerk of a leg or arm, my movements become smoother, easier.

The venom must be wearing off.

I force myself up, breaking through walls of resistance in each joint until I am upright over Storm's lifeless form. I kick him.

No response.

There's no doubt about it. He's dead. But how?

There's not enough blood on the ground to prove he bled to death.

What, then?

I replay everything that happened in the moments

before Storm's teeth sank into my leg: I put the bag over his head, then felt sorry for him and removed the bag. There was an exchange of blows, followed by my retreat up the tree and shooting the pellet into his mouth. That turned out to be a failed attempt to get his jaws shut so I could fall upon him with my blade. Instead, he bit me. End of hunt.

Then why do I live while he grows cold on the ground?

Did I land on his head?

No.

Slaycons have bones like stone. This tree could have fallen on his skull without giving him so much as a headache.

Was it the pellet? The little bundle that was supposed to make me smell of the forest?

I hobble like a stiff elder for a better view of the beast. A slaycon's face is normally a grotesque sight, but Storm's expression right now gives *hideous* a new definition. His eyes are rolled back. His mouth hangs open. A swollen tongue pokes the dirt.

Poison.

The pellet was poison. Powerful enough to kill a slaycon.

But it wasn't meant for him.

It was meant for . . . me.

I gag and nearly vomit with the realization.

Tamir. He is a gifted scientist in addition to being

a great warrior. He could have easily made a poison to guarantee my death. Storm would have been just as happy to eat a dead Singa instead of going through the trouble of killing me first.

And then there's Anjali.

She gave me the poison. This makes Anjali loyal to Tamir, one of his many secret servants. She also probably told him what I am.

I can't think about this right now. The sun is dipping below the tree line. I've got less than an hour to get back to the Border Zone gate with Storm's tail. Since I will serve the tail to Grandfather and Sariah's quadron tonight, I need to remove it quickly, before the poison infects the meat. Most slaycon meat is not worth eating, but the meat around the tail is sumptuous. My blade lies at the base of the tree. I hack through layers of skin, muscle, and sinew. It's a grisly job, and difficult to manage with a bad leg.

The tail removed, I kneel before the mangled stump and take a bite, washing it down with a mouthful of blood, and wait. If there is still poison in the tail, it should affect me in no time as it did Storm. Better to have one Singa die than to send Grandfather and the others to their graves, even if it means Tamir wins after all.

As I wait for death, my thoughts return to that other land, that beach, the music, the light, the winged creatures of every size and description . . . and the one who spoke to me, Daviyah, whose voice was many voices, the sound of it enlivening every cell of my body. My fingers trace the contours of my winged chest plate.

Was it a dream?

No. That place was so vivid, it makes *this* world look like a dream. Everything here is so dull and clunky by comparison.

Satisfied to still be alive and well a few minutes later, I limp to the riverbank and ease my damaged leg into the swift current. The water is so cold, it burns. I scrub the injured spot to remove clumps of blood and dirt. It hurts, but not nearly as much as it should. A gift of the venom still lingering in my veins.

Leaving my blade behind, I hoist the tail onto my shoulders and stagger to the Border Zone Fence, where Sariah and her quadron wait on the other side. I should feel victorious at this point, exultant at having rid the world of this evil Singa slayer. But the truth is, I didn't really kill Storm.

It was an accident.

Fortunately, Singas who survive the hunt are not allowed to say much about it, although a few facts will certainly be requested.

Storm's tail must weigh as much as I do. My back aches. My legs feel like twigs ready to snap. The wound throbs with every step, as though my heart has taken up residence in my ankle. I've drained my canteen, but my throat still feels like sandpaper. An angry stomach completes the chorus of complaining body parts.

I didn't expect this stage of the hunt to be a battle in itself.

Meanwhile, the sun surrenders to the encroaching darkness. I press on until the Border Zone Fence appears and I hear Sariah cry, "The prince! The prince approaches!"

Sariah roars and roars again. Mavrak, Biku, and Jimo join in. I'm supposed to roar in return, but I don't have the strength to even try.

"He is wounded!" Sariah cries, hastening to unlock the low gate built into the fence. She ducks through and sprints to my side, with Jimo and Mavrak in tow.

Sariah studies the scene below my knee. "Jimo, take the tail."

Jimo begins to ease the tail from my shoulders as though it were only a garden snake.

I step aside. "No."

I've made it this far. I can go another fifty meters to the gate in the fence.

"The Kahn has set up camp in Border Zone Eight," Sariah says as I collapse into the carriage. She's trying to keep a soldierly face, but her skittishness betrays her. She's clearly overwhelmed to find me alive. I only hope she's happy about the outcome, and not dreading the prospect of delivering the news to Tamir, if she's loyal to him like Anjali.

"Galil is there. He'll see to your leg."

It's a kilometer or so from the gate of one Border Zone to the next, and I'm content to melt into the cushions of the carriage. I don't miss many meals, and despite the piece of Storm's tail I swallowed, my stomach is about to claw its way out of my body in search of more food.

What will I share with Grandfather about the hunt? Should I tell him Storm died by accident? Should I reveal the attempt to murder me with the poison pellet? Should I share my vision of that beach and the light?

I conclude the answers to these questions are no, no, and definitely no.

Besides, Storm is dead and I live. Nothing else matters.

It's nearly dark when we arrive at Border Zone Eight. Grandfather wears a stern face as he waits outside the gate with Galil at his side, yet his eyes are shining.

Sariah hurries to open the carriage door. I slide out and limp to the back of the carriage, where the slaycon tail hangs over the storage box. I hoist the tail onto my shoulders, pivot, and let it fall at Grandfather's feet with a satisfying thud.

As instructed by Kaydan, I say the customary

words for this moment: "May the meat of my kill give strength to your body and to the Singa race."

Grandfather gives the expected reply, "Well done, youngling. Today you have begun your journey to become a Singa warrior." Then he hastens to add, "And what happened to your leg?"

Galil crouches to inspect the wound.

Grandfather's eyes narrow. "Just the facts, Leo."

Galil answers for me. "This is a slaycon bite!"

The Kahn's eyes enlarge, and my heart plummets to somewhere below my feet. No hunter has ever survived a slaycon bite. You'd think that would puff me up with pride, but no. It means I have some explaining to do about why I am not, at this very moment, being digested in Storm's belly.

"You . . . you were bitten by the slaycon and yet you live?" Grandfather asks, dumbfounded. He turns to Galil. "Is that possible?"

"Theoretically, yes," says the old scientist. "It is not the venom that kills, but the slaycon after the venom takes effect."

Grandfather searches my face, and I can see the conflict on his. He wants the details, but he knows it's safer for me to keep quiet.

Breaking the silence, he says, "We have the evidence we need. Leo lives and we will all feast on slaycon tail tonight!"

There are growls of affirmation, and the tension passes like an odor dispersing on the breeze.

"Come!" Grandfather commands, gesturing toward the open gate. "Our camp is set. The fire will be lit. There is food and drink for one and all." He glances at Galil. "See to the prince's wound."

Galil applies a layer of ointment and bandages my leg while Mavrak secures the karkadanns to the fence. Then our party dips through the gate into Border Zone Eight.

The terrain is similar to that of Border Zone Seven. The dark green tree line ahead stands out like an upside-down saw against a purple sky. Best of all, there are no slaycons here.

"Sire," Galil says to Grandfather. "Lord Leo should stay off his injured leg to allow the ointment to do its work. It is a long walk to the camp."

Before I can object, Grandfather orders me to mount Jimo's back. In a matter of moments, I'm reduced from Leo, slayer of Storm, to a cub riding piggyback.

Using only our keen Singa eyes, we follow a worn path through the Border Zone and cross the river by a series of boulders. The camp is not far from the Great Wall. A fire burns in the center of the site. The flames make our surroundings dance with color.

Biku removes her cloak, folds it, and lays it beside a boulder by the fire. I don't understand what she's done until Jimo drops to his knees and lowers me to the place.

"Sit here, Lord."

I'm reluctant to sit on a warrior's cloak, but Biku has moved away. I settle on the fabric, and the familiar feeling begins: a rushing sound in my head, blood pulsing in my ears as a fractal of fiction rolls onto my tongue.

Terrible timing.

I bow my head and release this unwanted guest to an audience of dirt and leaves. I strain to keep my voice at a whisper to prevent the vision from expanding beyond the space between my feet.

A warrior approached a sage and asked if Alayah forgives those who cause harm to others.

The sage replied with a question of her own. "Would you throw away your cloak if it is torn or develops a hole in the fabric?"

The warrior said, "Certainly not. I would patch my cloak and continue wearing it."

The sage nodded and said, "If you are that good to your cloak, will not Alayah also take care of you when you need mending?"

I look up and wince. The elderly sage from this little story kneels before me. She is in the phantom state, faded and wispy; present, yet not fully here. Her mouth curves into a broken-toothed smile. "You have a tear in the fabric of your fur," she says, meaning my injury. "Let me help you."

Jimo squats down beside me. "Are you comfortable, Lord? Would you like some water?"

The old sage is invisible to him.

I nod, grateful for the drink and for the distraction. Jimo removes the canteen from his belt. I drink eagerly, draining the whole thing in seconds, while the sage wraps her hands around my wound and mumbles strange words. I tremble and nearly choke on the water.

Jimo smiles. "You were thirsty indeed!"

I look at the canteen, then at Jimo with remorse.

"It's nothing," he says. "I can easily refill it in the river. Rest now. Soon we will feed." Jimo backs away to join the others.

"What do you want?" I hiss at the sage.

"The question is not what I want but what do you want?"

"I want to be left alone."

"That's exactly what he told me!"

I wince. Oreyon, the hunter, has returned, faded and phantasmal, unseen to all but me.

"We can't blame him," Oreyon continues. "He's young and still catching on, yes? Give him time."

"He has had enough time to amass an army! And

today he went to the Haven. I saw him there on the beach," the sage declares.

"Perhaps now he understands why we want to go back, yes?" Oreyon adds. "This world has its points of beauty, but everything here is so heavy!"

I try to move aside. They're not talking to me anyway. Oreyon lays a hand on my shoulder. For a phantom, he's incredibly strong. "You are supposed to be resting that leg, yes?"

I wiggle out from under his grip. "No!"

Conversation among the soldiers comes to an abrupt halt, and everyone stares at me. I struggle to my feet, embarrassed.

"Stay where you are and rest, Lord Leo," Galil urges. "The meat is almost ready."

Oreyon rolls his eyes as if to say, *See what I mean?*

I'm furious. These ghosts have no right to ruin my evening and keep me here like a criminal. Even though, technically, I am one.

"Aren't you going to thank me?" Oreyon asks.

I glower at him. "For what?"

"For giving you the idea to put your leg back in the hole to trick the monster!"

"Thanks," I grunt. "Now will you please go? This is a very important night for my grandfather. And me."

"We will, dear one," the sage says tenderly, "but we will not go far, and I'll be looking after that wound of yours." She is already beginning to drift away along with Oreyon.

As the hunter fades from view, he says, "Follow the Great Firewing. Let the Firewing be your guide, yes?"

The mood around the campsite is lively and cheerful. The radiance of the fire, the easy chatter of the soldiers as they butcher the tail, the stars flickering to life warm me as much as the flames. And these soldiers, so willing to sacrifice anything and everything for our safety and comfort. This might be the happiest night of my life. Grandfather's too, knowing the throne will pass to me.

Not to Tamir.

The thought of Tamir brings a sudden chill in spite of the fire's heat. What will be his next move? How will he respond when he learns the plan to poison me failed? What has Anjali told him? Perhaps my hunt was just a prelude to another battle brewing back home.

Grandfather and Galil emerge from the tent and take a seat on either side of me. Sariah passes out plates piled with slabs of raw slaycon meat. When everyone is served, all eyes turn to me.

I know what's expected. I'm supposed to take the first bite as a sign of my victory over Storm, before everyone else digs in. Kaydan prepared me for this, too.

I poke my fork into a hunk of meat and raise it high

overhead, preparing to thrust it into my mouth. I don't feel triumphant, only grateful to be alive, grateful to Grandfather and Galil and these loyal soldiers. Instead of taking a bite, I stand, expecting an angry burst of pain from my leg.

"What are you doing, Lord?" Galil objects.

He reaches for me, but Grandfather waves him off. I hobble to Grandfather and hold the piece of meat before his muzzle. His jaws part, and I slide the hunk of meat between pointy yellowed teeth.

I make my way around the fire and do the same for Galil, Sariah, Jimo, Biku, and Mavrak. This is a complete break from tradition, but everyone is too stunned to do anything other than accept my little gift. Besides, it would be Grandfather's place to stop me.

Once everyone is served, I return to my seat and take the last piece for myself. The meat nearly melts in my mouth and glides down my throat to an aching stomach that will surely beg for more. Too bad my plate's empty now.

One by one the others rise, each taking a turn to offer me not one, but two hunks of meat from their plates. Each Singa transfers a portion of his or her plate onto mine. Soon my plate is stacked with a small mountain of meat.

Grandfather comes last. He lowers to his knees, an outrageous posture for one who wears the crown, and empties his entire plate onto mine. Precious pieces slide off the edges and flop to the dirt.

In a choked whisper he says, "You will be a great Kahn."

To love the Kahn is good,
but a Kahn who loves you is better.
— *Sayings of the Ancients*

THE FIRE BURNS LOW. Hot coals glimmer beneath charred logs, pulsing orange, then white, and back to orange. Stars sparkle, sprinkled like salt across a boundless black tablecloth.

Jimo and Sariah take turns keeping watch while Mavrak and Biku sleep. I'm nestled in the crook of Grandfather's arm under deerhide covers. In the distance, we hear a drumbeat and voices riding atop the waves of sound.

"What is that, Grandfather?"

"That," he says with disgust, "is the drum and chant of the Maguar. Pay it no attention whatsoever."

"Tell me about the Maguar," I ask, trying not to sound eager. None of the forbidden books in Galil's secret reading room say anything about our enemies. They speak of "the Ancients," but not about the Maguar, or the Singa for that matter. All we know about the

Maguar is what the elders who fought in the Great War say about them, which isn't much.

"They are a superstitious breed, heads so full of stories and fantasies about their god, they wouldn't recognize a scientific fact if it bit them on the nose!"

"Why don't we have a god?"

Grandfather becomes cross. "We don't need one! We have our superior brains, logic, reason, science, inventions, books! The Maguar lack these things, and their beliefs fill in the gaps of what they cannot explain. To believe in something, to accept something as true without evidence, is pure folly, Leo.

"Consider the sun. The Maguar believe the sun is a servant of their god, which flies around our planet every day. What nonsense! The earth is not the center of the universe. Our sun is just one of the billions of stars we behold in the night sky."

"Could the Maguar be taught?" I ask.

"You could sooner teach a slaycon how to swim!" he says with a snicker. That, of course, makes me think of Storm's head bobbing up and down in the river, struggling to keep his snout in the air, all of it a trick to lure me to his side.

"The Maguar can't be trusted with knowledge. Respect them, yes, for they are as fierce as they are primitive; however, with our weapons and intellect, we have the advantage."

The way our elders talk about the Maguar, I imagine them as huge and monstrous, tossing aside even the mightiest Singa warriors like unwanted toys.

"How many Maguar have you fought?"

Grandfather chuckles darkly. "More than I care to count!" He leans forward and pushes back his robe to expose an old wound. "You see this scar? It's from the Great War. The scoundrel would have finished me off if I hadn't clung to my blade and felled him before he could sink his teeth into my neck. All of that is in the past. The wall and the fence protect our way of life now."

I want nothing more than to see a Maguar, from a safe distance. Their drumming continues, and the rhythm soon lulls me to sleep. In my dreams, I am flying through blue sky far from this world with its slaycons, enemies, military, walls, fences, and traitors; far from my disease with its freaky apparitions. I wrap myself in clouds, soar over mountain peaks, glide up steep cliffs, and float to wherever my mind directs me.

Until I am ripped back to earth by the shrill sound of Sariah's voice.

"Sire!"

Sariah and Jimo hover over us, blades drawn.

"Forgive me for waking you and the prince, but there is something you must see."

"What is it?" the Kahn says, groaning and rising.

"Come with us to the wall," she says, rousing

Mavrak and Biku with one foot. "To arms!" she barks. "Bring your bows."

She glances my way. "Perhaps the prince should stay here with Galil."

"Do you forget that today my grandson killed a slaycon and has begun his journey to become a Singa warrior?" Grandfather asks. "He will come with us!"

Sariah hesitates. "He is wounded, and his safety may be in question. All of us could be at risk."

Grandfather does not respond, indicating his mind is set and the discussion is over.

"Then he should be armed." Sariah spins a blade and offers the handle to me. It's a long blade, and I have to use both hands to keep it from slumping to the ground.

Grandfather grins. "Lead on, Captain," he says.

The warriors, two in front and two behind, guide us into a grove of trees and through a clearing to the Great Wall itself. Only keen Singa eyes can make out where the upper edge meets the night sky.

I've been this close to the wall just once before. Grandfather took me camping in the Border Zones for my tenth birthday, including a tour of the topside of the Great Wall. There I saw huge crossbows with arrows the size of small trees. Those weapons were designed to slay not the Maguar but much larger creatures unknown to our lands. From a watchtower, we peered far into enemy territory. I searched for the slightest showing of a Maguar pelt until my eyes ached. I saw only trees and hills and sky. It was, much to my surprise, just like our side of the wall.

As we draw closer to the patchwork of stones and mortar, Sariah raises a hand, two fingers pointing at a shape lurking against the wall. An icy tingle runs up and down my spine.

Mavrak and Biku quickly sheathe their blades and notch arrows to the strings of their bows. They fan out and slink closer to the dark mass while we follow. Grandfather steps in front of me. No doubt he's regretting my tagging along.

The shape is taller than a full-grown Singa and twice as wide. It does not move with our approach, which means the thing is sleeping, dead, or waiting to attack. It's like facing Storm all over again. But this time, I've got help.

Less than two meters from the wall, it's clear the shape is actually a tunnel leading to the Maguar realm on the other side.

My eyes drink in the sight of enemy territory. I gasp and nearly cry out with surprise as the call of a firewing bird pierces my ears. It's the young firewing from the story I told Anjali, perched on the branch of a tree less than a meter from my head. He's older and larger now, but not yet full grown, invisible to all but me.

"What's the matter, Leo?" Grandfather asks.

"Nothing," I say, turning aside.

"Does your leg trouble you?"

The phantom bird spreads magnificent red wings edged with gold and drops into the air. He floats through the hole in the Great Wall and settles on the Maguar land beyond. He stares at me, cocking his head from side to side.

"*Eliyah.*" Daviyah's voice fills my mind, voices within voices. "*Do not be afraid.*" My heart swoons. Before I can stop myself, I'm charging into the tunnel, desperate to reach him.

"Leo! No!"

Grandfather's words barely register. I'm inside the hole now. The view of the Maguar's domain opens up with each step. The drums have stopped.

Two arms wrap around my waist, and I'm hauled back to Singa territory by Jimo. I don't resist. For one thing, it would be pointless. A rabbit would have more luck escaping from the grip of a bear. For another, I'm ashamed of my disobedience, and I'd rather not embarrass Grandfather further. Jimo tosses me in front of Sariah, who can't disguise her disappointment.

"Lord Leo," she hisses. "We don't know who made that hole or what might be lurking on the other side."

I peer into the hole again. The firewing is gone. Thinking fast, I say, "We should inspect both ends of the hole, don't you think, Captain? If there is more rubble on the Maguar side, we will know the hole was made by them. If there is more rubble on our side, we will know it was made by someone over here."

"That would prove nothing," Sariah counters. "Even if there is more rubble on this side, the Maguar could have moved it over here after digging the hole to confuse us. They are primitive but not stupid."

"For the love of science!" Mavrak puts in. "What Singa in their right mind would dig a tunnel through the Great Wall? The very idea is illogical and preposterous."

"Nevertheless, the prince has a point," Grandfather says. "Jimo and Mavrak, you will go to the other side and make an inspection."

Jimo and Mavrak share an uncertain glance.

"The Kahn has spoken! Move!" Sariah orders.

The two warriors collect themselves and put a blade to each hand.

"Go through single file," Grandfather advises. "If anything is waiting to attack on the other side, it would be best if it did not kill you both at once. The second, at least, will have a fighting chance."

Jimo, who is older than Mavrak, walks ahead, because that is the Singa way. The young are valued more highly than the old.

A few steps into the gaping hole, Jimo and Mavrak are little more than shadows before disappearing altogether on the other side of the wall. They give no cry of warning, and there are no sounds of battle flaring up from a Maguar ambush. Several moments drip by and we hear nothing. Then, shapes stir in the tunnel and a single figure advances. Sariah has an arrow on a string, ready to sail.

"Identify yourself or I will shoot," she commands.

I believe her.

"It's us, Sariah," says Jimo. "All is well. Or so it seems."

Sariah lowers her bow as Mavrak crosses back into Singa territory, followed by the hulking frame of Jimo.

"There is more rubble on that side than this one," Jimo reports.

"Evidence that supports our hypothesis that the tunnel was made by the Maguar, from their side to ours," says Grandfather. "And this is a strategic location, exactly between the two watchtowers of Border Zones Seven and Eight. Jimo and Mavrak, go to each of those guard towers and make a full report. Tell them, by order of the Kahn, to repair this breach immediately, guard it, and organize an inspection of the entire wall at first light. We must know if this is a single incident or part of a broader campaign."

"The question," Sariah ponders, "is why and how the Maguar would punch a hole through the Great Wall and then leave it completely exposed, unguarded, and so easy to find."

"I'm wondering the same, Captain," Grandfather

replies. "There is no scent of Maguar here. My theory is they are trying to send us a signal, letting us know we are not as protected as we might like to believe."

Sariah nods. "That much is certain. We've known the Maguar wouldn't stay quiet forever. Perhaps their make-believe god has spoken or they have invented a new fiction about the future."

My ears perk up at the mention of fiction.

Grandfather shrugs. "No sense speculating about things we do not know. That will lead us to unreasonable conclusions as quickly as any story. Fiction is a dereliction . . ."

". . . of a scientific prediction!" we all respond together.

"Exactly so," Grandfather says. "For now, I will go back to camp with the prince. Sariah, you and Biku stay here until reinforcements arrive. If anything comes through that hole, put an arrow through its hide without hesitation."

"You will leave the Border Zones as quickly as possible, then?" Sariah asks.

It was more of a recommendation than a question, and Sariah appears uncomfortable at having come so close to giving an order to the Kahn.

Grandfather only smiles. "Yes, Captain. And we thank you for your concern."

"Strength and truth, my lord."

"Now more than ever, Sariah," Grandfather says, "strength and truth."

Sariah and Biku offer a quick bow and set to work arranging their weapons. I suppose if the whole Maguar Pride came charging through that hole, these two warriors could unleash a barrage of arrows and plug up the passageway with the corpses of our enemies. If not, there is no better death for a Singa than to die protecting our realm and the throne. And anyway, the Border Zone Fence would put a stop to a Maguar invasion. Singa archers from atop the wall and on the other side of the fence would bring them down.

Unless . . . the Maguar had found a way to breach the fence, too.

I tremble at the thought of wave after wave of Maguar flooding Singara to rob us of our peace, our loved ones, and our way of life.

For a time we walk in silence, Grandfather brooding and puzzling over this new development while I hold back a burning question. Soon it is too much to keep in.

"What's going on, Grandfather?"

"I wish I knew, Leo," Grandfather says. I can almost see doubt and worry crawling around his words like worms. "The whole thing is very strange. Twenty-five years of peace and now this?"

"May I offer an idea?"

"Of course. You may always speak freely with me, Leo."

"Maybe the Maguar don't want to invade our lands. Maybe they want something else."

"That is a very charitable thought, but if you knew the Maguar, you would not give them the benefit of the doubt. They are single-minded savages who crave vengeance and victory above all. With their kind there is only one response: a lethal one.

"We will not speak of this to anyone, Leo. If word of the breached wall reached Singara, it would cause quite a stir. Best to keep it under wraps for the time being."

I nod, demonstrating skill at holding my tongue.

"Good," he says before sinking back into deep thought.

The terrain lightens with the approaching dawn. Galil is already awake as we return to camp.

"Good morning, Galil," Grandfather says. "Have you seen, heard, or scented anything unusual this morning?"

"Only the sounds of birds, the smoke of our dying fire, and the usual sights and smells of a new day." He looks over our shoulders and the smile fades from his muzzle. "Where are the others?"

"I ordered them to stay and make a routine inspection of the wall."

It is the truth, but not the whole truth.

"We will return to Singara without them," Grandfather adds.

Galil cocks his head. "We will return to Singara *without* a military escort?"

"Until we reach the first army outpost beyond the woods, yes. Gather up what you need. We leave immediately."

We apply ourselves to the tasks of packing and tidying up the camp. I shake the dust off Biku's cloak, which served as my bedding, and hang it on a stubby tree branch. We carry what we can of our provisions and leave the rest for the others.

"Allow me to inspect your leg, Master Leo," Galil requests before we begin our trek to the Border Zone Fence. He removes the bandage as though unwrapping a delicate artifact. The ointment clings to the bandage and to my fur in long, gooey tendrils. He wipes the excess away, looks closely. Sniffs.

"It is healing well, extremely well, in fact. Far better than I would have guessed after only one night."

It's true. The throbbing is gone and the wound has closed, but the horrible memory of Storm's teeth pressing into my skin and bone is as present and painful as ever.

Galil produces a pair of scissors from his satchel.

"I'm going to cut off the dead skin. This might hurt a bit."

He is right about that, but I try not to let it show. I'm supposed to be soldier material.

"That's a good lad."

"Let's move," Grandfather says, sounding ever more like the commander in chief. Yet the toll of this night shows in his bent back and labored gait. And we still have a decent march ahead of us to the fence where the carriage and karkadanns await.

For me, it is a new day, one that I had not counted on seeing. The air is soft. Everything is awash in sweet, green freshness and glazed with morning light. If not for the threat of a Maguar invasion bringing the end of the world as we know it, I might feel as bright and carefree as those sun-drenched leaves dancing overhead.

Soon the Border Zone Fence is in view, rolling out of the ground like a giant metal serpent. Ten steps later I see the carriage. The karkadanns have spotted us too, their ears erect and snouts sniffing the air. Grandfather drapes an arm around my shoulder to use me as a crutch.

"Leo," he says as we lumber on. "Tonight we will feast at the castle with the senior soldiers of the Royal Army in honor of your triumph over the slaycon."

I feel a rush of pride, knowing how much this means to him, followed by a shiver of dread because I did not triumph over Storm in true warrior fashion.

"Then you will go immediately to the Academy." He stops and scans the horizon. "These are dark, difficult times for Singara, Leo. Tamir has grown powerful, and there are many who stand with him. His supporters are everywhere. Even at the Academy."

He turns to me, locking his eyes with mine.

"I should have reined Tamir in long ago. But because he is family, because he is my brother's son, I did not. And now the realm I will hand over to you is at risk of coming apart."

Grandfather's features are weighed down with regret and fatigue. I picture him falling asleep as soon as we touch the velvet seats of the carriage. Then he brightens, enlivened by a more hopeful insight.

"What do we have to worry about?" he says, slapping me on the back and urging us toward the fence. "If you can triumph over the Keeper's most vicious slaycon, a few troublesome Singas at the Academy won't be any problem for you!"

CHAPTER 8

By crawling a cub learns to stand.
— *Sayings of the Ancients*

GRANDFATHER DOESN'T SLEEP. He's too busy thinking. He hunches forward in his seat, head in hands, his mane a wilderness of tangles and disordered strands. Morning sunlight streams through the carriage window.

"Leo, there is something you must hear," he says at last, "something I did not wish to share among the others. There are facts about the Great War not recorded in the Kahn's History that every Singa-Kahn after me should hear. These facts prove why the Great Wall and the Border Zone Fence are necessities beyond all others. Never, never forget what I am about to tell you."

I sit on the edge of my seat, ears angled forward, whiskers twitching.

Grandfather breathes somberly, summoning his strength. Whatever he is about to say, it brings him no pleasure. "In the years before the Great War there was a fragile truce between the Singa and Maguar races. There were occasional skirmishes along the border between our lands, but all in all things were peaceful enough. One day, when your mother was just a cub, as was Tamir, the Maguar attacked without warning and without cause. This was the beginning of the Great War. They bombarded us in overwhelming numbers. We held them off, but the fighting was severe, and casualties were heavy on both sides. Day after day, week after week, the Maguar pressed on with their campaign, and though I am not proud to admit it, they began pushing us back, claiming our land for themselves. The enemy was winning.

"They might have conquered us entirely if not for the terrible strangeness that followed. I despair to speak of it . . . or even to recall it."

Grandfather shifts and rubs his temples. "The battle reached the place where the Great Wall stands today, which tells you that our lands used to stretch much farther than they do now. The Maguar swept forward, determined and unrelenting. That's when we saw him, the one we call the Abomination.

"Behind the first wave of enemy warriors, a solitary warrior stood on a platform carried by four of the largest Maguar I had ever laid eyes on. He was slender of build yet fearsome to behold. His face had been painted in the fashion of a great bird, and his mane was woven with firewing feathers. More feathers were attached to his arms, which he extended upward as though he might lift into the air. With one hand, he held a brightly colored staff. He was in some sort of trance, and yet he spoke with a commanding voice."

Grandfather appears to be in a trance himself as he reveals these details. He's looking at me, but his mind is far from this carriage.

"As he spoke, a horde of beasts appeared; slaycons and draycons, giant wolves and bears, serpents as wide as this carriage, and other horrible monsters unknown to this earth. I did not stop to count, but there were hundreds of hideous creatures flinging our warriors aside and blazing a trail for Singara with thousands of Maguar in their wake. All the while, Maguar warriors chanted, *'Damar ha shem! Damar ha shem! Damar ha shem,'* over and over as they fought on with renewed vigor. That dreadful chant, whatever it means, still rings in my ears and chills me to the bone. We were overwhelmed, overpowered by this new army of creatures. It appeared that all hope of protecting our realm, and our way of life, was lost."

"The Maguar on the platform, the Abomination, was he . . . a Spinner?" I interject, hoping there's no sign of the somersaults going on in my stomach.

"He was. More powerful than any Spinner I have ever seen before or since. There are rumors, seldom spoken, that such Spinners are born to the Maguar, but rarely."

"But the Maguar did not succeed," I say. "What happened?"

"Kaydan and I were the first to conclude that the Abomination on the platform was the cause, the conjurer, of those monstrosities. I ordered all of our arrows and blades to be concentrated on him. Naturally, the Maguar and the monsters did everything they could to protect their demon of a weapon. The battlefield was awash in blood and covered with the bodies of Singas and Maguar alike, though the casualties were heavier on our side. We lost many, many fine warriors in that effort, including my own brother . . . and my sons.

"It was General Dagan, only a young captain in those days, who felled the Abomination with one well-placed arrow. With his death, all the beasts he'd conjured vanished in a flash, as if they had never existed. At that precise moment the earth shook. It was the same earthquake that created the crack in the central hall of the castle. The quake spooked the Maguar as much as the death of the Abomination and the disappearance of his monsters. They all turned tail and retreated to their lands. We gave chase, bringing down as many Maguar as we could before they reached unknown territory, and we dared pursue them no farther."

"So you ordered the construction of the Great Wall

and Border Zone Fence, not only to keep the Maguar out, but any beasts conjured up by another . . . Abomination?"

Grandfather lifts his chin. "For twenty-five years the wall and the fence have protected us from another invasion and the horrors of their sorcery. This is why we have always dealt swiftly and harshly with Spinners. Most Spinners are harmful only in their ability to pollute facts with fiction. Some Spinners, however, like that painted and feathered demon from the Great War, have the power to turn fiction into facts."

My stomach tightens. I look away, terrified he might see a glimmer of the enemy Spinner in me. If that ever happens, everything will be ruined.

. . .

We exit the shadows of the forest and roll into the light of an overcast morning. Galil stops the carriage at the army outpost, dismounts from the driver's bench, and opens the door for the Kahn and me. As Grandfather climbs out, the karkadanns stamp and paw the earth in expectation of the food and water that will soon be theirs.

The soldiers stationed here bow respectfully to Grandfather, but their attention is on the carriage. They wonder if he is alone, whether the prince has enjoyed victory over the slaycon or if he is being digested in his gut. Although the outcome of my hunt is old news to us, it has not yet reached this outpost, let alone all of Singara. Grandfather is not blind to the soldiers' curiosity.

"Leo, perhaps we should take a moment to stretch our legs before we continue the journey home."

That's my cue.

I pop into the open carriage doorway, prompting cheers and roars from the soldiers. Grandfather beams and even I permit a smile.

A captain offers his quadron as an escort back to Singara. Grandfather accepts and draws the captain away to determine the best route into the city. There's the simple matter of getting into and through a city bursting with curiosity over my fate.

And then there's Tamir.

No telling what he's been plotting in our absence.

"Will we go through the main city gate?" I ask when we're on our way, this time with Galil joining us in the carriage.

"I do not think that would be wise," Grandfather says. "The city will be in an uproar as soon as it becomes public knowledge that you have proven yourself in the hunt. We will enter discreetly, quietly, through Needle's Eye, closer to the castle."

The Needle's Eye is a crack in the city wall that surrounds Singara, made by the earthquake that ended the Great War. The opening is just large enough for one Singa to squeeze through.

"Not through the Mountain Pass?"

The Mountain Pass, an escape tunnel cut straight through several kilometers of mountain rock from the castle courtyard to the southern edge of the city, is available to only a few top-ranking warriors.

"The Mountain Pass would be the most direct route, but it's too obvious and too confined, and therefore too dangerous. Tamir would expect us to go that way. It's possible he would trap us in there and see to it that we never come out."

After the failed attempt to murder me, most likely orchestrated by Tamir and Anjali, I'm sure he's right.

"He seemed so concerned about my safety two nights ago, on the eve of my hunt."

Grandfather sours. "Fables and fantasy! He only wanted to delay your hunt to keep you from being confirmed as my heir. Listen to me, Leo. Tamir may be your elder cousin, but all you are to him is an obstacle to the throne. He's more dangerous now than ever. Fear him as much as the Maguar."

"Have you considered that Tamir may have some of his soldiers stationed near the Needle's Eye?" Galil asks.

"I have, Galil. And I have made arrangements."

Galil lowers his voice. "And have you further considered that the quadron with us right now may be loyal to Tamir as well?"

Grandfather leans forward and gestures for us to do the same. Our heads meet in the center of the carriage.

"For the time being we must assume that any soldier unknown to us could be with Tamir, even our escorts; however, I do not believe these soldiers, if they are disloyal to the throne, would do anything to reveal their treachery. Not yet. The situation is too fragile for Tamir to act boldly. We have that to our advantage."

"I think our advantages are few at the moment, dear Kahn," Galil says. "Once the Pride learns that Leo has killed his slaycon, their opinion of him will be strengthened. If Tamir wants to make a move, he would do it before we reach the castle, perhaps even before we reach the city."

Grandfather bows his head and releases a long and weary breath. I can't remember ever being at Grandfather's side and not feeling completely safe. My thoughts drift to Sariah and her quadron, some of our most trusted and skilled soldiers, now many kilometers away guarding the wall. What else could Grandfather do but leave them there, putting himself at risk to protect the whole city?

That's what Kahns do.

"Do you see what one troublesome, power-hungry Singa can reduce us to, Leo?" Grandfather explodes. "Sneaking around our realm like frightened mice! I have put up with Tamir for too long. Tonight, I will deal with him once and for all!"

No sooner is this pledge spoken than we feel the carriage veer off the main road to Singara onto a less traveled, bumpier trail to the south. Grandfather's head perks up. He looks out the little round window in the carriage door.

"This is the road to the Mountain Pass!"

"It is as we suspected," Galil says evenly.

Grandfather smacks the carriage wall to get the driver's attention. "Halt!"

Instead of slowing down, the carriage speeds up.

"Stop this carriage now!"

The carriage rolls on, towed by the now charging karkadanns. Grandfather puts one hand on the hilt of his dagger and the other on the handle of the door. He pushes, but the door holds fast.

We're locked in.

"What the devil?" Grandfather snarls, shaking the handle and throwing his full weight behind the door. He kicks it furiously, pounding again and again, like a trapped and desperate animal.

"It is no use, Sire! You know how strong and secure this carriage is. We will not get out that way. But there is another."

Galil points to the floor, and Grandfather wastes no time rolling back the carpet at our feet to uncover a little trapdoor. It's barely large enough for an average-size Singa to stick his leg through. He opens the hatch to reveal the ground streaming by.

They turn to me.

"Leo," Grandfather begins, but I know what he's

going to say. "You are the only one who can get through this hatch. Go down, climb your way to the front, and pull the pin connecting the carriage to the team of karkadanns. When you pull that pin, the karkadanns will be free of the carriage. You will have a split second to leap onto the pole between them. The karkadann team will spirit you away while the carriage slows to a stop. Get yourself to the Needle's Eye. General Kaydan will meet you there and take you back to the castle."

It's a good plan. The only problem is I have no idea how to find the crack in the city wall known as the Needle's Eye. And I have a larger concern on my mind.

"What about you and Galil? The quadron outside will—"

"We can handle these traitorous vermin," he says with a wink. Galil doesn't look so sure about that. "You must be brave, Leo," Grandfather continues. "Think and act like a Kahn. Don't bog yourself down with worries about me. Get to the Needle's Eye. Find Kaydan. He will protect you far better than I can."

I stare at Grandfather, impressing his features upon my mind in case this is the last memory I have of him. He cups my jaw with one hand.

"You are so important, Leo. Do take good care of yourself." Grandfather resumes his stony, authoritative face. "Go! Now!"

I take a deep breath and lower my feet through the hole when Galil lays a tender hand on my arm.

"The laws of gravity and motion suggest you have a better chance of survival if you go in headfirst. With your face up toward the bottom of the carriage, you can shimmy your way to the front, along the center beam. Your claws will serve you well on this little journey."

Galil, ever the scientist, sounds like he's reciting a math formula. On the other hand, his delivery concentrates my mind and sweeps fear aside. He produces a scarf from a hidden pocket of his robe.

"Wrap this around your muzzle. It will help you breathe down there."

With the scarf tied on, I slide onto my back and dip my head through the opening. At first I'm blinded by the cloud of dirt kicked up by the carriage wheels and pounding karkadann feet. To my left, through the haze, Singara comes into view, the high outer wall wrapped like a belt around the sprawling city. This carriage is bound for the mountainside, to the opening of the Mountain Pass, where Tamir will surely be waiting for us. The Needle's Eye, that sliver of an entryway in the city wall, must be close at hand.

I wiggle one arm and then the other through the hatch and dig my claws into the wood of the carriage's center beam. I extract my legs, pressing my toe claws into the underside of the carriage and wrapping my tail around me to keep it from getting shredded on the ground. I must look like an ant clinging upside down to a blade of grass.

I move forward, claw by claw, toward the pin connecting the carriage to the pole that runs between the
karkadanns. The front axle provides a better way to
hang on while yanking the pin free.

But the pin doesn't come free. It's wedged in place,
unwilling to move.

"Leo!"

I look back along the base of the carriage and find
Galil's head sticking out of the hatch. If this wasn't a
make-one-wrong-move-and-die type of situation, the
sight of his plump, upside-down face poking through
the hatch would be wildly funny.

"You must unclip the pin from the bottom!" he
bellows.

My fingers find the clip below the pin and pop it
open. The pin bounces up and down like a cub jump-
ing on his bed. Galil nods encouragingly. With a good
yank the pin slides out, and the pole connected to the
karkadanns begins to drift away. Remembering Grandfather's instructions, I pump my legs and shoot out from
under the carriage into the light of day between the
karkadanns.

The driver notices me right away and calls out to
his companions.

"The prince! The prince is escaping! Get up here
with arrows!"

The two soldiers riding on the back of the carriage
crawl forward over the roof. The carriage, separated

from the team, slows as the karkadanns continue their charging pace. The driver grips the reins and quickly finds himself drawn forward until he is teetering over the growing gap of ground.

"Whoa! Whoa!" he commands, but the karkadanns show no sign of breaking their stride. Just to be sure, I slap their rears and yell to keep them moving. With a yowl, the driver is yanked to the ground, releases the reins, and flops about like a fish out of water before becoming completely still. It's a sickening sight and a comforting one.

That's one less traitor for Grandfather and Galil to deal with.

The other soldiers watch helplessly as their prized captive is whisked away. One of them notches an arrow to the string of his bow.

I crouch down, using the karkadanns as shields, wondering if this is really happening: Singa soldiers attempting to kidnap the Singa-Kahn, the prince, and the Royal Scientist? And now they're shooting at me?

The first arrow zings harmlessly overhead. The second implants itself in the rump of one karkadann. He screeches and quickens his pace, forcing his partner to keep up.

All the better for me.

We're speeding up.

The carriage is slowing down.

The reins have been flapping about since the driver

took his nosedive into the dirt. I put one rein in each hand and attempt to guide the karkadanns off the road leading to the Mountain Pass and toward the city wall. My arms tremble with the strain of steering these beasts, which are not at all interested in a cross-country adventure.

We barrel several hundred meters into a field where a herd of goats graze under the care of a lone shepherd. The animals scatter at our approach, dodging and leaping and bleating like . . . well, like a bunch of frightened goats.

They part in two waves on either side of the shepherd. He is a tall, sinewy Singa with hunched shoulders.

That's a good sign. Elders are more likely to be loyal to the Kahn.

The shepherd is surprisingly relaxed in the face of two stampeding karkadanns. He holds out a hand as if willing them to stop, which they do, less than three meters from pounding him into the ground. The old Singa approaches and strokes the neck of one beast, as a mother might caress the cheek of her cub. Though his clothing is humble and his frame is withered with age, the shepherd's bearing is noble. Noting my royal chest plate, he bows respectfully.

"Greetings, good shepherd," I say, although I just want to fall on my knees and beg him to take me to the Needle's Eye and find Kaydan as quickly as possible.

"Good morning, Lord Prince. I am happy to know

you have triumphed in your hunt. Yet, this is an unexpected way to make your return to Singara. Where is the Kahn?"

I hop down from between the karkadanns.

"The Kahn sent me ahead. He will be along . . . shortly," I say, trying to sound unconcerned.

The goats trickle back to their master, still bleating with unease.

"May I be of some assistance to you, Sire?"

I take a deep breath, weighing my next words carefully.

"Needle's Eye," I say. "I need to get to the Needle's Eye and find Kaydan."

The shepherd tilts his head. "Kaydan?"

I may have said too much.

"Can you take me? Now?"

"I can, though perhaps it would be best to wait until nightfall, when we will be less visible? My dwelling is not far and I can tell you who—"

"There's no time. Grandfath—the Kahn is in danger. Kaydan will know what to do."

Without another word, the shepherd grabs the bridle of one karkadann and walks in the direction of the city wall.

"What about your goats?" I ask.

"They know my voice. They will follow."

The shepherd begins to sing, using words I have never heard before. The goats fall silent and glide through the grass like a cape streaming out behind their master.

When his voice fades away, I ask, "What language was that?"

"It is the Old Language."

The Old Language is just a rumor and not mentioned in the official record of the Kahn's History, but I'm not going to argue the point.

"It was a song of praise to Alayah, blessed be the name," he says, as if he doesn't know or care it is forbidden to speak that name.

"Alayah is known by many different titles," he continues. "One of them is the Lord of Lights. A closer translation into our language would be the 'Light of Lights,' which is the title of that song. It says the light of Alayah burns within every creature. We come from the light and we return to the light. A beautiful image, don't you think?"

The Light of Lights.

My mind drifts back to that beach when I died . . . or something.

"How do you know so much about the Maguar's god?"

"Alayah does not belong to the Maguar, my lord," the shepherd replies. "All living things belong to Alayah: the earth, the sky, the Singa and the Maguar, me and you."

The goats resume their bleating, and the shepherd

launches into another song. As before, they calm down in a hurry.

The city wall is fast approaching.

Where is the Needle's Eye?

All I see is the unbroken surface of the wall, built from the same mountain rock as the Great Wall. I'm about to question the judgment of this old Singa, who speaks about Alayah as easily as he talks about his goats, when he makes a quick right turn.

What was not clear as we approached the wall head-on now becomes obvious: There is a long crack stretching from the top of the wall to the bottom, just wide enough for someone to wiggle through and enter the city. I'm so relieved, I could do cartwheels.

"The Needle's Eye," the shepherd announces, blocking the way.

"Thank you," I say, hoping he will move aside.

"One question, Lord, if I may."

I wave my tail, urging him to get on with it.

"What task is more urgent: to claim the throne *or* to discover who you are?"

What's that supposed to mean?

"I know who I am. Please, let me pass."

The old shepherd bows. "Of course. I will tie up the team of karkadanns and leave them here. May Alayah light your path until we meet again."

I disappear into the wall.

The crack opens to an empty street. I'm blinking

away the dust, getting my bearings, when a muscular arm wraps around my waist and a rough hand closes over my mouth. I am yanked into an alley formed by the city wall and the back of a house. I thrash and try to scream, but it's pointless. I've got nothing on this brute.

From the shadows of the alley, a female soldier advances.

Anjali.

I double up my thrashing and muffled screaming. She tried to get me to take poison, tricking me into believing that the pellet would make me smell like the forest.

She's the last Singa I ever want to see. Second only to her boss.

"Relax, Leo," she orders. "Don't make a sound."

I keep squirming and scratching and hollering muted cries into the hand around my muzzle.

"Leo, stop struggling," says the Singa holding me in a grip of steel. "We are here to help you." The armor on this soldier's arms is maroon, the color reserved for generals. And the voice sounds an awful lot like—

"It's me, Leo. Kaydan. Would you kindly remove your teeth from my hand?"

I didn't realize I was biting him. Sure enough, there's the taste of blood, as well as flesh and fur, between my teeth. Kaydan puts me down, and I see tiny rivers of red winding around his knuckles and fingers.

"Sorry, Kaydan. I didn't know."

His eyes brim with relief. "It's good to see you, Leo. Alive and well." This tenderhearted moment is short-lived. "Where is the Kahn?" he demands.

I direct my words to Kaydan only, ignoring the silent traitor at his side, and reveal the facts as quickly as possible. As each detail emerges, Kaydan's temperature rises, until he's hissing with rage.

"Stay here with Anjali. Do *not* leave this place until I return! Do you understand?"

I nod. I'm really not used to being spoken to like that, even by Kaydan. And I don't know how to explain that Anjali is no better than the traitors he is so worked up about.

"Where is your blade?" Anjali asks.

Kaydan doesn't wait for my reply. He removes the dagger strapped to his thigh and turns the hilt to me. "Take this."

Kaydan storms out of the alley and calls for more soldiers from somewhere up the street. I watch them squeeze into the Needle's Eye, then hear the thumps and snorts of the karkadann team whisking them all away to Grandfather and Galil.

"How are you?" Anjali inquires.

I thrust Kaydan's dagger toward her face. The tip stops just shy of her nose. "Are you going to take me to Tamir now?"

Anjali appears more disturbed by the pointed question than by the blade. "What?"

"I know you stand with him."

"Are you out of your royal mind, Leo?"

"That pellet you gave me. You said it was supposed to make me smell like the forest. Remember? That was poison. You tried to kill me!"

"Poison?"

The dagger shakes in my hand. "You found out what I am and then you tried to kill me!"

"First of all, lower your voice and the dagger," she growls. "Second, I wouldn't help Tamir do anything but fall on his own blade!"

"Then why did you help him get that bundle of death to me?" I'm still yelling. I don't care.

"Don't get your tail in a knot. I got that pellet directly from Galil. Unless you think he's with Tamir, there must be some other explanation." Her tone softens. "Think for a minute. Did anything out of the ordinary happen after you left the Kahn's den yesterday morning?"

"I went back to my own den. Then I went down to the central hall and into the courtyard to Sariah and her quadron. Nothing happened!"

"Did the pellet ever leave your possession, even for a few seconds?"

"No, it was . . ." The dagger, suddenly heavy, sinks to my side.

"What is it, Leo?"

"On my way out of the castle, I was skipping over

the crack in the floor of the central hall. There was a soldier . . . I don't know his name. I bumped into him. The pellet fell on the floor, and he gave it back to me."

Anjali growls. "I'll bet my tail and whiskers *he* knocked into *you* and picked my pellet out of your pocket while dropping a different pellet, the poison one, onto the floor."

It makes sense. Unless Anjali is lying to cover her own tracks. I don't know what to believe.

"If it was poison," she considers, "why are you still alive?"

I freeze. I hadn't counted on her asking that.

Anjali's eyes expand. "Did you get your slaycon to eat the poison?"

I look away. My ears burn. My legs feel like jelly.

"You poisoned Storm with it, didn't you? Leo, that's brilliant!"

"No. You don't understand," I protest. "It was an accident."

"There are no accidents in nature, Leo. Some of science's best discoveries happen because of so-called accidents!"

"I didn't exactly triumph over Storm like a real warrior."

"A kill is a kill. Let the evidence speak for itself. You live. Storm is dead."

"No one believed I would survive. Not even me. I

guess that's why Tamir thought I would eat the poison and clear his path to the throne."

"Tamir's plan totally backfired, though, didn't it? Instead of clearing his way to the throne, he gave you the means to secure your birthright by poisoning your slaycon and—"

"That just makes Tamir more desperate and dangerous than ever," I say, cutting her off.

"Forget about Tamir. You survived the hunt. That's all that matters. You are going to the Academy, and you will be the Singa-Kahn one day!"

"What if I don't want to be the Singa-Kahn?"

I didn't mean to actually say it, but once the truth is spoken, there's no reeling it back in. Then, more truth comes spilling out of my eyes, blazing little trails of sorrow down my cheeks and muzzle. All of the pent-up stress of the past twenty-four hours pours out of me in a sloppy rainstorm of tears.

I slump to the ground, back against the wall, head in my arms.

Anjali crouches next to me, drapes an arm over my shoulders, and wraps her tail around my waist. When I pull myself together, she says, "Kaydan won't be back for a while yet. How about a you-know-what to pass the time?"

I groan. "I told you, it doesn't work like that. They just come when they want, not when I want . . . which is never."

"Why don't you just make one up, then?"

I can think of a thousand reasons not to, starting with the most obvious. "Remember what happened right after the story about the firewing birds? Do you think it was just a coincidence that a firewing appeared on my head and flew away?"

"I got it. I'm not stupid."

"It's dangerous, Anjali. I'm dangerous."

Anjali appears foolishly unafraid.

"Look," I continue, "suppose I'm forced to tell a story about a slaycon. A slaycon is bound to appear in this alley. With us. Maybe even Storm himself will come back from the dead. Would you like that?"

"Sure. It's better than sitting here with nothing to do."

I sigh and tip my head against the wall. "And I thought I was the crazy one."

We sit a while longer, watching shadows lengthen in the street.

"Why don't you have a quadron, Anjali?"

It's a random question, but one I have wondered about. A soldier as skilled as Anjali is clearly captain material.

"Right now my orders are to protect you. I'll get a quadron later. I have time. I'm in for life."

All Singas are required to spend six years in the military after two years of training at the Academy. At the age of twenty-one we are free to return to civilian life, mate, raise a family, and pursue whatever trade or craft we wish. A few, like Kaydan and Anjali, give all that up and remain soldiers their whole lives. I want to ask Anjali more, but someone is squeezing through the Needle's Eye.

Anjali springs up and draws her short blade, signaling for me to stay back. She relaxes as Kaydan ducks into the alley.

"The Kahn is well," he announces before I can ask. "And Galil. Their captors are defeated and on their way to a locked cage. Galil and the Kahn will enter the city through the main gate disguised as common Singa folk and meet us at the castle."

Kaydan pushes past us, lifts the top of a barrel, and pulls out three red military cloaks. He tosses one to each of us and keeps the third for himself. How did those get in there?

"Put this on and draw the hood over your brow."

"Anjali, you will take the forward position, followed by Leo. I will take the rear. We should have little trouble if we stay among other Singas. Tamir is still too concerned about his reputation to strike openly in public. Let's move."

Anjali turns to me with eyes that ask, *Ready?*

I give a quick nod. She whirls around and leads us into the bustling city streets.

CHAPTER 9

Walling evil out has a tendency to wall it in.
— *Sayings of the Ancients*

L EO," KAYDAN WHISPERS as we turn down the
first empty street. "I am curious to know the facts
of the past twenty-four hours, including how you killed
that devil of a slaycon. For now, tell me how you found
the Needle's Eye. It's almost impossible to see from the
other side of the city wall."

"An old shepherd guided me."

"A shepherd?"

"He seemed to know you."

"Ah," Kaydan says. "I know only one shepherd."

"Who?" I can't imagine Kaydan spends much time
with their kind.

"The captain of my quadron during the Great War
became a shepherd. He was, and probably still is, one of
the greatest warriors in Singara. He would probably be a
general alongside me if . . ." Kaydan's words trail off. I'm
not letting him stop there.

"If what?"

"If he hadn't quit the army right after the Great War. It is something of a mystery. As soon as the Great War ended and the Maguar fled in defeat, he went missing. In the chaos of battle, he was presumed dead. He appeared a day later and requested the Kahn's permission to be released from duty. The Kahn granted his wish, in gratitude for his service in the war, but with great remorse. Since then he has been a shepherd, dwelling among the Border Caves. All of this is recorded in the Kahn's History."

Referring to the Kahn's History is the official way to conclude a list of facts to assure listeners that their ears have not been polluted by fiction.

"Shanti?" I wonder aloud. I remember this collection of facts from my own study of the Kahn's History: a brave warrior named Shanti who quit the Royal Army immediately after the Great War.

"The very same," Kaydan affirms. "It was a great loss for the army. He was not only an exceptional soldier, but wiser than any Singa I have ever known."

The fur on my back lifts. Daviyah said I would meet a wise Singa. Could it be?

"I need to rest a minute, Kaydan."

"We are only a kilometer from the castle, Lord. It would be best to press onward."

"Please. Just for a moment. I feel dizzy."

"Actually, General, we're only eight hundred and seventy-two meters from the castle from this exact point," Anjali corrects, coming to my aid. "A short break won't set us back too much."

Kaydan grunts and leads us across the street to a little eatery where meat and drink can be purchased for a few coins. I have never been in a place like this. There is a polished wooden bar lined with stools near the kitchen, and six tables with chairs in the main dining area. It smells of old wood and fresh, savory meat. The eatery is empty except for an elder sitting at the back corner table and the owner of the place, who is cleaning and stacking dishes behind the bar.

Kaydan surveys the scene and judges it safe enough to enter.

"Greetings, good soldiers!" calls the owner. The elder in the corner stirs as if roused from sleep. "What can I do for you?"

"We only wish to sit and rest like this kindly elder here," Kaydan says, gesturing to the eatery's sole patron.

"These chairs are for paying customers only," the owner responds. "Even for noble military folk such as yourselves. But I can assure you we have the freshest meat, the ripest plant foods, and the best drink in all of Singara."

"Very well," Kaydan agrees. "We'll have a plate of deer livers and three pints of wheat water." Wheat water is a grainy fortified brew, engineered to give energy and strength in addition to quenching thirst.

Kaydan sniffs the air, turns to Anjali and me, and whispers, "Keep your cloaks and hoods on, heads down. Don't talk."

As we seat ourselves, a quadron of soldiers enters and finds a table across the room. Kaydan and Anjali share a troubled glance. It can't be a coincidence that these soldiers entered immediately after we did. We're being followed.

Anjali's back is to the quadron, but Kaydan studies each one. I keep my head down as instructed. "You know them?" Anjali mumbles.

Kaydan draws a little circle in front of his muzzle with one finger, to indicate he recognizes them by face.

"Friendlies?" she asks.

He shrugs. I guess it's hard to say where anyone's loyalties are these days.

At that moment, the old Singa in the back rises and walks toward us. Her steps are slow and unsteady. Kaydan's right hand snakes to the dagger strapped to his leg, the same weapon I waved in Anjali's face. Will he cut down this frail creature in her tracks?

The elder passes our table, stumbles, and plunges toward the stone floor. I lunge forward, wrapping my arms around her shoulders, and we both end up in a heap, with me serving as her landing cushion. Kaydan lifts the elder and places her in a nearby chair, never taking his eyes away from me.

"Are you all right? Are you hurt?"

I'm fine. After being bitten by a slaycon and shot at with arrows by traitorous Singas, this little tumble with somebody's grandmother was a breeze; however, my cloak has been flung open, revealing my winged chest plate. The hood has fallen away too.

"The prince!" the elder cries. "The prince lives!"

The soldiers across the room get on their feet, looking jittery. Kaydan is one step ahead of everyone, switching gears to take control. Anjali helps the elder up and urges her to make use of the door.

"Have you no respect for the throne?" Kaydan snaps at the quadron. "Bow to Lord Leo, our future Singa-Kahn!"

All four bend forward, pushed down by the force of Kaydan's order if not by sincere loyalty. That's enough to lift Kaydan's suspicions even higher. His nostrils flare. His tail sways over the floor. I know that look. And I'm glad I'm not them. Anjali positions herself in front of me at Kaydan's side.

"In the name of the Kahn, lay down your weapons." He says it so slowly, each word could be a sentence unto itself. Peeking through the narrow space between my protectors, I look upon the quadron for the first time. The sight of the captain makes me gasp. He's the one I bumped into before leaving the castle, the one who exchanged Anjali's pellet for the poison. The fur on my back sticks up for the second time in only a few minutes. And I'm ashamed for suspecting Anjali of high treason.

"Get behind the bar, Lord," Anjali says without turning around.

I race behind the bar and peer to the side to see what's coming.

Anjali's arms are relaxed, which means she's preparing to draw a blade or two in the blink of an eye. Two against four would be bad odds in most cases, but Kaydan is well known for defeating quadrons all by himself in training exercises.

And he has Anjali.

For a moment nothing moves. Even the dust seems to hang suspended in the air. The owner of this eatery squats behind the bar next to me, no doubt worried about a battle reducing his business to a pile of bloody rubble.

"As you wish, General," the captain says at last. "We mean you and the prince no harm. I am happy to see that he lives and—"

"Shut your talk hole, put your blades on the floor, and move to the back wall," Kaydan demands.

"Do it now!" Anjali growls. "Slowly."

Asking warriors to give up their weapons is like asking them to rip out their claws or cut off their tail. But Kaydan leaves no room for discussion. The captain reluctantly unsheathes his long blade and lays it on the floor, followed by his short one and the dagger. His companions follow suit. Anjali advances, drawing her long blade to cover them.

"And your aero-blades," Kaydan says. "Do you take me for a fool?"

The aero-blade is a ringlike weapon that warriors wear on their back. They are designed to be thrown short or long distances with great speed and deadly results. The four soldiers unhook their aero-blades.

This is the most delicate moment of all.

With a flick of their wrists, four aero-blades could fly in our direction. Kaydan could block one or two with his blade, but four? I guess that's why Anjali looms over them with her long blade, ready to chop any hands and arms moving in the wrong way.

I release a breath I didn't know I was holding as the rings of metal clang on the floor.

"Tell me your names, Captain," Kaydan growls.

"I am Mandar," the captain says with a hasty bow. "This is Holu, Jatari, and Nora. And we are loyal Singas."

"I will remember your names," Kaydan says, "and if you are loyal, you have nothing to fear. Now move back."

The quadron shuffles to the far corner of the room.

"Kind sir!" Kaydan calls to the owner of this eatery. "I trust you remember how to handle a blade from your days of soldiering."

"It has been many, many years, General," he says.

"Not to worry. Gather up their weapons and lock them in your kitchen, except one, which you will put in your own hand to prevent these four from leaving over the next hour. Then, and only then, will you let them go free. Under no circumstances are you to return their blades. Is that clear?"

"It is, Master Kaydan," the owner says, making his way around the bar to the heap of discarded metal. He scoops it all up and delivers it to the kitchen. He returns with a long blade in one hand and a plate of food in the other. "And . . . would you like to take your order of deer livers with you?"

Kaydan's only answer is to head for the door. Anjali waves her tail for me to follow. Out in the street I ask Kaydan how he knew that quadron was loyal to Tamir.

"I didn't know," he says. "But I don't take chances. Your safety is all that matters."

Kaydan sets a swift pace for the remainder of our journey to the castle. Anjali strides alongside me.

"Anjali . . . that captain . . . Mandar . . . he was the one I bumped into, the one who gave me the poison pellet."

Her eyes narrow. "So Kaydan's instincts were right. Always are."

"Should we tell him?" I ask.

"If we do that, you'll have to tell him everything about the pellet."

Forget it. As much as I dislike secrets, I don't want Kaydan to know Storm died after swallowing poison meant for me. Mandar would be locked away in a prison cage where he belongs, but I might end up repeating the hunt.

Upon arriving at the castle, Anjali and Kaydan deliver me to the bath for a good wash and then to my den, instructing me not to open the door for anyone except them or the Kahn himself. The door is hefty and the bolt is strong. Just to be sure, Kaydan assigns Anjali to keep watch while he consults with the Kahn.

Grandfather said he would deal with Tamir's treachery tonight. And that was before our quadron escort attempted to kidnap us.

Grandfather will have to move swiftly and carefully. Tamir has many followers, perhaps more than we imagine. Dealing with him too harshly could drive a deeper wedge into an already divided realm.

I'll get my answer soon enough. Right now, all I want to do is fall into bed, bury myself in the sheets, and sleep for the rest of the week.

CHAPTER 10

It is a double grief when a firewing bird is killed by an
arrow feathered from its own wings.

— *Sayings of the Ancients*

I DREAM OF THE GREAT WAR, twenty-five years
ago.

Or, more accurately, the moments right after
the war.

The ground rumbles from the aftershock of the
earthquake. Singa soldiers give chase to retreating
Maguar warriors. Behind me, a much younger version
of Grandfather weeps over the body of a fallen soldier.
The soldier's armor bears the royal sign of outstretched
wings, which means he is one of the Kahn's sons, one of
my mother's elder brothers.

With the enemy on the run, the battlefield is
quickly vacated, revealing a plain littered with the broken and bloodied bodies of Singas and Maguar alike.
Besides Grandfather, only one Singa soldier remains
behind. He moves toward a platform covered in feathers and surrounded by the corpses of several massive

Maguar. I follow, curious to know what beckons the soldier, my feet sliding a bit in the blood-slick grass.

Then I hear it: the frightened whimper of a cub. I bound closer as the soldier lifts the platform and discovers a little Maguar underneath. He is dirty and blood-smeared and no more than seven or eight years old. The soldier is astonished. He sheathes his blades and kneels before the little enemy.

"What is one so young doing on the field of battle?" The youngling is terrified. "It's all right. Don't be afraid. I won't hurt you."

"*Abba!*" the cub cries.

"I am not your *abba*. I am Shanti."

The cub holds a fistful of bright firewing feathers. "*Abba!*"

"The feathered one, the Spinner, was your father?"

The cub sobs, "*Abba, Abba, Abba . . .*"

Abba, his father, is nowhere to be found. His slain body must have been collected by the retreating Maguar, who forgot the Abomination's young son trapped under the platform.

But why is he here at all? Why take such a delicate young creature into the crush of war?

Shanti wraps the quivering cub in his cloak and carries him away, fading into the morning mist.

• • •

I'm pulled out of the dream by a fist pounding on my door.

"Lord Leo." It's Anjali. I'd know her voice anywhere, even half asleep through a door ten centimeters thick. "The Kahn requests that you join him and all the senior warriors in the feeding hall. I will escort you."

"Just a minute," I say, rubbing sleep from my eyes, stretching this way and that. The images of the dream are still fresh in my mind, as fresh and vivid as any fiction that might have invaded.

I check myself in the mirror, sorry to find that a few hours cocooned in silk bedding has not transformed me into a fierce-looking warrior. I'm still the same scrawny piece of fur on a bony frame that I was yesterday.

I unbolt the door and find Anjali standing perfectly still like some life-size hall decoration.

Seeing her makes me feel both safe and insecure. She proved her loyalty in her willingness to fight and die to protect me, but she also knows what I am. What if she can't keep my secret and lets it slip that the prince is a diseased Spinner?

I slide past her and head down the hall.

"Did you sleep?" Anjali asks, falling in behind me.

"How long was I in there?"

"Three hours, seventeen minutes. Or eleven thousand eight hundred and twenty seconds."

"Do you count everything, Anjali?"

"Can't help it. My brain never shuts off. Makes me the perfect Singa, don't you think?"

Light is dimming throughout the castle, activating our night vision. The interior of the castle shifts into shades of gray, but everything remains clear. We bound and jump our way down the leaping platforms to the central hall.

General Kaydan chats with General Dagan by the entrance to the feeding hall while dozens of senior soldiers file in. The fireplace hosts a bright blaze. The candelabras are lit. Both bring color back into my eyes.

"Good evening, Lord Prince," General Dagan says, bowing gracefully. Dagan killed more Maguar in the Great War than any other Singa, including the Abomination. Countless kill marks are etched into her aged blade scabbards. Her face itself is a carving of sharp edges, hard lines, and battle scars. "And congratulations on a successful hunt. You have done Singara a great service by killing Storm."

"Thank you, General."

"Kaydan will be your guard now," Anjali says dolefully. "Senior warriors only at this dinner."

She'll hear all about it soon enough. Whatever happens tonight will be the talk of Singara for a long time to come.

Grandfather sits with two of his four generals at the high table overlooking the hall. To his left are three empty chairs for Kaydan, Dagan, and me.

I cross the length of the hall and ascend the four steps to the high table. Kaydan and Dagan remain on the floor. I keep my eyes on Grandfather, searching his face for clues about what he might say or do tonight, but his expression is locked up like a strongbox. With each step the room quiets, until my final footfall is so noticeable, it might be echoing off the far wall.

Grandfather turns his large and stately head and winks at me. His mane is groomed and he's dressed in his finest robes. He is every centimeter the Singa-Kahn.

Once I'm seated, the swell of conversation rises, washing the strained silence away. Kaydan takes his place next to me. Flanked by these two great Singas, I feel secure as well as fragile, like a dandelion between two mountains.

I search the room for Tamir and can't locate him anywhere. Maybe that's what everyone is talking about: the obvious absence of Tamir.

The Kahn rises and roars. Hundreds of commanders and legionnaires respond with a collective, room-rattling roar before settling onto rows of benches at the tables.

"Welcome, senior soldiers of Singara," Grandfather calls. "As you all know, Leo, my grandson and heir to the throne, has proven his worth in the hunt. Tomorrow he will begin his training at the Academy, and when he has graduated he will be ready to rule as the Singa-Kahn. Tonight we feast in his honor and drink to a prosperous and united Singara! Let all loyal Singas rise and recite the Singa creed."

When everyone is on their feet, the Kahn places two fingers on his temple and everyone in the room does likewise. I cringe at the words that are about to come. "We are the present and future glory of Singara," he begins.

"We are the crown of creation, the most evolved and advanced species on earth." Every voice joins in. "We believe only in reason, evidence, and the way of science. We will protect and defend our race against all threats, be they enemies of flesh and blood, dangerous ideas, or fictions of any kind. Therefore, Spinners are as much a threat to our way of life as the Maguar. We pledge to report all Spinners at once, even if they are family; even if, nature forbid, I am one of them."

I exhale, grateful this ritual has passed.

Grandfather claps his hands, and servants enter bearing trays of raw meat, fruit, vegetables, and drinks for the hungry masses. The room erupts with applause and the thunder of fists banging on tabletops. Before the cacophony dies down, the main doors open, and Tamir storms into the hall with a few soldiers in tow. Silence descends as though a wind has swept through the room and sucked out all the sound.

"Greetings, nephew," Grandfather says. "I see you have decided to join us after all."

Tamir bows. "It is an honor, dear Kahn. And congratulations to you, Prince Leo."

Grandfather looks flustered. Whatever he plans to do or say to his mutinous nephew, Tamir isn't going to make it easy for him.

"Please be seated. You and your . . . followers."

Tamir bows again, but not before a shadow of anger passes over his face.

"Feed! Be filled!" Grandfather says. "May this meal strengthen you and Singara!"

I select hunks of meat from different animals and pile them onto my plate. I surround them with helpings of plant foods. For a time, there is little to hear beyond lips smacking, teeth tearing and chewing.

Grandfather bellows, "Who will be the first to raise their mug and offer a toast to the prince and future Kahn?"

"I will," Kaydan says, rising and lifting his mug. "Lord Leo, you have killed one of the most vicious slaycons in all of Singa history, against whom so many others have failed. By your hand, Storm is dead. Or should I say, the storm has passed?"

That yields some laughter. It's rare for Kaydan to use humor. I'm sure it's a calculated move to lighten the atmosphere. He doesn't twitch a finger or move an eyebrow without some strategy behind it.

"The Kahn has feasted on Storm's tail, and the slaycon's body now rots in Border Zone Seven. His death,

Lord Leo, means Singara will be in strong hands when you receive the throne of your grandfather. Let us drink to the prince and to the future of Singara!"

Approving snarls ripple around the room as hundreds of mugs tip to the ceiling. Other toasts follow. The string of speeches begins to feel like a loyalty contest, each senior soldier trotting out bigger, grander expressions of praise to outdo the last.

It goes on for a long time.

Tamir is the last warrior to speak. "Lord Leo, son of my cousin, your mother, had she lived to see this day, would be radiant with pride at your accomplishment. As for your father, whoever he is, wherever he is, he would certainly be proud of you as well. For all we know, he's in this room right now!"

Grandfather growls.

"Do not be alarmed, Uncle," Tamir says. "I mention Leo's unfortunate family background to allow his victory to shine all the brighter. A diamond is more noticeable on a pile of dung than in a box of jewels, is it not?"

Tamir refocuses his attention on me, and I feel more like dung than diamond.

"Cousin, no one expected you to survive your hunt, especially against an opponent like Storm. You have defied all of our predictions and perhaps even science itself. I'm sure one day you will share the facts of your hunt for our official record. For now, we can add your victory to the long list of mysteries that grow up around you like weeds."

"Are you going to toast to the prince or not?" Grandfather snaps.

"So allow me to join my comrades," Tamir continues, "in commending you on your kill. I wish you well at the Academy, where you will meet my eldest child, who is a second-year cadet. I'm sure you two will be fast friends, in addition to being blood kin."

It's been a few years, but I've met Tamir's daughter, Amara, several times. She's about as warm, caring, and congenial as her father.

"And so, young cousin, though you will be gone from our sight, you will not be far from our hearts. We eagerly await your return in two years' time because, as the Kahn has said, then and only then will you be ready to rule in his place. Let us drink one last time to the prince!"

There are grunts and growls of support around the clunking of mugs, which I can barely hear over my own heartbeat.

When I lower my mug, Grandfather is on his feet.

"Nephew!" he shouts. There is a flash of something old and dark and terrible in Grandfather's eyes. The room plummets into silence again.

"Sit down!"

Tamir scowls and parks himself on the nearest bench.

"Tamir is my brother's son," Grandfather says after a thoughtful pause, as though this is new information. "My brother who so wanted to be the Singa-Kahn, who felt he would be a better, stronger ruler. Although he was the firstborn, our father passed the throne on to me. My brother never got over it. He was headstrong and ambitious and a fine warrior, but because he was bent on glory and anxious to prove himself more worthy of the throne than I, he got himself killed in the Great War, although you can be sure he wanted that fate for me.

"And, alas, he left behind a son who inherited all of his blind thirst for power: Tamir."

I wish I could say the room has gone from respectfully quiet to deadly still because of Grandfather's ability to screw Tamir to the wall with words. But the real trouble is this: Everything Grandfather said about his brother is not recorded in the Kahn's History, which puts Grandfather dangerously close to spewing fiction.

Several soldiers reveal their loyalty to Tamir with poorly stifled grins. Tamir makes no effort to conceal his delight. His face is a picture of triumph. He has only to say what we are all thinking to cast doubt on Grandfather.

"Uncle, I don't recall reading that in our official record of history. Was it added recently?"

Grandfather sighs. "Tamir, what is the first oath of every Singa warrior?"

Tamir does not answer.

"Fellow warriors of Singara," Grandfather chides. "Suddenly, Tamir has nothing to say!" Laughter echoes through the hall. "Surely, Tamir, you know what oath you have sworn above all others? Has it been so long since you learned it?"

"Everyone here knows that well enough, Sire," Tamir replies coolly. "Why treat us like cubs?"

"I agree, even cubs know the first oath," Grandfather says. "My question is, do you?"

Tamir grimaces. "A warrior's first oath is to protect the Singa-Kahn, the Pride, and our land, even at the cost of his or her own life."

"Have you done that, Tamir? Would you protect me at the cost of your own life?"

Again, Tamir does not respond.

"Do you think anyone in this room is ignorant of your scheming? Do you think anyone here would be surprised to learn that you have attempted high treason on this very day?"

"High treason?" Tamir says, sounding genuinely astonished. "Fables and fantasy! What evidence do you have for this charge?"

"I have three traitorous soldiers in prison right now, ready to confess that you ordered them to kidnap Galil, the prince, and me on our way back from the Border

Zone. You instructed them to bring us to you for execution in the Mountain Pass."

"This is outrageous!" Tamir thunders. "Are we to accept the words of three soldiers held at blade point simply to tarnish my character and reputation?"

"I do not need the help of any Singa to call your character and loyalty into question," Grandfather says evenly. "But let this gathering note that Tamir has not denied the charge of high treason. He has only challenged the testimony of his followers."

Murmurs of support sound from many, but not all, around the hall. Still, the Kahn is gaining the advantage. While Tamir casts about for something to say, Grandfather delivers a crushing blow.

"Do you deny it, Tamir? Or would you like to offer a *story* of your own instead?"

With that, Tamir is backed into a corner. Saying anything other than admitting his guilt would be telling a fiction. Naturally, he changes the subject.

"You dare to suggest I am ignorant of the first oath, but what about you, Uncle? You sit here feasting and toasting to your weakling grandson while there is a breach in the Great Wall that puts our whole realm at risk! Right now the Maguar could be crossing into our lands, and you are doing nothing about it! It is you, and not I, who is guilty of breaking the first oath!"

Instantly, the room erupts into chaos. Warriors hiss and slash the air with their claws. There are shouts and roars and calls to arms. No one knows what to believe or what to do. Only an onslaught of Maguar warriors bursting through the doors and windows could make the hall more frenzied than it is right now.

It could happen. I've been so focused on saving my own pelt, I forgot about the hole in the wall and the threat it poses to Singara. Even Kaydan's pelt trembles with anxiety.

Grandfather alone is relaxed. He takes a long drink from his mug, releases his mightiest roar, and hurls the mug across the room into the fireplace, where it cracks and splinters in a spray of sparks.

"Silence!" he howls. "In the name of all that is good and right and true, be quiet and compose yourselves! Are we a room full of cubs frightened by our own shadows, chasing our own tails? Or are we levelheaded warriors guided by logic and reason?"

"Is there a breach?" inquires a commander from the far side of the hall.

Grandfather straightens his back. "That is a fact; however, it is contained and secured, and there is no evidence of Maguar activity inside."

"And why did you not make this known sooner, Uncle?" Tamir asks, a smile playing at the corners of his mouth. "Surely such news is worth sharing with your senior soldiers at least. Or is your memory slipping in your old age?"

"There is nothing wrong with my memory, Tamir.

I have been too focused on the threat growing inside Singara to be concerned about a little hole in the wall. In fact, my memory tells me I have put up with your schemes for far too long." Grandfather narrows his eyes. "You are dismissed, Tamir. More than that, you are hereby relieved from serving in the Royal Army. Be grateful your punishment is not more severe."

The air crackles with tension. Tamir prepares to say something, but Grandfather closes the door on that possibility.

"And if anyone in this room is loyal to Tamir, and not to me or to the prince, why not stand with Tamir now?" he challenges. "Make your allegiance known before one and all."

Every Singa stays rooted to his or her place. Kaydan searches the assembly for signs of wavering or fidgeting that might give more traitors away.

"You see, Tamir, you stand alone. You will now remove your weapons and leave this hall. Alone."

"I will go, Uncle," Tamir says through gritted teeth while unstrapping the short blade and aero-blade from his back. "And let it be known that you have dismissed the most loyal servant of Singara!"

He throws both blades to the floor and unbuckles the long blade at his side.

"'Strength and truth! Strength and truth!' Isn't that what you always say?" Tamir sneers. "Yet there is no strength in living like cowards, hiding behind our pathetic wall. We beat the Maguar in the Great War, but you didn't allow us to finish the job. And here you condemn us to live like penned-up vermin inside your fence, with our rusting weapons and crumbling armor! *That* is the truth!"

The long blade joins the other weapons on the floor, and Tamir unfastens his dagger.

"All of that metal from the mines of the Great Mountain wasted on your fence, metal that could have been used for new and improved blades and armor, as well as for new and better weapons I was creating, more powerful than any blade and faster than any arrow. Weapons that could exterminate the Maguar once and for all!" The dagger clangs to the floor and Tamir is defenseless. Somehow he manages to keep his claws withdrawn despite his mounting rage.

"Stop!" Grandfather commands. "Shut your mouth this instant before I rip the jaw out of your rebellious head!"

"But you put an end to my research and experiments!" Tamir says, pushing forward with his case. "And because of that, you threw away the key to our future prosperity. I am the son of a once-great Pride, but you prefer to have us live like cowards on our little corner of the planet, when we could be running free across the endless lands held by our enemies."

"Dagan, Kaydan! Destroy this piece of filth!"

Tamir's eyes shift to Dagan.

"With pleasure," Kaydan says, launching himself over the high table and pouncing to the floor. Four other warriors close in while Tamir carries on with his rant.

"We won the war and lost the world! Because . . . *you . . . are . . . weak!*"

Kaydan hisses and thumps Tamir on the side of the head, raking his face with extended claws. Tamir makes no effort to defend himself, and the blow sends him staggering to his knees.

"You are weak, Uncle, but you are a tower of strength compared with your runt of a grandson."

Kaydan hits him again with such force, I want to look away.

Another blow follows.

And another.

Within seconds, Tamir is sprawled out on the stone floor, unconscious. Kaydan draws the short blade from his back and twirls the weapon in his hand so the tip is angled downward, preparing to drive it into Tamir.

"No!" I shriek. "Stop!" Kaydan hesitates and turns to the Kahn.

Grandfather looks at me, then at Kaydan. "Untail him," he says coldly.

A soldier lifts the end of Tamir's tail and pulls it tight. Kaydan's blade flashes and slices through the flesh connecting Tamir's tail to his backside. Though unconscious, Tamir yowls with pain.

"Get him out of here," Grandfather says, collapsing

into his chair. "Lock him up." Four warriors lift Tamir and carry him out of the hall.

As for me, my mind is whirling as though I've been hit by Kaydan's blows along with Tamir. My head tips up, and my vision is reduced to a shrinking circle of ceiling as if I am sinking into a thick and inescapable swamp.

"Leo!" Grandfather cries.

It's the last thing I hear.

CHAPTER 11

A wise leo will always find a way
even when there is nowhere to go.
— *Sayings of the Ancients*

LIKE TAMIR, but for different reasons, I too am carried out of the feeding hall. I spend the rest of the night in bed, writhing in a semiconscious, dreamlike state. With my defenses down, a fiction tumbles out and plays itself over and over:

There was a Kahn who had one son and one daughter. The Kahn urged both children to learn to read and study as much as they could to gain wisdom. But the boy ignored his father's advice. When he was grown, the prince saw the error of his ways. He decided to travel outside their realm to find the wisdom he lacked. Without sharing his plans with anyone, he took a bag holding his savings of gold coins and set off on his quest.

After traveling a long time, he saw a shepherd in a field and asked if there were any wise folk in the area.

"Why do you seek wise folk?" asked the shepherd.

The prince reported that he was on a quest for wisdom. The shepherd offered to give the prince a bit of wisdom for every gold coin he paid him.

The prince agreed. The shepherd said, "My first piece of wisdom is this: You are the son of the Kahn; whenever you are outside the castle and someone offers you a chair, do not sit down right away. Move the chair a little to one side; this is my first piece of wisdom for you. Please pay me with one gold coin."

The prince handed over one gold coin.

The shepherd said, "Here is the second piece of wisdom: The son of the Kahn should never bathe at the common bathing place, but in a private place by himself. Another gold coin, please." Again the prince paid him.

The shepherd said, "Here is my third gift of wisdom: The son of the Kahn must learn to restrain his anger. If anything makes you angry, take a deep breath and do not take action too quickly or you will make a terrible mistake." The shepherd held out his hand for another gold coin.

The prince handed over the coin, sorry to see his money disappearing so quickly.

The prince decided to return to his home, feeling bad for having spent his gold on useless advice. On his way there, he stopped at a marketplace and entered a shop. The shopkeeper invited him to sit on a chair positioned on a rug. The prince was grateful for the chance to rest and was just about to settle into the chair when he remembered the shepherd's words. He moved the chair and pulled the rug to one side and saw that it had been spread over the mouth of a deep cage built below the floor. If he had sat there, he would have been trapped and at the shopkeeper's mercy.

As he continued his journey, he saw a bathhouse and thought how good it would be to bathe before returning home. Remembering the advice of the shepherd, he avoided the common bathhouse and went to a private place along the river. After bathing, he resumed his journey. Soon he realized he had left his bag of coins beside the river. He returned to the spot and found them untouched. He again applauded the wisdom of the shepherd. If he had gone into the public bathhouse, surely someone would have seen the bag and stolen it.

Finally, he arrived home, reaching the palace late at night. He went to his lair without waking anyone. Beside the door he saw a cloak, a long blade, and pieces of body armor. The sight enraged the prince. He took the blade in one hand and pounded on the door with the other. "Who is in the lair of the prince?"

It was the prince's own sister sleeping in his

lair because she missed her brother so much. His sister was half asleep and did not recognize the voice of her brother. She opened the door and found him ready to strike her down.

"Wait!" she cried. "Let me step into the light and then, if you wish, you may strike me down."

Remembering the shepherd's words about restraining anger, the prince agreed. When he saw it was his own beloved sister, he wept with gratitude because he had nearly killed her.

I awake with a jolt and a throbbing at the back of my head. A figure dressed in a scientist's robe sits next to me, his familiar scent tickling my mouth and nostrils.

"Galil?"

"Do not move too suddenly, Lord."

"How long have you been here?" I ask, wondering if he heard the story and saw the words spin into a vision.

"Only a few minutes."

"What happened?"

"You fainted."

I fainted in front of the senior soldiers just after Tamir's tirade about my weakness? I guess I did have the last word after all, and it turned out to be living proof of his point. I touch the back of my head and feel a tender little robin's egg poking through my fur.

"You will be fine, Leo. I'm less interested in the bump on your head than the slaycon bite on your leg."

I forgot about that.

"It has completely healed," Galil says with a raised eyebrow.

I guess that's why it slipped my mind.

"There is not a scratch on you. How do you explain that?"

I shrug.

"I would like to study your condition further, but there is no time. You need to get to the Academy."

The Academy? "Is it tomorrow?"

Galil laughs. "It is always today, Lord Leo. Tomorrow is nothing but a fiction we permit to tell ourselves about the future. But yes, it is the day after yesterday, when you took your tumble at dinner."

I sit up, wincing and woozy.

"Slowly, Leo. Slowly."

"Where is Grandfather?"

"The Kahn is meeting with the generals, except for General Kaydan. He is waiting for you at the castle gate to escort you to the Academy."

"Is there a crowd? Outside?"

"No. The whole city is too disturbed by fears of a Maguar invasion. There is also much talk about how you saved Tamir, but not his tail, from Kaydan's blade. At any rate, the streets are nearly empty. Even so, Kaydan will take you through the Mountain Pass."

Fear blazes up within me.

"It's all right, Leo. Tamir is no longer a threat. Your way to the Academy and to the throne is secure. Just to be sure, Kaydan has ordered a search of the pass. And he has a company of soldiers waiting on the other end."

Relieved, I swing my legs over the side of the bed, hop to my closet, and grab my backpack. I toss it on the bed, where an impression of my body is still visible on the sheets. My eyes sweep to the mirror mounted on the wall. Instead of my own reflection, I see the prince from the story, the one who learned wisdom from the shepherd. He's holding something out to me. Gold coins. He tips his hand, and the coins clang and ping their way to the floor on his side of the mirror.

I shudder and turn away, only to find the same ghostly prince sitting on my bed next to Galil, who is unaware of his presence.

"There is no need to pack," Galil says. "You are not allowed to bring anything into the Academy except yourself. You will enter wearing nothing but your own fur and exit when you are a warrior."

Nothing but my own fur?

I stare blankly, wondering if I heard that right.

"At the Academy, everyone is treated equally, hence the start in your natural state. Even though you are the future Singa-Kahn, you will not be treated that way. Always bear in mind who you are, even if no one else does. Going to the Academy is your chance to learn the Science of War, but it is also an opportunity to show you are fit to rule, to gain the loyalty and confidence of others."

The story prince stands. "This is wisdom. Listen to him."

I have a feeling Galil wants to say something else, something more than just a few pointers about the Academy. If there's one thing I've learned in the past few days, it's how much we say by saying very little. What was it that Tamir said last night? That mysteries sprout up around me like weeds? It was only one phrase in a flurry of verbal arrows flying between Grandfather and Tamir, but the same could be said of our world.

I wonder if and when I will learn the whole truth.

I bid farewell to the healer and bound down the leaping platforms to the central hallway. As I hit the floor, the wisdom-seeking prince from my last story appears again. Startled, I lose my balance and tumble to the polished floor tiles.

"My name is Kensho," he says. "I am ready to serve you."

"I don't need anything from you," I grumble.

He holds out a faded hand. "May I help you up?"

I wave him off and climb to my feet.

"Speak my name if you ever need advice or guidance."

"Here is some advice for you," I say, rubbing my backside. "Don't scare me like that again!"

He bows and vanishes.

Outside, the air is crisp and cool. There are more soldiers than usual bustling about the castle courtyard. They sharpen blades, engage in fighting drills, and carry supplies to the top of the castle wall, where a good number of archers are stationed. The news of a breach in the Great Wall and fears about a Maguar attack have raised everyone's anxieties.

Kaydan waits at the north side of the courtyard in full military dress, complete with his familiar weapons, aging battle armor, and cape. If I didn't know better, I'd think he was marching off to war instead of delivering me to the door of the Academy.

I'm just glad he's on my side.

"Good day, Lord Prince."

I smile up at him while my eyes dart around the courtyard, taking in all the activity. I was already on edge about leaving Grandfather and the safety of the castle. The ramped-up military presence isn't doing anything to calm my nerves.

"You have no reason to worry, Leo," he says. "Getting to the entrance of the Academy is the easy part. Come, we have a decent hike ahead of us through the Mountain Pass. After that, I have two karkadanns and a company of soldiers waiting to escort us the rest of the way."

Kaydan crosses the courtyard to a metal door where the castle wall meets the mountain rock. He produces a key from his belt and fits it into the lock. After a few turns and clicks, the door opens and slides out of sight. Kaydan steps into the gloomy interior and I follow. He yanks the door back into place with a definitive clack. The darkness is deep, even for Singa night vision. Kaydan is little more than a shadow before me. He removes a torch from his satchel and lights it. The little fire illuminates the passageway and Kaydan in a bright sphere of color. I estimate the tunnel to be two meters wide and three high, seemingly endless beyond the reach of the torch light.

"It's two kilometers to the end," Kaydan says. "Shall we begin?"

He turns and heads down the corridor with long, confident strides.

We walk in silence. The only sounds are our footfalls, our breath, and the occasional trickle of water tumbling down the rock walls, gathering in puddles on the floor.

"You must have some questions about last night," Kaydan says after a time, his voice bouncing around the tunnel.

"All that Grandfather said about his older brother wanting to be the Singa-Kahn — is that true?"

"If your grandfather said it, I accept it as truth."

"And what Tamir said about winning the war against the Maguar but losing the world?"

"The ravings and ravages of a power-hungry mind,"

Kaydan replies with despair. "Tamir thinks the Great War should have ended only with the death of every last Maguar, even their cubs. He still believes we ought to attack and exterminate them before they have the chance to do the same to us. It shows how little he knows about the Maguar . . . and their devilry."

"You mean it's impossible to wipe them out?"

"It might be possible, but it is not prudent. We would lose many, many warriors, and for what? We have all we need on our lands. We live peacefully and prosperously."

"If we are so peaceful and prosperous, why do we need such a strong army?"

"Because, Leo, prosperity depends upon ferocity. We must remain vigilant to protect our way of life against all threats from beyond the Great Wall. And within it."

"Do you think Tamir made the hole in the wall?"

"That is my hypothesis. How else would he know about it? And don't you find it striking that the hole was made in Zone Eight, where you and the Kahn rested only two nights ago? That can't be a coincidence. Thankfully, you were unharmed, but it gave him a reason to press for a new war against the enemy."

"What did Tamir mean by new weapons?"

Kaydan sighs. "As you know, your elder cousin is not only a fine warrior, but also a brilliant scientist. He was working on new weapons against which the Maguar would have no defense. Or so he said."

"What kind of weapons?"

"I have seen them only once. A metal tube shoots a metal ball at an opponent—so fast, it is invisible to the eye. He has developed two models: one that fires a ball the size of a cauldron, but more accurately than a catapult, and a smaller one that can be carried by a soldier."

"How is the ball launched?"

"It requires an exploding powder found in the deepest part of the Great Mountain. It is an unstable substance, and Tamir has not found a way to control it. Besides that challenge, the construction of these weapons will require a lot of metal. Since we have so little metal to work with, Tamir wants to take down the Border Zone Fence and reuse it for his purposes."

"But without the fence we are less protected and more vulnerable."

"That is why your grandfather opposed the idea. With Tamir disgraced and imprisoned, that will be the end of it."

I can tell our little question-and-answer session has ended as well. Kaydan is about as fond of lengthy conversations as I am. I still have one more thing on my mind, and it takes a few minutes to get my mouth to spit out the words.

"Kaydan . . . you knew my mother, didn't you?"

Kaydan halts and I ram into his back, taking in a

mouthful of his cloak. Treelike Kaydan hardly seems to notice.

"I knew her very well. Mira was was as strong and ferocious as any warrior. And she inherited her father's gift with words. She could cut an opponent down with her tongue as fast as with a blade. But when she smiled, it was, well, the world was made anew. Your grandfather was so proud of her. She would have been an excellent queen. Those . . . are the facts."

Kaydan's mind is a long way from this gloomy corridor. He has time traveled across an invisible landscape to a point at least fourteen years earlier. It's the most anyone has ever said about my mother. I'm hanging on every word.

"I had hopes that we would be . . . that she and I might . . ." Kaydan's voice falters, and I hardly recognize him. "Alas, it was not to be."

There goes any chance that Kaydan could be my father.

Actually, I'm relieved. I like the way things are between us. Why complicate it with the stress and power struggles of parents and cubs? Besides, there's little evidence we share any genetic material.

"Don't ask me who your father is," he concludes bitterly. "That secret died with her."

And that's it.

I can almost hear Kaydan slam this book of memories shut and return it to an out-of-reach shelf in his heart. He recomposes himself into the tough, calculating Singa I know and love. We resume our trudge into the unyielding darkness of the Mountain Pass.

Unyielding, that is, until it ends at another metal door built into the mountain rock. Kaydan takes a different key from his belt and slides it into the hole at the door's center. With a loud clack, the door slides away.

Daylight drenches the tunnel, stabbing my eyes. Moist, salty air fills my mouth and nostrils. The ocean can't be more than a few kilometers south of here. Overriding the seaside fragrances are the scents of soldiers, leather, weapons, dried meat, and karkadanns— the smells of home.

"Greetings, General Kaydan," says an approaching soldier with purple armor on his arms. "Strength and prosperity to our Kahn."

"And to all who serve him," Kaydan answers. "Greetings, Company Commander Gunari."

The two warriors clasp forearms while a dozen or so soldiers look on.

"Allow me to introduce Prince Leo," Kaydan announces, not only to Commander Gunari but to the entire company. "Grandson of Lord Raja Kahn and our future Singa-Kahn!"

Every soldier in the company, from Commander Gunari to the very last, drops to one knee and bows his or her head.

To me.

Kaydan whispers, "These are truly loyal Singas, are they not, Leo?"

If not, they're putting on a very convincing show. My pelt tingles from this display of devotion. Even the surrounding sounds of nature seem to hush out of respect for the moment.

Kaydan bends to my ear. "Leo, you must tell them to rise or they will kneel all day."

"Please," I say, embarrassed by my small and scratchy voice. "Rise . . . um . . . noble warriors . . . of Singara."

When everyone is back on two legs, Commander Gunari says, "It is a great honor to meet you, Lord Leo."

"Were you . . . at the dinner last night?" I'm not just making small talk. I want to know if he witnessed Tamir's speech and everything that came after, including my crash to the floor.

"No, Lord. Battalion commanders, legionnaires, and generals only at that event. I am just a humble company commander."

"Nonsense!" Kaydan exclaims. "Commander Gunari is one of the finest commanders in Singara, regardless of his rank and experience. Graduated from the Academy at the top of his class, what, four years ago?"

"Five, General Kaydan."

"Time grows swifter wings with each passing year!" Kaydan says. "It is so good to see you, Gunari." Kaydan turns to address the whole company. "I have called you here today because you are among the most trusted warriors in the Royal Army. You are also among the very first to see the prince after his hunt, in which he executed the most brutal slaycon in Singara using only a dagger and a slingshot!"

The soldiers exchange looks of surprise. I cringe and squeeze out a smile.

"This is an important day," Kaydan continues, "a day that will be recorded in the Kahn's History. The day Prince Leo begins his training at the Academy!"

"Only three kilometers to the Academy, Lord Leo," Commander Gunari says. "We have two karkadanns here for General Kaydan and you."

The commander interlocks his hands as a stepping place and launches me into the saddle. He draws us away from the Mountain Pass and into a plain of tall waving grass, heading to the seacoast at the southernmost part of our realm, home to the Royal Academy of War Science. The soldiers form an oval around me, with Kaydan in the lead. Gunari orders a young soldier to serve as my escort.

"What is your name?" I ask.

"Nolan, Lord," he says, avoiding my eyes.

I rarely get to talk with someone who is more uncomfortable speaking than I am. I recall a bit of advice Grandfather once gave me on the Science of Conversation: Ask questions about the other, because most folks enjoy talking about themselves and appreciate someone taking an interest in them. As long as they stick to the facts and avoid personal stories.

"What part of Singara are you from, Nolan?"

"The north side, Lord. My parents are blacksmiths."

"Do they make weapons for the military?"

"The military is our largest customer, but we also make everyday things such as tableware, tools, and the like. Ours is the largest shop of its kind, and we employ many Singas," he adds with a note of pride.

"And how is business?"

"As you know," he says, choosing his words carefully, "there is little fresh metal since the construction of the Border Zone Fence. We rarely have the privilege of crafting a new blade from fresh ore. We have to make do with used or discarded material."

That's a touchy topic, so I steer the conversation in a different direction. "When did you graduate from the Academy?"

"A year ago."

"With Anjali?"

"Yes," he says. "Very skilled, that one. A natural with a blade."

"So you know her?"

"Her adoptive father works in our business. Like me, Anjali has been handling and testing weapons her whole life."

"Adoptive father?"

"She was found as a little cub wandering the streets of the city. No one knew where she came from. And she was too young to know anything about herself except her name."

I'm tempted to inquire about Anjali's brother, the Spinner, but instead I ask, "Why doesn't she have a quadron of her own?"

"She did, but then she was called up to serve in the castle as soon as she graduated, which is a high honor. Most Singas stay with the quadron they join at the Academy, but not all. When I was in the Academy, your cousin Amara was in my quadron."

I wince at the sound of her name. "I imagine Amara will make a fine soldier."

"In the skills of soldiering, she is almost unrivaled," Nolan agrees. "But—if I may speak freely with you, Lord—she has too much of her father in her. Like him, Amara believes your grandfather, our good Kahn, should never have ascended the throne. She is well connected and has ways of getting information from outside the Academy. When she learns her father has been disgraced and dismissed from the military, she will focus her anger"—he looks me square in the face—"on the most obvious and available target."

CHAPTER 12

A friend is someone who helps carry your burdens.
— *Sayings of the Ancients*

THE GRASSY PLAIN TURNS ROCKY. Sea breezes grow stronger. We climb a slope and pause to take in the ocean sparkling in the sun. I comb the horizon for something that might be a military school. But there are no Singa-made structures; nothing except mountainous, jagged rock cliffs plunging into the ocean.

"Where is it?" I murmur to Kaydan.

"Not far," he says, urging his karkadann onward.

The ground dips to the sea, making the cliffs seem higher with every step. The uneven terrain is peppered with boulders and difficult to traverse. Ravens fly overhead in wide, lazy circles, mocking our cautious plodding.

I'm starting to wonder if something is terribly wrong. This place is deserted. Where could there be a campus teeming with soldiers in training anywhere near here?

My karkadann rounds one last rock formation ten meters from the ocean. Gunari waits by a tidal pool at the base of the cliffs. He cuts an impressive figure against a vast blue background of sky meeting water. The wind fills his mane. Soldiers gather along the edges and stare thoughtfully at the pool.

Kaydan dismounts, and I slide down from my beast to the stony ground. The tidal pool is about three meters wide. Shallow edges reveal rocks beneath the water, but the center is dark and deep. A flat mirrored surface reflects somber soldiers and lacy white clouds.

I look up at Kaydan with a furrowed brow.

"We're here," he declares.

Before I can ask where "here" is, Gunari clears his throat. "Lord Leo, by the hunt, you have proven yourself worthy to train at the Royal Academy of War Science. This pool is the entrance. At the bottom you will find a tunnel that leads to a similar pool on the other side of this cliff." He gestures to a mass of rock stretching high into the sky. "When you emerge from that second pool you will be just a few paces from the Academy. First you must remove all clothing and anything that adorns your body. At the Academy, everyone is equal."

Kaydan nudges me and I strip down, clutching my winged chest plate to my hips. I'm shivering as much from embarrassment as from the ocean air. All the soldiers respectfully keep their eyes trained on the pool.

"I can take care of that," Kaydan offers, removing

the chest plate from my quivering fingers. "The Kahn will treasure it beyond all else while you are at the Academy, I assure you."

"Lord Leo, do you want to become a soldier to serve our Kahn and protect our lands?" Gunari asks.

I am a royal, the future Kahn. Serving and protecting are what I was raised for. I straighten my back. "Yes. More than anything."

"Remember that," Gunari says sternly, "when you get to the other side."

I lean in to Kaydan. "Is there anything down there I should know about?"

Kaydan knows I'm stalling. Singas like to keep their fur clean by scrubbing with water, but we despise being submerged in the stuff. Kaydan tips his head toward the pool, advising me to get on with it.

"Strength and prosperity to the Kahn!" I yell, hoping to stir up some courage.

"And to all who serve him!" the soldiers chant in one voice.

I grunt and fling myself into the center of the pool. There's a crashing sound, followed by a thud as I'm wrapped in frigid, salty water. After a return to the surface for one last breath, I wiggle and kick and pull my way to the sandy bottom.

The shock of cold and the weight of the water dislodge a seed of fiction from the folds of my mind. It thrashes about in my mouth like a caged animal. As usual, I'm nauseous and dizzy and struggling to keep my jaw shut. This time there is the additional threat of drowning if the fiction gets free.

There is a glimmer of light ahead, a flashing beacon poking through a dark blob. That must be the tunnel to the next pool. I worm into the passageway and pull myself through while the ball of fiction expands and threatens to split my head open. The second pool is narrower than the first. I squat down and propel myself to the surface, then gulp air into aching lungs. As soon as my mouth opens, the fiction barrels out. It's all I can do to tread water as the words conjure up a vision expanding into the space over the pool:

A sage was meditating beside a river when a youngling interrupted her. "Teacher," he said, "how do I find the light of Alayah?"

"Through wanting."

"But I want Alayah more than anything in the world. Why hasn't it worked?"

The sage snarled, grabbed the youngling by the scruff of his neck, and dragged him into the river. After holding the youngling under the water for a minute or so, the sage pulled him out and tossed him onto the riverbank.

The youngling coughed up water and gasped to catch his breath. When he had recovered, the sage spoke. "Tell me, what did you want most of all when you were underwater?"

"Air!" the youngling gasped.

"That's right," said the sage. "And when you want Alayah as much as you wanted air, you will find what you are looking for."

The story concludes and the vision evaporates. I'm relieved to find myself totally alone.

Almost.

As usual, a character is left behind. The sage, life-size and wraithlike, crouches at the edge of the pool. She is the same story-being who appeared with Oreyon, the hunter, by the fire in Border Zone Eight. Covered in her tattered robe, she reaches for me.

"Take my hand!" she commands.

Forget it. She'll probably try to drown me, too. Even if she weren't a phantom, she's too old and frail to pull out a soaked youngling.

"Give me your hand!"

I ignore her and kick to the side of the pool. There's a place to insert my foot, but I slip and my muzzle slaps a rock.

I yowl.

The sage's annoyance turns to amusement. My second attempt is more successful. With trembling arms and legs I break the surface and tumble onto the ground, shuddering from the cold.

The sage lingers over me, shaking her head. "Foolish, foolish youngling. If I didn't need you to send me back, if you weren't so important, I would throw you right back into that pool!"

Here we go again with the "sending back."

"I didn't ask you to come here," I stammer, breathing hard, "and I don't know how to send you back."

"You don't need to *know*. You only need to be *willing*. When the time is right, you will learn. I will wait with the others." Her arm makes an arc as if to suggest an audience.

I look around. "What others?"

"Those who have come into this world because of you, of course! They are all still here, and let me tell you, most of them are very frustrated with you!"

This elder is crazier than I am. "I don't see anyone."

"Because you commanded them to disappear, and so they have! They stay hidden, waiting for you to speak their name and to call them into service. Or to be sent home. But you have done neither!"

"I suppose you want me to know your name?"

She bows. "My name is Vishna."

"And I can call on you whenever I want a lecture?"

Vishna flashes her broken-toothed grin and

straightens to her full height. "I have a bit more to offer. How do you think your leg healed so quickly?"

"That was you?"

"I could have healed you much faster if you had spoken my name. In this halfway state," she adds, gesturing to her airy, transparent form, "my healing arts are more limited."

"I'll keep that in mind. I'm okay for now. You can go."

"As you wish, Eliyah. Remember Vishna if you need someone with my skills, but know this: When you say my name, I will be visible and real to one and all."

And then she is gone.

I look around and take stock of my new surroundings. I am on a narrow shelf of land between tall rock walls on my left and the sea to my right. Behind the place where Vishna stood, a path snakes around the bluff. There is an old, weatherworn sign bolted to the cliff with an arrow pointing down the path. The sign reads:

ACADEMY THIS WAY.

Maybe it's because I grew up in a castle, but this shabby little sign hardly seems worthy of the Royal Academy of War Science.

I shake the water from my head, arms, and legs and

squeeze out my tail. I follow the slender path around the cliff until it dead-ends at yet another soaring wall of rock.

Did I miss something?

I search for a door or a ladder. I press my hands to the surface of the cliff where the path ends and push, half expecting an entrance to appear. None does.

I lean against the rock wall, my wet fur smearing the surface. A few letters, carved into the rock, are made visible by the water stain. I wipe the area with a damp forearm. Two sentences emerge.

> Looking for something?
> Give a roar and help is yours.

My roar isn't anything to roar about. My dignity won't even allow me to try. I could call for Oreyon or Vishna or even Kensho and ask them to roar for me, but that carries the risk of making them visible. How would I explain that to whoever from the Academy might be watching right now?

I have no choice.

"Please help me with this," I whisper to no one in particular.

I breathe deeply, tilt my head skyward, part my jaws, and—

On most days, my roar sounds like a squeaky door. This time there is a crack and boom of thunder. For a moment, I'm pleasantly shocked by what my vocal cords have produced, ripening just in time for my entrance into the Academy. Then a second blast of thunder sounds, not from my mouth but from black clouds rolling in over the sea. There is nowhere to take shelter on this barren chip of land; I'm going to get thoroughly drenched.

Again.

"Better get up here!" a gruff voice calls.

A thick rope drops from the cliff and whacks me on the head. It sways like the tail of some unseen beast above.

I grab the rope before it can vanish as quickly as it appeared.

A whoosh of wind, herald of the coming storm, fingers its way through my pelt and urges me to climb. I reach the top, some twenty meters up, and roll over the cliff's ledge.

I'm not alone.

There is a broad, stocky Singa, not much older than me, dressed in deerskin leggings and torso cover, with a short blade strapped to her back. A patch of fur has been ripped off her upper arm and shoulder, exposing damaged skin.

"Who are you?" I pant.

"I'm 24-2."

Her name is a number?

I gesture to her wounded arm. "What happened there?"

"Slaycon."

"Did it bite you?"

She scowls. "If it bit me, I wouldn't be standing here, would I?" She tosses me a pair of deerskin leggings, identical to the ones she's wearing.

"Put those on," she says flatly.

Remembering my state of undress, I scramble into the leggings and tie them off. A good fit.

"Where is the Academy?" I query. There's not much to see except the ocean on one side and more rock cliff on the other, with another rope dangling from a ledge far above.

She coils the first rope and lays it by a metal ring anchored to the cliff. "This way." She trots to the rope hanging from the next ledge and begins to ascend. In spite of her size and wound, she's a good climber.

"Now you," she calls from the ledge. I grasp the rope, lift my feet off the ground, and go nowhere fast. Getting out of the pool and that last climb have sapped the strength from my spindly arms.

"Coil your legs around the rope and hold on!" 24-2 bellows.

Thunder echoes from across the sea, and the rain begins.

I twist the rope through my legs and lean against

the line, its bristly surface poking my cheek. Moments later, the rope wobbles and the rock wall flows downward as I steadily rise. I can't see 24-2 because of the ledge, but I know what's going on.

She's hauling me up.

I'm grateful. And afraid.

Does she have help up there? What if she gets tired or has to let go? Suppose the rope slips out of her hands? I'd drop like a stone and leave this world as a bloody splat mark on the ground, washed away by the rain.

Before I can contemplate my military career ending before it starts, I see the next ledge within arm's reach, and I'm dragged over the lip onto solid ground.

"One more climb," 24-2 says, coiling up this rope and nodding toward yet another rope hanging from a section of cliff.

"I need to rest. Just give me a minute."

24-2 tilts her face to the angry sky. "No time." She grabs me, lifts me over her head, and lays me across her rain-soaked shoulders. I'm too tired to complain. She takes the rope and, hand over hand, begins our ascent. I close my eyes and hope no one sees me enter the Academy like a cub on his mother's back.

This last cliff top comes quickly. And not soon enough.

She pauses at the precipice. "You first."

I scramble up 24-2's shoulders and throw myself

onto the level ground, accidentally stepping on her wound in the process. She yowls and snarls.

"Sorry," I whimper.

24-2 hefts herself over the edge, coils the rope, and lays it near the anchor, just as before. Our fur is matted to our bodies. Water drips from our muzzles. I check our surroundings, searching for more ropes to climb and finding none. We've reached the top, a table of land a hundred meters above the ocean. Behind us is a triangular peak of rock, punctured by a short tunnel.

Thunder shakes the earth and clouds unleash their cargo in great sheets of water.

24-2 hastens to the tunnel. "Over here!"

I follow and we huddle together, waiting for the squall to pass.

"Won't last long," 24-2 says. "Storms that start fast end fast."

Soon there is only drizzle spiraling in the wind as the storm blows off to drench some other piece of land.

Exiting the passageway, we come to the rim of a vast circular canyon. It's like standing on the edge of an enormous bowl or, better yet, on the edge of a gargantuan, upside-down tortoiseshell. The sloping sides are sheer canyon rock. The bottom is a patchwork of fields with a cluster of buildings at one end, newly washed by the rain. Looming high over this little village is a fortresslike structure built into the canyon, much like the castle of Singara. Hundreds of cadets are sprinkled over the fields in company groups, practicing combat drills. Their weapons flash in the sunlight poking through the retreating storm clouds. At the far end of the canyon, a waterfall plunges into a misting pond. Except for the castle I call home, this is the most magnificent place I have ever seen.

24-2 smiles faintly, amused by my dumbstruck expression. "Welcome to the Academy," she says. "We've been waiting for you."

CHAPTER 13

Small minds are conquered by misfortunes;
great minds rise above them.
— *Sayings of the Ancients*

I WATCH 24-2 PICK UP a conch shell and raise it to her lips.

"What's that for?" I ask as a horrible sound, something like a dying karkadann, erupts from the shell. Far below, all cadets cease their exercises. More pour out of buildings. Every head tips up.

To us.

Looks like I won't be making a quiet, subtle entrance. Maybe no one does.

Cadets swarm around the central path stretching from the castle at one end of the campus to the waterfall at the other while 24-2 jogs to a ladder. The top of the ladder is at our feet, and the bottom rests on a ledge fifteen or twenty meters below. She descends and waves her tail for me to follow.

I'm impressed by the Academy's simple security system. No one can climb up from the seaside without someone throwing down the series of ropes. Even if an invader managed that, without these ladders leading into the canyon, they would be stuck at the top, with no way down.

We descend ladder after ladder after ladder.

On the final ladder, I notice the cadets, perhaps five hundred in all, positioned like statues on either side of the central path. Several dozen adult instructors, identifiable by their royal armor and taller stature, fall in behind their students. The cadets wear deerskin leggings like mine, and perhaps torso covers. The standard weapons are strapped to their backs, hips, and legs.

24-2, having reached the ground, growls to get my attention. Her whiskers twitch with impatience. I descend half of the wooden rungs and pounce to her side.

"Walk three meters behind me," she instructs. "When we get to the path, just keep walking no matter what."

"No matter what, what?"

"It's called the gauntlet," she says over her shoulder, as if that clears it up. "It's how we welcome new recruits. I did it last week; don't flinch, don't stop—just keep walking and you'll be fine."

She reaches the rows of cadets and waits. On the steps of the great house, at the opposite end of the path, an instructor roars: "Weapons, ready!"

Weapons?

Simultaneously, each cadet draws a weapon or two and assumes a combat stance, facing the path.

I don't like the look of this.

24-2 walks down the path between the lines of waiting cadets. No one moves, and my hopes are momentarily lifted. Then I pass the first cadet. She huffs a little roar and thrusts her blade at my head. I instinctively dodge the attack, and a cadet from the opposite line sweeps my leg, sending me crashing to the ground.

"Get up!" he barks.

I rise blearily and resume my march. The next cadet comes at me with his blade, this time a jab to my ribs. I bend my body around the blade, and a different cadet from the opposite line once again sweeps my leg and drops me.

"Get up!" this one says. I lie in a cloud of dust, wondering how anyone makes it to the other end. The instructions I got from 24-2 come back to me: "Don't flinch . . . just keep walking."

I wobble up to my feet and shake the dirt from my pelt. Eyes closed and using only my sense of smell to keep me on the path, I take a step. To my left, a cadet snarls, and I feel a breeze pass over my muzzle. With another step, a blade whistles behind my head and down my back.

Step by step, cadets from both sides of the line

attack, coming within centimeters of my body but without nicking my pelt or whiskers. I quicken my pace and the attacks accelerate like a mini cyclone of wind and metal.

All at once it stops. I open my eyes and find myself standing before the instructor, who glares down at me from the fortress steps. He is tall, with thick arms, a barrel-like chest, and almost no neck whatsoever. As with most soldiers, his armor is old and battle worn. 24-2 stands in the shadow of this mountainous soldier. Next to her is a scruffy, lanky cadet with sharp features and a short mane that sticks out in every direction.

"Where are your manners, newcomer?" the soldier growls. "Bow in greeting to your superiors."

I've never bowed to anyone, not even to the Kahn. I'm used to everyone bowing to me. I bend awkwardly at the waist.

The soldier rolls his eyes, unimpressed. "Get down on one knee."

I take a knee, my body still aching from those two tumbles.

"Rise, cadet, and tell us your name."

"My name," I say with as much nobility as I can scrape together, "is Leo, prince of Singara, grandson of Raja Kahn."

"No!" He scowls and leaps to the ground before me. "That is not your name here! Your name is 24-4 because you have been assigned to the fourth position of quadron 24. If you ever speak your birth name again, you will be punished. What is your name, cadet?"

"My name is Le—" The expressions of 24-2 and her companion stop me cold; 24-2 shakes her head.

"My name is 24-4."

"And I am Jakal," the soldier says. "Chief instructor of the Royal Academy of War Science. Your quadronmates, 24-2 and 24-3, will take you to Alpha," Jakal commands.

24-2 steps forward along with the other cadet, who must be 24-3. He bears a scab-covered wound across his chest like a sash. The injury appears to be a week or two old. Slaycon, no doubt.

"Come on," 24-3 says. "Let's get this over with."

Two cadet guards open the doors of the fortress. Unlit candelabras dangle in a spacious foyer. A set of leaping platforms, mirror images of each other, curve to a balcony.

"She's up there," one guard directs.

Before we bound up the platforms, 24-3 studies me thoughtfully. "Are you really who you say you are?"

"Don't I look like a prince?"

"No, not really," 24-3 says.

How fortunate, I say to myself, echoing Oreyon, the hunter. If I don't look like the prince, I have a better chance of blending in and avoiding trouble.

"Listen to me," 24-3 counsels in a low whisper. "Prince or not, you have to watch your step with Jakal and Alpha. If you cross them, they will put a foot so far up your dirt hole, you will cough out a big toe."

On the balcony level, we find a Singa sitting behind a bulky desk. She wears an elegant bejeweled garment, a combination of light armor and ceremonial dress. Pen in hand, she works with brisk, alert movements, too intent on her stack of papers to take any notice of us.

We lower ourselves to one knee.

"Come," she says without looking up. "Who do we have today?"

We approach the desk in a clumsy little line.

"We are the three newest recruits. Quadron 24," 24-3 offers. "Or we will be a quadron when we have a captain."

Her pen stops midstroke. She peers over the edge of the paper in her hand. "Did you say 24?" Her muzzle is frosted with gray, matching her silver eyes—the sort of eyes that can shut you up fast with a single look. Like now.

24-3 nods.

"From Company F, is it?"

He nods again.

"Ah yes," she says, shifting her attention to me. "You must be . . . the fourth. Welcome to the Academy, 24-4."

"Thank you," I reply. "Who are you?"

It seemed like a simple question, but my two companions simultaneously jerk their heads at me. Their expressions are inflated with fear.

"Who am I?" she says, eyebrows raised. "Who am I? Well now, let me see." She glides around her desk until she is towering over us. "I am the mistress and master of the Academy. I am the mind and heart of this canyon, the law and the judge. I am the shaper of Singara's military might, the author of our present and future glory. I am the creator of captains, commanders, legionnaires, and generals. I can make your time here as gentle as an afternoon breeze or a mountain of misery. I can cover you with meat for dinner or withhold food and drink for as long as I like. I can make you stand up all night in the rain or let you sleep all day. I will teach you discipline, honor, duty, and how to move like a cold wind through the tumult of war. That's who I am! You may call me Alpha.

"Everything you learn here is based on centuries of research in the laboratory of battle. You have already received your first lessons in the Science of War. To get into the Academy you had to rely on someone else, and to arrive at my house you had to trust your fellow cadets. Remember, you have a far better chance of survival when you depend on others and have complete trust in your captain, your quadron, your company, and every Singa who pledges to fight and die for the Kahn."

"When will we be assigned a captain?" I ask.

"Tomorrow, at first light," she replies curtly. "Now let's get to the real purpose of your visit to my fortress. Like all new cadets, you are here to see why we train so hard, the reason why a strong military is so important to our way of life. You are here to behold our enemy from beyond the Great Wall: the Maguar."

What? The Maguar? Here?

I exchange stunned glances with my companions, our fear scents filling the room as an invisible cloud.

"It is quite safe," Alpha assures us. "Follow."

Alpha guides us to a heavy door built into the canyon rock at the back of her fortress. She takes a key from around her neck and fits it into the lock. "Before I show you what is on the other side of this door, you must swear, upon your lives, never to speak of this to anyone beyond the Academy. Is that clear?"

More secrets. Nevertheless, we all bob our heads affirmatively. I would pluck out half my whiskers just to see a Maguar.

"Good." Alpha turns the handle and leans on the hefty door. Instantly, a rank scent invades my nostrils. Every hair on my pelt pops up like a porcupine quill.

"Mark that scent well," Alpha says. "There is no scent more important to remember. Keep your distance.

Come no closer to the cage than I do. The creature is swift and cunning. And one other thing: Do not look him in the eye. He will take it as a challenge."

We enter a cavelike chamber lit by three skylights in the ceiling. One half of the room is divided by thick bars. A dark shape crouches against the back wall.

Alpha bangs on the bars with a wooden stave. "Get up, Maguar! Meet some new cadets."

The figure stirs and groans. The sound of chains dragging on the stone floor joins the sluggish movements of an awakening creature. He rises to full height, and we behold the enemy warrior: huge and fearsome, with a dark striped pelt and a splash of white across his muzzle and neck. He approaches the bars, growling and regarding us with contempt.

"Here is the enemy from beyond the Great Wall!" Alpha says triumphantly. "Behold his bloodthirsty mouth. Note his broad shoulders, large hands, and claws. Each of you killed a slaycon using weapons. This brute could rip a slaycon apart barehanded. Imagine tens, hundreds, thousands of beasts like him pouring into Singara to rob us of our liberty and loved ones and everything we hold dear. This is why we train so hard. This is why a strong military force is a necessity beyond all others. This is why you are here, to join in the great tradition of protecting our way of life!"

"How long has he been locked up in there?" 24-3 asks in a thin voice.

"He was captured on the border just after the Great War, before the Great Wall was built. He was a young warrior in those days, but he was as large and as formidable as he is today."

So this poor Maguar has spent twenty-five years, most of his life, in captivity, behind these bars.

"Do not pity him," Alpha says, noting our sagging whiskers and drooping tails.

"Can he talk?" I probe.

The Maguar's eyes shift to Alpha.

"Of course. They have their own primitive language."

"Can he speak our language?"

"Yes, but he is forbidden to do so."

I'm drawn to the creature and take two steps forward before I know what my legs have done. Alpha gasps as the Maguar's arm, quick as lightning, thrusts out from behind the bars, reaches behind my back, and smashes me against the cage. He crouches and presses me to his face, inhaling my scent.

"Let him go immediately or you will not eat for a week!"

"*Yoda'at mi atah,* infidel?" the Maguar rumbles.

He gives me a final sniff, licks my neck, and drops me like a bag of sand.

"*Et yoda'at mi et?*"

I scramble away. Alpha pulls me back to hasten my retreat. 24-2 and 24-3 check me for wounds and find none. The Maguar slinks back into the shadows of his cage.

"You okay?" 24-2 asks.

"That thing's meaner than a bag of rattlesnakes," 24-3 adds.

"You will suffer for this, Wajid!" Alpha snarls.

"Suffer already," he replies mournfully.

Wajid! That's who Daviyah told me about. His former servant!

"Well, 24-4," Alpha says when we are safely on the other side of the door. "You have not only seen one of our enemies—you have come closer to a Maguar than any Singa, save those who fought in the Great War. I trust it is an experience you will not forget."

"What did he say to me?" I ask.

"How should I know?" Alpha snorts. "I do not speak their gibberish."

"He called me infidel. What does that mean?"

"It means 'unbeliever.' We are all infidels to them."

Alpha escorts us to the entryway of her fortress. Before letting us go she says, "One more thing. Assist me in protecting the purity of our army and keep an eye out, or better yet, keep an ear out, for Spinners. It is always our duty to do so, but at the Academy we must be especially vigilant. In my experience Spinners are the quiet ones, reluctant to open their mouths lest the disease expose them. Every Spinner is found out, eventually. Better now, better here, than after they graduate and enter the Royal Army, don't you agree?"

I shiver, not knowing which is more chilling: my close encounter with Wajid or this.

"We will," I declare for all of us, topping it off with a little bow.

Alpha smiles for the first time. "All the best to you, younglings. Train hard. Our realm and everything we hold dear depend on it."

We tumble into the fresh air of the canyon, blinking in the late-afternoon sunlight. The fortress door closes behind us, and I say, "I want to go back in there. Tonight. And I'll need you both to help me."

The shortest distance between two leos is a story.
— *Sayings of the Ancients*

THE CAMPUS IS EMPTY. The scores of cadets who lined the central path only fifteen minutes ago have vanished.

I part my jaws and taste the air. "Where is everyone?"

24-3 is panicky. "We're late for feeding time!"

"Feeding time?" I protest. "It's only the sixteenth hour."

"We eat early on gaming days," 24-3 explains, charging down the steps of Alpha's fortress with 24-2 in tow.

"What's gaming?"

He runs away. "We have to hurry or there won't be any food left!"

"Wait!" I yell, but they don't. My quadron-mates make a beeline for a large building a hundred or so meters off, most likely the feeding hall. We sprint by pastures packed with antelope, goats, and deer that scatter at the sight of us. "You haven't told me your real names!"

24-3 slows a bit, permitting 24-2 and me to catch up. "We're not supposed to use names around here, remember?"

"You know my name. It's only fair for you to tell me yours."

He searches the area for onlookers. "Everyone back home calls me Stick."

"Because you are skinny?"

"Because he has sticky fingers," 24-2 explains. "He's a thief."

"I can't help it if other people's stuff clings to my hands!" Stick argues.

"Good thing I don't have anything to steal," I say.

"Yes," 24-2 agrees. "It is."

"What about you?"

"My sister is Zoya," 24-3 reveals as we trot up to the feeding hall.

"You two are brother and sister?"

"Twins," Stick says. "Not identical, though."

I figured that. They are about as identical as a boulder and a sapling.

Stick opens the feeding hall door and pokes his head inside. "We're in luck. Still a bit of meat left."

The feeding hall is similar to the castle's. I cast

my eyes around the vaulted ceiling, the stone fireplace, and the rows of tables and benches, tightly packed with feasting cadets. It all brings a tender touch of comfort and a prickly pinch of homesickness. Instead of the Kahn reclining with his four generals at the high table, Jakal is sitting with four head instructors. And somewhere, in the sea of faces, is Tamir's daughter and my cousin, Amara.

Stick, Zoya, and I weave to a table of cadets at the far corner, which I take to be their company . . . *our* company. Stick snags a piece of meat from every table we pass. All it takes is a growl from Zoya to discourage anyone from lashing out at Stick for his thievery. Few in this hall are as large and fearsome as Zoya. For every two pieces that Stick devours, he tosses two over his shoulder for Zoya and me until we slide onto the benches of our table. The cadets around the table gawk at me, nudging one another.

"He doesn't have any wounds!" one of them says.

"Maybe he had someone do his hunt for him," another says with a sneer.

My ears burn. Most cadets at this table sport slaycon injuries, like Zoya and Stick. That means they are all somewhat new to the Academy as well. I guess companies are made of the most recent arrivals until they reach sixteen members. I am the fifteenth. Our captain will make us complete.

Jakal rises from his chair and the room quiets. "We have a new cadet among us today. I call on him to stand on his bench, introduce himself to his fellow cadets, and announce what company he trains with."

Zoya prods me with an elbow. I climb on the bench and clear my throat as though I'm about to make a grand speech. My voice comes out in an airy whine. "My name is Leo, grandson of Raja Kahn and prince of Singara . . ."

That's what I meant to say. In fact, I only manage "My name is Le—" when Stick erupts in a coughing fit that blocks out everything else.

Zoya leans across the table. "Use your Academy name: 24-4!" she snarls as if I'm the dumbest Singa on the planet and putting the whole company at risk.

"My name is 24-4 and I am proud to serve with . . . um . . ."

"Company F!" Stick whispers.

"Company F."

"Welcome, 24-4. Who would like to present blades to our newest cadet?" Jakal asks the assembly.

"I will," comes a voice, strong and clear, from the other side of the hall. She is older and larger than the last time I saw her, but there is no mistaking Amara. A hot lump of dread sizzles in my throat.

"Ah yes, 10-1," Jakal says breezily, as though he expected her. "Both of you, come forward."

Amara and I approach the high table. Jakal hands

Amara a set of used blades in worn leather scabbards: a long blade, a short blade, a dagger, and an aero-blade. Her nostrils flare. Her eyes narrow with rage.

"The words, 10-1," Jakal says.

"On behalf of your fellow cadets, I welcome you and wish you well in your training," Amara says mechanically to contain her anger. "Our safety and prosperity depend on all of us serving together as one. These blades represent the Pride of Singara. Train with them, become one with them, and use them only to protect the Kahn, the Pride, your company, your quadron, and your own life. If you surrender your blades, you surrender your honor and your duty to protect the throne."

Instead of placing the blades in my arms, she drops them in a clatter of metal and leather. I manage to catch the aero-blade and the short blade, but the dagger and long blade tumble to the floor like dead limbs. Amara squats with me to scoop up the fallen weapons. Our heads are so close, our whiskers interlace.

"I know what the Kahn did to my father!" she says, nearly spitting.

"It could have been worse," I reply. "He could have lost more than his tail."

"The Kahn will regret letting him live."

I've got nothing to say in response to that. Grandfather wanted to kill Tamir on the spot. He's alive because of me. I guess that part wasn't shared with Amara. It might not matter anyway.

Amara turns to Jakal. "Permission to offer another word of greeting, Commander."

"Granted. But keep it short, Captain."

Amara addresses the assembled cadets, and a shiver of alarm climbs my spine. "It is no secret who 24-4 is, or that he and I are cousins," Amara begins. "The cadets have talked about little else since he arrived. He and I share the same great-grandfather, Jamar Kahn. His grandfather and my grandfather are brothers, his grandfather being the *younger* brother. My father and his mother are cousins, his mother being the *younger* cousin."

Without saying it directly, Amara is questioning Grandfather's claim to the throne over his older brother and, therefore, my right to become Kahn after him. Not only does Tamir have his heart set on the throne, Amara does as well.

The head instructor seated next to Jakal leaps to his feet. "Cadet, these facts are not recorded in the Kahn's History! Are you a diseased Spinner? I'll have your tongue!"

Jakal glowers at the instructor, staring him back to his seat.

"I am not a Spinner," Amara says calmly. "And it should come as no surprise that these facts are not recorded in the Kahn's History. It is, after all, the *Kahn's* History. But history can be changed, just as Kahns change."

It is a bold idea, but murmurs of support spread around the hall as Amara marches to her table. I clutch the blades to my chest and hurry back to Company F.

Blood thumps in my ears, followed by the sound of rushing wind. The affliction is back. A lump of fiction is creeping through the coils of my brain, preparing to roll onto my tongue and overtake me. I need to get out of here. Fast.

"I think I'm going to be sick," I whisper to Stick. "Where is the dirt shack?"

"Outside. Go through the kitchen."

Jakal calls on a cadet to read a chapter from *The Science of War*. That gives everyone just enough distraction for me to make my exit. I dump my blades on the bench and dash through the kitchen into the twilight, the fiction thrashing about in my mouth. The air around the dirt shack is predictably foul. The next building is a barn and I slip inside. Surrounded by an audience of lumber and tools, spiders, and the smell of dingy old things, I open my aching mouth. The words flow and a bright swirling vision fills the dusty space.

Once there was a mother sheep who decided to take her lamb to the northern plains, where the grass was rich and abundant and where many sheep grazed during the summer.

I watch, fascinated and resentful, as the scene unfolds: the beautiful sheep and her little lamb, the sunlit valley, a flower-strewn meadow surrounded by sturdy trees.

As the mother sheep and her little lamb made their journey, they encountered Rukan, a huge and ferocious wolf.

"Good morning, Madame Sheep," said Rukan the wolf. "Where are you off to?"

"Mr. Rukan!" replied the terrified sheep. "I am taking my little lamb to graze on the rich and plentiful grass of the northern plains."

"How tragic," said Rukan. "Because, as it happens, I am very hungry, and I'm going to eat you both."

"Oh, please don't, Mr. Rukan," cried the mother sheep. "Not now. In the autumn, we will be fatter and make a much more satisfying meal. Wait a few moons and eat us then."

Rukan liked the idea. "Certainly you are right, Madame Sheep," he said. "I will not eat you now, as long as you promise to meet me at this very spot on your return journey in the autumn."

So saying, Rukan pranced away while the sheep and her lamb continued their journey. Soon they forgot their frightful encounter with the wolf. All summer they feasted on the rich grasses of the northern plains. When autumn came the mother sheep was as fat as she could be and her little lamb had grown into a handsome youngster.

As they returned south, the mother sheep recalled her agreement with Rukan the wolf, and she became increasingly seized with dread. When they approached the very place where they had encountered the wolf, along came a large rabbit, hopping down the road.

The rabbit noticed how sad the mother sheep appeared and said, "Sister Sheep, how can a sheep as healthy as you with such a handsome lamb be so sad?"

"Brother Rabbit," said the mother sheep. "Ours is an unhappy story. Last spring, as we came to this very road, we met Rukan the wolf, who was about to eat us. I persuaded him to wait until we were both fatter after feasting all summer on the rich grass of the northern plains. The wolf agreed and promised to meet us on our return. I fear that we shall soon be killed and eaten!"

"This is indeed a sad story!" replied the rabbit. "But do not despair, Sister Sheep. I can handle that wolf."

The rabbit reached into his bag and dressed himself in a fine new robe and put a royal hat on his head. He took out a large sheet of paper and tucked *a pen behind his ear, climbed upon the back of the sheep, and directed them down the path.*

When they came to the appointed place, Rukan was waiting, looking fiercer and hungrier than before. The rabbit called out in a tone of authority, "Who are you and what are you doing there?"

"I am Rukan the wolf, and I am going to eat these two healthy sheep according to our agreement made in early summer. Who are you?"

"I am the royal rabbit. I am on a special mission from the Kahn to collect ten wolf skins as a present to his wife. How fortunate that I should find you. Your skin will count as one!"

With that, the rabbit took his pen and sheet of paper and wrote a very large "1" in clear view of the wolf.

"If you don't mind waiting here for a minute or two," said the rabbit, "hunters are right behind us, and they will gladly remove your skin and fur."

Immediately, the wolf turned and fled. The mother sheep thanked the rabbit for his kindness, courage, and quick wit, and she and her lamb continued their journey home.

I exhale, grateful the story is done and for the privacy of this barn. This place could come in handy next time the disease overtakes me.

My relief is short-lived. Something stirs under a tarp.

Something big.

I fling open the barn doors and retreat into the night. A dark shape rises up in the barn's dim light, snarling and shaking dust from its pelt. The beast leaps through the door, knocks me down, and straddles me.

He is massive, five times larger than a slaycon, with powerful legs, coarse black fur, a bushy tail, teeth like daggers, and bright blue eyes.

It's Rukan, the wolf from the story. He is in the halfway state: ghostlike and visible only to me. Instead of biting off my head, which he could do in half a heartbeat, Rukan licks my face. Although nothing about him is completely solid, his tongue is still damp and bigger than a door. That's twice I've been licked today.

"Stop that!"

Rukan whimpers and dips his head. "My apologies, Lord. Instincts. I can't always control them."

I scramble back on all fours, spooked by such courteous words coming from this terrifying creature.

Rukan takes a step in pursuit. "You have nothing to fear from me. You are the master, and besides," he says with a chuckle, "eating you would make it very hard to fulfill my mission to serve you. What is your bidding? Give me a task, some noble purpose, and it will be done. I am yours to command!"

Rukan rests his snout on the ground, tail wagging like a puppy's.

"I don't really need any help at the moment."

The great wolf jerks up with disbelief. "Then why was I sent here? Think carefully now. I can smell a few foxes and snakes nearby, and I'm not talking about actual foxes and snakes, but Singas with the hearts of foxes and snakes. If you ever need help with one of those, you must call on me, and I will handle the problem properly!"

"Thanks, but I'm fine."

"Fine!" the great wolf howls. "No one is fine here! If only you could see this world as I do. All of you are half-blind! How Alayah puts up with you is beyond me!"

His snout spins in the direction of the feeding hall. "Someone's coming! Say my name! Make me solid and visible and allow me to demonstrate my skills!"

"No! That would be the worst thing. You need to go. Please!" I hiss.

Rukan bows his great head. "As you wish, Lord. You will remember my name, won't you? Rukan . . . Rukan . . ." He fades away.

I breathe easier until I pick up Zoya's scent riding on the evening breeze, followed by her gruff voice in my ears.

"Who are you talking to?"

CHAPTER 15

Joy and peace are the fruits of sacrifice.

— *Sayings of the Ancients*

ZOYA CARRIES MY BLADES under one arm. "You okay?"

I climb to my feet, brushing my backside. "Just tripped. That's all."

She hands over my weapons. "Put these on. We're supposed to be in the arena right now. For gaming."

"What's gaming?"

"Happens once a week. A company gets to demonstrate their progress in the Science of War. Tonight, we're up. It's our first time."

We jog through the training fields to an area encircled by bleacher benches at the far end of the Academy. Torches perched on posts light the space. Alpha and the head instructors are gathered on a platform overlooking the arena. Signs jut up from the benches, designating where each company is to sit. The section for Company F is empty because the cadets lined up in the center of the ring. Jakal is with them, frowning at the two late-comers.

Zoya points to the empty benches. "Sit there. Cadets don't game on their first day. It's the one bit of mercy you'll find around here."

Zoya trots into the arena. The crowd of cadets stomp impatiently, hundreds of feet banging out a steady rhythm, louder and faster, until the canyon vibrates.

Jakal roars, and the stomping dies away.

"Good evening, Alpha! Good evening, instructors, and welcome, cadets of the Royal Academy of War Science!" Jakal bellows. "Tonight's gaming gives Company F, our newest batch of cadets, the opportunity to demonstrate progress in the Science of War. A series of challenges has been arranged in the arena, and these cadets will prove themselves worthy of the blades they carry." Jakal turns to Company F. "Is your company ready, Commander?"

"Ready!" a stout cadet answers.

"Then let us begin."

For the next hour Jakal pushes Company F through a long string of basic fighting drills, such as the double draw, the act of drawing two blades at once, and several "kata," sets of fifty or more moves the company must perform together. From a lifetime of observing soldiers train at the castle, I'd say Company F is not terrible. They are not good, but definitely not terrible.

After all, some of them have been here for only a few days.

At one point, Jakal has each cadet show his or her skill with all four weapons in rapid succession. He introduces an array of targets set on wooden posts pounded deep into the earth and demonstrates the test. Jakal bounds over a starting line and sprints forward. He unhooks his aero-blade from his back and flings it at the farthest post. The circular blade whistles through the air and sinks into the wood. Still in motion, Jakal draws his long blade and slices a cabbage sitting atop the post to his right, cutting it neatly in half. A moment later, Jakal's short blade flashes in the torch light and is thrust into a bag of sand on yet another post. Returning both the long blade and short blade to their sheaths, Jakal leaps and executes a perfect flip while drawing his dagger. He lands astride a log, driving his dagger into a circular target painted on the bark.

The crowd of cadets cheers and roars.

"Now you!" Jakal orders Company F.

Our stout company commander leads off. His sprint toward the collection of targets is more of a waddle, prompting hoots of laughter from the audience. His aero-blade misses its goal. The long blade hits the post but fails to connect with the cabbage on top. He has to stop running to draw the short blade before plunging it awkwardly into the bag of sand. Skipping the leap and flip, he marches to the log, places the handle of his dagger between his teeth, and whips his head to the log, driving the blade into the target.

The commander appears to have knocked himself out with that final blow. After an uncertain moment, he pops up, waving and bowing as though he has just defeated four Maguar. Only Company F cheers the creative finish. Everyone else hisses with disapproval, scratching at the air with extended claws.

As the rest of Company F take their turns, the commander's performance looks better and better, each of them having a harder and harder time managing the series of challenges.

Zoya goes last.

She doesn't bother throwing her aero-blade. She thumps the post holding the cabbage with her forehead, causing the vegetable to fall to the ground, where she crushes it underfoot. She slashes the sandbag with her claws and watches the contents drain out. Finally, she picks up the log and uses it as a battering ram against the aero-blade target.

Company F surrounds Zoya with shouts and roars of praise. Zoya remains stone-faced.

Jakal enters the ring carrying a bowl. "Commander, in this bowl are slips of paper, one for each company at the Academy, except Company F of course. The company you choose will face Company F in several rounds of Judoko."

Jakal holds the bowl well above the commander's

head. The commander has to teeter on his toes to reach inside, sparking more snickers and cackles. Finally, he extracts a paper and hands it to Jakal. Out of the corner of my eye, I catch Amara rising from the crowd, as if she already knows the outcome. Perhaps this is a charade, and *all* the pieces of paper in the bowl say . . .

"Company C!" Jakal announces.

Energized, Company C leaps from the bleachers and pours into the ring, led by Amara.

"Company F will face Company C in three rounds of Judoko," Alpha says. "The winners of those rounds will go on to a final round."

Judoko is a combat game in which two opponents face each other in a ring. The ring, about five meters wide, is made of curved branches fastened together and secured to the earth with pegs. Two blades stick out from the ground at opposite edges of the circle and behind the two challengers. The first to reach the blade behind his or her opponent wins. Claws are not permitted. No attacks are allowed until each player is ready, signaled by crouching down and touching the ground with one hand. Beyond that, there are no rules. It's a game of strategy, skill, strength, and speed.

Within minutes, almost every cadet of Company F has been defeated by the far more experienced, and less weary, Company C. Only Zoya, a natural fighter and the largest cadet anywhere, and Stick, the stealthiest and fastest, remain standing at the end of three rounds.

For the final round, Amara selects 10-2, a brawny member of her company, to challenge Zoya and keeps Stick for herself. Zoya eyes Amara hungrily, as if she would happily take on both opponents at once.

Zoya and 10-2 square off. They squat low, fingertips brushing the dirt, growling at each other, tails swaying.

The brawny 10-2 surges forward, plowing into Zoya's middle and forcing her down. He backflips over Zoya, but Zoya locks her hind legs around 10-2's waist and uses their combined momentum to launch herself upright and on top of 10-2. Zoya slams 10-2 to the ground, sits on his torso, and bashes him in the head with one fist, knocking him momentarily senseless.

Instead of bounding off to retrieve her blade like any other Singa would at this point, Zoya grabs 10-2 by the foot and drags him along. He revives in time to see Zoya seize her blade and claim victory. The audience applauds and roars for the winner.

10-2 shakes the sting of defeat from his muzzle, looking woozy and weakened.

The combatants return to the center of the ring for the next match. Before Zoya can signal her readiness by touching the ground, 10-2 delivers a spinning back kick into Zoya's gut. She crumples, growling and moaning. 10-2 saunters across the ring and claims his blade. The crowd boos, scratching the air in protest of 10-2's cheap shot.

Alpha rises. "10-2 has battled dishonorably and

is hereby disqualified from this competition! I declare 24-2 the winner!"

Now it's Stick's turn to face Amara.

As they move to the center of the ring, the difference between them is obvious. Amara is a year older, confident, and powerful. Stick is almost as new to the Academy as I am. He is shorter than his opponent, bonier, and scruffier. Within a heartbeat of the first round, Amara conquers Stick, sweeping his leg and pressing his face into the dirt. She glides easily over Stick's prone body, leaps, seizes the blade while still in the air, and lands with a dramatic fighting pose.

Only Company C expresses approval for this brutal and overdone victory. Amara plants the blade and returns to the center of the ring. In the next round, Amara permits Stick to have the first attack. He propels himself past Amara, but before he can tuck into a roll, she grabs him, spins, and thumps him to the dust. Amara claims the blade as Stick forces himself up.

I can't bear to watch any more of this. I'd rather be Stick than witness what happens next. I wonder if that is even possible.

"Wait!" I yell.

Hundreds of eyes shift to me.

"Wait," I repeat, confirming to myself that I'm actually doing this. I hop from the bleachers and face Alpha and the head instructors. "I request permission to take 24-3's place in the final round."

Alpha, and all the Academy with her, is stunned.

"I accept!" Amara says.

"Very well," Alpha agrees. "I will remind you, 10-1, this is only a training exercise; 24-4 has much to learn."

I enter the ring. Amara crouches in a ready stance. "You are no match for me. You have no reach, no strength. You are as foolish as your grandfather. You will never be the Singa-Kahn, even if you do make it through the Academy."

"Send that fox out of the ring with her tail between her legs," someone from Company F yells.

Fox? What was it the great wolf said? Something about Singas with the hearts of foxes? What was his name?

Just before my fingers touch the earth, I say it.

"Rukan."

"What?" says Amara.

She is answered by a howl from outside the arena. Alpha jumps to her feet as Rukan soars over the bleachers and lands behind me. Everyone yowls with terror, making it completely clear that this giant wolf, from his daggerlike teeth to his long, bushy tail, is visible to one and all. Whatever happens next, it's my fault. I am responsible. I said his name. I made him real, solid, present.

I swivel to face Rukan, shaking uncontrollably. His snout is centimeters from mine, warm breath pumping on my face. I have no fear of the beast. I'm horrified by what I've done and deathly afraid of what Rukan might do.

"What are your orders, Lord?" he whispers.

Alpha, Jakal, and the instructors draw their blades and leap into the ring. Amara scrambles to the blade behind her.

"Pick me up in your mouth and toss me aside," I mumble without moving my lips. "Give a show of battle, but don't hurt anyone. Then go."

Rukan growls and snatches me up in his great mouth. With a flick of his head, Rukan launches me into the crowd. I land, in time to see Amara roar and leap over Alpha and Jakal, blade in hand, to attack the giant wolf.

It's a brave move.

And a stupid one.

Rukan snatches her in midair between his teeth and flings her aside. She too crashes into the crowd. Alpha and the head instructors surround the fearsome intruder and attack. Rukan's skill as a fighter is quickly revealed. He kicks and twists and snaps his jaws, toying with the soldiers.

"Attack! Attack!" Jakal yells to one and all.

Cadets from every section of bleachers draw blades and dive into the battle, swinging wildly and unsuccessfully at Rukan. The giant wolf seems to enjoy having more foes to play with. Jakal and two other instructors unhook their aero-blades. It would take at least ten aero-blades to bring him down, but a few well-placed throws could do some damage.

"Run!" I shout to Rukan over the din of battle.

Rukan spins, charges straight for Jakal, and knocks him to the ground. The wolf surges out of the arena and jumps into the waterfall.

Dozens of cadets give chase until Alpha calls out, "Stop! There is no need to pursue the beast. He will not survive what awaits him beyond the falls."

Alpha scans the disheveled crowd. "Is anyone hurt?"

Everyone checks themselves for wounds. No one breathes a word.

"Do you mean to tell me this vicious monster did not harm or wound one Singa?"

"Where did the beast come from?" an instructor wonders.

Jakal and Alpha exchange an uneasy glance. Alpha stares at the waterfall for a long moment. "Such a creature has not been seen since the Great War," she says thoughtfully, "commanded by a demon of a Maguar."

She must mean the Abomination, the enemy Spinner who nearly defeated our army and destroyed Singara. Alpha and Jakal both fought in the Great War. They saw what he did. No wonder they're so freaked.

What have I done? I've put myself, my company, and the entire Academy at risk.

A different instructor asks, "If this is the work of the Maguar, is it the beginning of an invasion?"

Alpha surveys the campus of the Academy from the training fields to the top of the canyon walls. "If it were a Maguar invasion, there would be hordes of unnatural creatures storming the Academy right now. Why there was only one, and why the beast did us no harm, is a mystery beyond all science and reason."

Alpha sheathes her blades. "Jakal will return to Singara to make a full report to the Kahn and his generals. Meanwhile, we will double our guards and watch for any further sightings of enemy devilry. Sleep with your blades close at hand. That is all. You are dismissed."

The spooked and skittish crowd of cadets drifts toward the bunkhouses. On the way, I pull Zoya and Stick aside and remind them about going back to see Wajid, the captive Maguar, in Alpha's fortress. I want to talk to him now more than ever.

Stick refuses. "We just got attacked by a giant wolf sent by the Maguar and you want to visit the only Maguar around?"

"That's exactly why we should go," I argue. "He might have the answer to the mystery of the wolf. If Singara is in danger, I can't just sit around and wait for something else to happen."

Obviously, I know where the wolf came from, and I'm not too concerned about an attack from the Maguar, not even from the hole in the Great Wall. I mostly want to ask Wajid about the Abomination and Daviyah.

Could they be one and the same? No use mentioning any of that to Stick and Zoya. Too many questions will follow. Questions I can't answer.

Stick struggles with my proposal. "How are we going to get in there?"

"What better challenge for a thief than breaking into Alpha's fortress?" I say encouragingly.

"Maybe," he replies, "but there are lots of guards, and the locks are tough."

"If you won't help me, then maybe Zoya can." I look up at her. "How about it?"

She says nothing at first, then murmurs, "There is another way."

"How? Where?" I ask.

"Tonight, when the rest of our company is asleep, I'll wake you both. Stick, can you get your hands on twenty meters of rope?"

"You know I can."

We arrive at the little village of bunkhouses, simple wood-and-stone structures, each with a small front porch, all built in tight rows under the watchful eye of Alpha's house. We shimmy through the bustling throng of cadets. I have no idea which bunkhouse is ours, so I hang close to my companions, fearful I might lose them in the thicket of Singa fur. We stop outside one bunkhouse as the rest of Company F ambles in for nighttime napping.

"So you're in?" I press Stick. "You'll do it?"

"You took my place against Amara. I guess I owe you," Stick concedes. "I still don't know if that was brave or stupid."

I shrug and smile. "Thanks to that wolf, we didn't have to find out."

CHAPTER 16

Bravery is not the absence of fear,
but action in the presence of fear.
— *Sayings of the Ancients*

I DREAM.

At first I'm in the central hall of the castle following the crack that runs the length of the floor. I pass through walls and floors as the crack expands deep into the Great Mountain. Now I'm in a sloping cave, trailing a soldier bearing a torch. He stops suddenly and turns, eyes aflame with curiosity and fright.

I'm also filled with fear. The soldier is Tamir.

He sniffs the air before continuing his descent. He senses someone's presence but he can't see me. Relieved, I edge forward, my gaze drawn to Tamir's tail gliding over the rough, rocky way. If he still has his tail, I must be looking into the past again, before he was disgraced.

The cave opens to a large chamber. A strange, gray powder lies in piles and swirls in the air. As Tamir enters the chamber, his torch illuminates the far wall, which is not made of rock. It has the appearance of metal, smooth and reflective, but supple as skin. Tamir kneels reverently and extends a hand.

"Such power," he mumbles to himself while stroking the expanse of flesh. "Soon you will be free, my friend. Your countless years of imprisonment are coming to an end. You will have your revenge. Together, we will conquer."

A moaning sound rattles the earth, and I realize this mass of flesh is only a small fraction of an impossibly huge and terrible beast trapped in the rock.

"Soon," Tamir repeats. "Very soon."

. . .

I'm roused by a shake on my shoulder as I lie curled in my hammock. Two figures loom over me, one wide, one narrow. I almost scream when a hand clamps around my muzzle, so tightly it feels like my teeth are being crushed.

The larger one leans down. "It's us."

Zoya's raspy voice catapults my brain into wakefulness. Recalling our plan, I relax, and Zoya removes her hand. Stick has a long rope coiled around his shoulder. I roll off my hammock and we file out the door.

A not-quite-full moon illuminates the campus and casts sharp shadows of the bunkhouses, trees, and even ourselves—not a helpful situation when you're trying to be stealthy. I'm about to suggest waiting for a darker night when Stick mutters, "Follow me." He slips off the porch, melting into a shadow beyond the moon. He moves on, wearing the darkness like a cloak. He's so quiet. A leaf would make more noise falling on the forest floor than his footsteps. He escorts us through the village of bunkhouses, clinging to the darkest places.

Just when I've lost track of where we are, Stick hunkers by a wall. "We're here. This is the south side of Alpha's house."

I look up. The stone wall is capped by a tiled roof, reaching high into the night sky.

Stick nudges Zoya. "What's the plan?"

"We go up to the roof and lower Leo through one of the skylights into the room with Wajid's cage."

Stick's eyes nearly leap out of his head. "We're going to lower the prince of Singara into a cage with a Maguar?"

"Shut it!" Zoya scolds. "Do you want to wake up every cadet in this canyon? If you'd rather go knock on the front door, be my guest."

Stick sighs. "I hope you know what you're doing, Zoy."

"Our first challenge will be climbing up the roof without being seen," Zoya muses.

She's right.

On that moon-drenched roof, we'll be about as obvious as pee on snow. Someone is bound to see us. Before I can spend another moment worrying, a cloud passes over the moon, covering everything in a gray gauze. Singa eyes are sharp, even in the dark, and the less light there is, the less pronounced our golden pelts will be up there.

"That will help," Stick says, staring at where the moon used to be.

"Bend down," Zoya orders. "I need a boost."

Stick hunches over as if they have performed this maneuver a thousand times. Zoya steps on her brother's back and hoists herself onto the roof. She pulls us up one by one, as though we are cubs. The roof stretches upward in a gradual slant before meeting the canyon rock. The place where the rock and the roof meet is where Wajid's cell must be. We'll know for sure when we find the skylights that offer the only view of the outside world he's had in two and a half decades.

The roof tiles make for easy climbing. We reach the place where the roof merges with the canyon rock. Gradually the scene brightens.

Zoya's ears go flat with dread. "The cloud is moving away."

Seconds later the canyon is bathed in a fresh wave of milky moonlight.

And so are we. Anyone looking in this direction would see us in a heartbeat.

"Over here." It's Stick's voice, but he has vanished. "On your left. Under the ledge."

Zoya scoops me around the waist and pulls me

beneath a rock overhang next to her brother. I'm sitting on Zoya's lap, feeling safe and extremely awkward.

"There!" Stick exclaims. We follow the line of his outstretched arm to a dark rectangular blotch a few meters up. "I'll bet my tail that's one of the skylights over Wajid's cell. But the canyon rock is too sheer. Nothing to climb on."

"I counted three skylights when we were in there," I say. "All at about the same height, spaced evenly apart."

Stick nods. "Me too. That means the others aren't far away. I wouldn't be surprised if one of them was directly above this ledge."

"That would give us a way up," Zoya offers hopefully. "And a base of operations for lowering Leo down."

We stare at the blazing moon, and Stick voices what we are all thinking: "Sure would be nice if another cloud came along."

But there are no clouds in sight.

"We've come this far," Stick concedes. "Might as well keep going." He turns and for the first time sees me sitting on Zoya's lap, one of her thick arms draped protectively over my waist. "Don't you two make a cute couple!"

"Give me the rope," Zoya snaps. "I'm going up."

Stick drapes the rope over Zoya's shoulders as I wiggle off her lap.

"Remember what I taught you about moving quickly and quietly?" Stick asks.

"Keep your joints loose. Don't tense up. Flow like water," Zoya recites. "Got it."

She lunges into the moonlight and scurries up the rock overhang, unleashing a landslide of pebbles, followed by a river of dirt.

Stick winces. "Not exactly what I meant by 'flow like water.'" We peer down into the Academy grounds, looking for any responses to the disturbance.

All is quiet.

From above, Zoya whispers, "Now you."

A rope dangles over the ledge and sways invitingly at us.

"You first," Stick urges. "Be quick about it. The less time you are out under that moon, the better."

I grab the rope and scuttle up to Zoya. A moment later Stick appears and we all crouch together.

"Look," Zoya says, pointing uphill.

We crane our necks toward the rectangular opening yawning into the night, three meters above.

"I knew it!" Stick crows.

"If you get on my shoulders, 24-4 can climb us like a ladder." Zoya links her hands together. "Up you go."

Stick allows Zoya to lift him to her shoulders. Perched there, Stick's chin is level with the opening of the skylight.

"Can you see anything?" I ask.

"Not much from this angle. But I can smell him. It's Wajid's cage for sure."

Zoya links her hands again and boosts me into Stick's arms. He guides me into the skylight's shaft. I hold on to the edge to keep from sliding down. Stick takes the rope, drops the end to his sister, and tosses the rest into the shaft. We both listen for the rope to smack the floor.

It doesn't.

That means the rope isn't long enough to reach the bottom.

"If the end of the rope is too far from the floor, you may have to have your little chat while holding on," Stick counsels. "Safer that way."

I grasp the rope and lower myself feet first, into the skylight shaft. The shaft is less than two meters long. Without warning my legs are dangling in empty space, signaling the beginning of my descent into Wajid's prison. His scent wraps around me like giant hands.

No doubt he can smell me, too.

I'm relieved to find the tip of my rope dangling only a meter from the floor and well outside the bars of the cage. I shimmy my way to the bottom, heart banging against my ribs. The stone floor is cold underfoot. The air is damp.

"Wajid!" I say in a half whisper, suddenly aware I have no idea how to formally address a Maguar, let alone have a conversation with one.

No response. There are no sounds at all. My eyes

adjust to the gloom, and I can see into nearly every portion of his cage.

"Wajid!" I repeat, louder.

I expect him to come charging out of the darkness, hungry for another chance to attack the same Singa who got too close just a few hours ago.

I creep to the bars, raking the cell for any sounds of life. A fresh dose of moonlight brightens the chamber, including the gleam of metal on a length of discarded chain at the back of the cage.

Wajid's chains. But no Wajid.

My pelt stands on end. I squeeze through the bars and examine the chain and ankle cuffs that once bound Wajid to the wall. Where in the name of science has he gone?

Did he escape?

Was he set free?

A name floats to mind. One given to me before I left the castle, the prince from the story who sought wisdom. Didn't he say he could provide answers?

For the second time in only a few hours I speak a name, daring to call forth one of the strange visitors who have haunted and pestered me my whole life. I'm either desperate, or I'm losing my mind altogether.

"Kensho."

Nothing happens.

"Kensho!"

I feel ridiculous.

"Over here," a voice squeaks from the back of the chamber, barely more than a pin drop.

I whirl around and find two eyes glowing back at me on the other side of the bars. "What are you doing out there?"

"You ordered me not to scare you ever again," he says, stepping into a beam of moonlight.

"That's . . . very nice of you."

He bows. "How may I serve you?"

"There was a Maguar here, held captive for twenty-five years. He was in this cage only yesterday. What happened?"

Kensho smiles knowingly. "He escaped."

"How?!"

He ambles to the bars and studies each one. "This one," he says at last. "Give it a shake."

I cross the cell and wrap my hands around the bar. He nods encouragingly. I jiggle the bar. It rattles, loose at both the top and the bottom.

Kensho's eyes sparkle. "Can you lift it?"

I raise the bar into its mounting in the ceiling, and the bottom comes out of the floor. I push the bar outward. The top slides free and the bar begins a rapid descent.

Not good.

With a deafening clang, the bar bounces on the floor.

Kensho frowns. "That was unwise."

Together, we return the bar to its place.

"You should go," I say to Kensho.

"So should you," he replies, already fading away.

I bound across the chamber and scramble up the rope to the skylight. There are voices on the other side of the door, guards alerted by the falling bar.

"What's wrong?" Stick queries. I wedge my feet into the corners of the skylight's shaft and signal for him to keep quiet. I pull the rope up hand over hand, at a feverish pace. The door swings open, and two Singa soldiers burst into the cell chamber as the last meter of rope slithers into the skylight shaft, out of sight. The soldiers are shocked to discover that Wajid is missing. They rush from the chamber, calling out an alarm.

I hand the tangled mass of rope to Stick and climb into the night air.

"What was all that noise?" Stick asks. "Did he attack you?"

"He wasn't there."

Stick and Zoya narrow their eyes and cock their heads. For the first time, I see the family resemblance.

"Wasn't there?" Stick probes. "What's that supposed to mean?"

"It means he wasn't there. It's that simple."

"There is nothing simple about that! He's been locked in a cage for twenty-five years!"

"We need to get back to the bunkhouse as fast as possible."

"Were you seen?" Stick asks.

"No, but I think I have a few things to learn from you about stealth."

"Doesn't everybody?" Stick says, draping an arm around my shoulders. "Don't worry, I'm going to transform you both into sneaking thieves as my gift to the military. Starting now. Let's go."

CHAPTER 17

He who is destined for power
does not have to fight for it.
— *Sayings of the Ancients*

A BUGLE ANNOUNCES the rising sun. It seems only moments ago that we wrapped ourselves up in our hammocks following the late-night visit to Wajid's cell. The rows of cocooned bodies around the bunkhouse twist and stretch.

Our company commander's voice jabs my ears. "Quadron 24!" The three of us lift our sleep-heavy heads. "Your captain has arrived. She is outside. I suggest you go and welcome her."

He looks troubled. Something isn't right about this.

My stomach tightens.

Stick leaps to the floor, licks his hands, and attempts to smooth out his scruffy mane.

"Don't bother," Zoya teases. "It's a lost cause."

We step onto the front porch, watched closely by a dozen sets of half-open eyes. Waiting on the ground is no cadet but a fully armed and armored Singa soldier.

"Hey, is that . . . ?" Stick asks.

"Anjali?" I finish.

"Good morning, Lord Prince," she says with a bow.

"You know her?" Stick asks, astonished.

"What are you doing here, Anjali?"

"She was undefeated at Judoko when she was at the Academy!" Stick gushes. "And she's going to be our captain?" He nearly trips down the front steps.

Zoya, scowling, remains on the porch with me.

"I'm position three," Stick yammers on, "and my lemon-face sister up there is our number two."

"I know," Anjali replies. "I know all about you."

"Oh," Stick says, enthusiasm draining from his face.

"Could you two leave us alone for a minute?" I ask.

"Let's go, Stick," Zoya says, returning to the bunkhouse. She opens the door to reveal the rest of the company scrunched together and listening. Zoya saunters through without breaking stride, and the cadets scatter like cockroaches.

"She's a confident one," Anjali observes as I pull her away from the bunkhouse and the eager ears of Company F.

"Why are you here, Anjali?"

"I've finally been assigned a quadron."

"Why this one?"

"Don't cough up a hairball. I'm here to help you."

"I don't want your help. I want to do this on my own."

"You're not off to a great start." Anjali draws closer.

"Alpha told me what happened at gaming last night. And there's more: Wajid has disappeared. The leadership of the Academy is in an uproar. Things at the castle aren't much better. And all the trouble starts when the prince arrives? Are you trying to stand out?"

"You think having a Singa soldier as my captain is going to make me stand out *less*?"

"Listen, Leo. Alpha thinks the wolf's appearance and Wajid's disappearance are linked. The fact that both happened on the day you showed up has her wondering. But she trusts me. I can protect you."

"I can protect myself."

"How? Will you conjure up another wolf? A slay-con? What's next? And have you figured out that Jakal is in Amara's pocket? You need someone on the inside of the Academy who can face up to them both, someone who knows your secret."

I wince. That's exactly why I want her gone before she blows my cover. If she won't leave willingly, there might be only one other way. I call over my shoulder, "Cadets! Assemble! We have an intruder."

Cadets, not only from our bunkhouse but also from those surrounding ours, file out into the misty morning air, their faces marked by curiosity and concern.

Anjali gives a half smile. "This isn't going to work."

"This warrior has been sent here by mistake," I explain to the mob. "She needs help finding her way out."

Thirty or more cadets close in on Anjali. None of them is armed, so I don't think much harm will come to her. I just want to wipe that smirk off her face before sending her home with her tail between her legs.

Anjali holds up her hands. "Wait!"

Or maybe she will just give up now and leave in peace.

"This isn't a fair fight," she protests.

Anjali does a perfect double draw with blinding speed. She tosses the long blade to Zoya, the short blade to our commander, and hands the dagger to a cadet from a different company who looks eager for a fight. Everyone flinches as Anjali unclips the aero-blade from her back and hurls the metal ring over our heads. It whistles in flight and sinks into a post on our bunkhouse porch.

"Now it's a fair fight," she concludes. "Let's do this."

Suddenly I'm at the back of a mob descending on Anjali like a pack of starved rats. There are growls and roars, arms and legs whirling along with an occasional flash of metal. In less than a minute Anjali is the only one standing, and somehow she has reclaimed all three of her weapons.

She strolls through the wreckage of groaning bodies. "They'll be fine," she says, hardly winded. "Not a drop of blood on these blades." She climbs the porch steps and looks over the fallen masses.

"Company F! Assemble!" she orders.

A few dusty pelts begin to stir.

"Company F! Assemble!"

Fourteen cadets rise with difficulty and form two scraggly lines.

Anjali shakes her head with disappointment. "Who is responsible for this company?"

Our commander limps forward.

"And you are?"

"21-1."

"You are relieved from command. I am in charge now."

21-1 bows, but I can tell he is as wounded on the inside as on the outside. It pains me to see his pain. But there's no stopping Anjali now.

"All of you, go inside, get your blades, and be on the training fields in five minutes!"

Nobody moves.

Anjali snarls and pounces from the porch to the ground. "I said *go!*"

The company lumbers up the steps and files into the bunkhouse.

Satisfied, Anjali addresses me. "What were you saying about me needing to leave?"

"So you're not only our captain but company commander and instructor, too?"

"I have the Kahn's permission to make changes like that."

"Are you going to take Alpha's job next?"

"If you say so." She winks. "When you're the Singa-Kahn."

"Why stay where you're not wanted?"

"You know," Anjali says, dislodging her aero-blade from the porch post, "most cadets would be thrilled to have a Singa soldier as their captain. Company F will be the envy of the Academy."

"I'm not like most cadets," I argue.

"And that's why I'm here. Get your blades," she says, marching off to the training fields. "Time to make soldiers."

CHAPTER 18

Without experiencing grief,
we cannot respond to the pain of the world.
— *Sayings of the Ancients*

ON THE EVENING of her third day at the Academy, Anjali informs Company F she will feed in Alpha's house instead of with us in the feeding hall. Her wrinkled brow and tight mouth spell trouble.

"Has something happened?" I ask as we walk to the feeding hall. It's my first chance to speak to Anjali in private since she arrived.

"Jakal came back from the castle this morning with General Dagan."

"So?"

"So nothing, I hope. Except . . ." Her voice trails off.

"Except what?"

"I trust Dagan about as far as I can throw her. Kaydan thinks she is loyal to Tamir. I feel some darkness creeping in like a shadow walking before her."

"Will you tell me what you can after feeding?"

"Of course, but not in front of the others." She

waves her tail toward the feeding hall. "You'd better go. Try to stay out of trouble until I get back." She winks, pivots, and jogs down the path to Alpha's house.

Jakal is not in the feeding hall, and neither are any of the head instructors who normally join him at the high table. They must be with General Dagan at Alpha's house. Only a handful of regular instructors prowl the hall.

After we have fed but before the evening's chapter from *The Science of War* is read, Amara and her company slither through the room and surround our table. Zoya growls out a warning as Amara ambles up behind me. The instructors pretend to take no notice. No doubt they are in Amara's pocket too.

"What do you want, Amara?" Stick demands.

Amara places her hands on my shoulders and rubs them. "Just a little quality time with my cousin. We so rarely have an opportunity to visit."

Heat pours off Zoya's body. She scratches the underside of our bench, just to give her claws something to do.

"If you want a Judoko rematch, that's no problem," I say, hoping to cool things off.

Amara grunts. "We've been in a Judoko match for our entire lives, cousin." She leans low and says, "And you are out of moves. Everything is about to change."

Her claws sink into my pelt, causing me to wince and tremble.

Zoya gives her brother a pleading look.

Stick nods and Zoya powers off the bench, tackles Amara, and pulls her to the floor. Amara kicks and screeches, but without success. Zoya has her pinned to the floor like a butterfly to a corkboard.

"Get this fat karkadann off me!" she roars.

Three of Amara's company-mates tug at Zoya's arms and neck. A fourth joins in the effort, and together they manage to separate Zoya from Amara long enough for Amara to unleash a barrage of blows to Zoya's belly and slaycon-injured shoulder. Zoya screeches with pain. Stick hurdles over the table and knocks one of Amara's company-mates away, giving Zoya time to drive a foot into Amara's chin.

Then we are all on our feet, lashing out like wild animals defending their last scrap of territory. Amara's company is at the end of their training, ready to become full Singa soldiers, while we are at the beginning. Three days of training with Anjali aren't making much difference.

We're getting pummeled.

All the other companies leap on top of the surrounding benches and tables, stomping and cheering, but no one offers to defend Company F. Fortunately, no one's rushing to help Amara's company, either.

Zoya and Stick are the last ones standing. When Stick is knocked to the floor and can't get up, a surge of rage reenergizes Zoya. She hurls one attacker at four others, then stoops to check on her brother. Seeing he's not seriously hurt, she jumps back into the fray, snarling and swinging at everyone in her path. Zoya is not a graceful fighter like Anjali, but she's effective. It takes six cadets from Amara's company to bring her down. She struggles under their weight, refusing to give up, when a high, shrill sound slices the air.

"Enough of this!" Alpha has returned, flanked by Jakal, Anjali, and General Dagan. "On your feet, all of you!"

Alpha and Dagan walk briskly to the high table as each company drifts back to their assigned seat. Anjali weaves through the crowd to my side. Her face is unreadable, like a wooden mask, but her cheeks and muzzle are stained with tears. Try as I might to get her attention, I cannot; her gaze is locked on Alpha.

The Academy leader reaches the high table and rests her fingertips on the surface, eyes downcast.

Anjali was right. Something is very wrong.

Have they figured out who conjured up the great wolf? Have the Maguar actually attacked?

Alpha's voice trembles. "We are . . . honored to have General Dagan visit the Academy tonight. But she brings difficult news."

Alpha steps back and General Dagan glides forward. "Our great leader and lord, Raja Kahn, is dead. He took his last breath this morning."

The words hit me like a blacksmith's hammer. My

heart shrivels. The room begins to swirl. Anjali puts a hand on my shoulder.

Dagan isn't finished.

"The generals have appointed Tamir as regent and supreme military commander until the prince has completed his training and is ready to claim the throne, which Tamir will surrender when the time comes."

My brain strains to contain these impossibly heavy announcements. Grandfather is dead . . . Tamir is in charge . . . appointed by the generals.

Including Kaydan?

Where is Kaydan? He is the senior general. *He* should be sharing this news, not Dagan.

"Steady yourself, Leo," Anjali counsels.

"Kaydan," I stammer. "Where is he?"

Anjali squeezes my arm. "Say nothing. Do nothing."

"As his first act as regent," Dagan continues, "Supreme Military Commander Tamir has declared war on the Maguar to punish them for a recent act of aggression against our lands."

Does she mean the hole in the wall or Rukan? Or both? Am I partly responsible for giving Tamir a reason to go to war?

"It will take weeks to prepare for a full-scale invasion. To ensure we have more than enough warriors ready, Tamir has declared that all cadets in their second year of training are now full soldiers in the Royal Army."

Half the room explodes with cheers at the prospect

of war and early release from the Academy. Meanwhile, I'll be stuck here as Tamir marches us into an unnecessary battle with our enemies.

After the shouts and roars die away, Dagan says, "I will return to the castle tonight with the prince so that he may pay his respects to the Kahn's body."

Every hair on my back rises.

"I'm coming with you," Anjali says through gritted teeth. "No matter what she says."

That gives me an idea. "I will go, General. But surely neither you nor Alpha would refuse having my quadron accompany me."

Dagan looks like she might protest, but Alpha cuts in.

"Of course your quadron will go with you," she declares. "All cadets and soldiers stay with their quadrons. Isn't that right, General?"

"Very well," Dagan grumbles. "Gather your things and be at the falls in ten minutes."

I lean toward Anjali. "The falls?"

"Yes. You think there is only one way in and out of this place?"

CHAPTER 19

Branches tied together in a bundle are unbreakable.
— Sayings of the Ancients

L ISTEN TO ME as if your life depends on it,"
Anjali says on our way to the bunkhouse. "Because
it does."

We're moving in quadron formation, like a four-
pointed diamond, cutting through the twilight: Anjali
in the back, Zoya just ahead, Stick to her left at the forward position, and I opposite Zoya.

"You have only begun to learn how to move and
fight as a quadron, but each of you shows potential."
Anjali slows our pace. "Obviously this quadron is unique
in one way. We have the rightful heir to the throne
among us, and that means our goal is to protect Leo,
even at the cost of our lives."

"Then we are no longer a quadron," I gripe. "A
quadron fights as equals and defends itself to the end."

We huddle in a tight circle outside our bunkhouse.

"I know," Anjali says. "But Tamir isn't calling you
back to the castle for you to pay your respects to the

Kahn's body. He has been disgraced, untailed, and he wants revenge. Our lives are at risk as soon as General Dagan leads us out of the Academy. She is loyal to Tamir, let's not forget."

"You think her orders are to kill Leo, and all of us, as soon as we leave the Academy?" Stick asks.

"I doubt that," Anjali reflects. "Tamir will want the pleasure of having Leo see him as supreme commander first and perhaps try to persuade Leo to back him."

"That won't happen," I say.

"Why does he want Leo's support anyway?" Zoya asks.

"Tamir doesn't have all Singas behind him," Anjali explains. "But if the prince makes a public statement affirming Tamir as temporary ruler, it will unify the kingdom under Tamir's leadership."

We enter the bunkhouse and strap on our blades. I take my short blade, normally worn on the back, and buckle it to my side, then fasten my dagger to the opposite hip. The long blade and aero-blade will stay behind. Half as many weapons make a little Singa like me twice as free to move.

As we leave what has only just begun to feel like home, Stick asks, "What's our plan once we get to the castle, assuming we live that long?"

"I haven't figured that out yet. Just remember, I am your commanding officer, and you will do exactly as I say."

"Spoken like a true captain." The voice takes us all by surprise. Not even Stick heard or smelled anyone. "Words that should be taken to heart." A lithe figure approaches from the shadow of the bunkhouse. Anjali puts a hand to her long blade.

"You won't need that, Captain. Not now."

"Alpha?" Stick exclaims.

Anjali is as stunned to see the Academy leader strolling alone among the bunkhouses as the rest of us. Alpha ascends the porch steps and rests her steely eyes on me.

"I know you sneaked into Wajid's cage. Your scent was all over the chamber."

"You did what!" Anjali explodes.

"It was foolish . . . and impressive," Alpha says. "What I want to know is why. Why did you risk your safety, and getting caught, only to discover he had escaped?"

"I wanted to know more about our enemies." It's not a lie, just not the whole truth.

"And you had nothing to do with his escape?"

"No!" I answer before Anjali pops her lid again. "He was gone before I got there."

Alpha considers this and nods slightly. "I believe you, 24-4."

"Where did Wajid go?" I ask.

"Back to his kind. We followed his trail until it disappeared. Wajid was very intelligent for a Maguar. He had been planning his escape for years, waiting for the right moment, until his task was complete."

Stick's ears twitch. "What task?"

"Wajid claimed he was sent to Singara by the Maguar right after the Great War to find someone. Twenty-five years is a long time to wait. But I wonder if he found the one he was looking for when he came upon you, 24-4."

"I've been alive for only half that time," I argue. "It's not logical."

"Perhaps, but what other conclusion can we draw, given the evidence? I've never seen him take such a strong interest in any other cadet. And then to escape right after?"

Stick cocks his head. "So Wajid was sent as a spy to find and kill the next Singa-Kahn before he takes the throne?"

"Finding and killing the next Singa-Kahn was not his mission," Alpha says. "I'm sure of that. Wajid didn't know that the one he was looking for, the one he found, is also the prince."

Anjali folds her arms. "So what does he want with Leo?"

Alpha shrugs. "The Maguar mind is not driven by reason. But now Tamir has strong reasons for war: the hole in the Great Wall, Wajid's escape, and the attack of the giant wolf. No doubt the beast was sent by the Maguar to distract us while Wajid fled."

My stomach turns. As I feared, I am partly responsible for the coming war. Speaking the names of story creatures and bringing them fully into our world leads to nothing but trouble.

Anjali knows Wajid had nothing to do with the appearance of the wolf. She's concerned about something else. "Does Tamir or Dagan know about Wajid's mission? Did you share your theory that Leo is the one Wajid was looking for?"

"I have not shared that theory with anyone until now. The prince's life is in enough danger as it is."

Anjali is relieved. I wish I could say the same.

"Thank you, Alpha." Anjali bows. "We are in your debt."

"Farewell, soldiers of Singara," Alpha says. "Remember your training."

.   .   .

Anjali leads us to the waterfall at the far end of the Academy, where General Dagan waits with two karkadanns. Moonlight sparkles on the cascading water. The serene beauty is a welcome relief from the ugliness brewing in our realm.

"I did not count on having so many travelers tonight," Dagan shouts over the rumble of water. She hoists herself into the saddle of a karkadann. "The rest of you will have to walk."

I glimpse at Anjali before mounting. She nods, and

Zoya makes a step with her hands to launch me into the saddle.

Dagan waves her tail toward the falls. "You know the way, Anjali. Why don't you lead us?"

Anjali hesitates. Being in the forward position puts Dagan and me out of her sight. From a strategic point of view, that's not good.

Dagan notes Anjali's reluctance and sighs wearily. "How old are you, Anjali?"

"Sixteen."

"I am two and a half times your age and a general of Singara. In fact, I am second in command under Tamir, and my orders are to deliver the prince safely to the castle. I intend, upon my honor as a soldier, to fulfill those orders. And I expect you to fulfill mine."

Anjali shifts uneasily.

Things have gotten tense in a hurry. If Anjali doesn't follow Dagan's orders, she risks punishment, which would leave me far less protected in the long run. Trusting Dagan might be the only choice we have.

Anjali grabs the bridle of my karkadann and directs our party to the waterfall. Stick and Zoya walk on either side, Dagan bringing up the rear. The mossy path is laden with puddles, like little mirrors scattered on the ground. Mist from the tumbling column of water lays a glittering curtain of moon-kissed droplets over my fur. Ten more steps and we will be under the falls and completely drenched. Zoya and Stick look as uncertain as I do, which tells me they haven't experienced the waterfall as a way out of the Academy either. The karkadanns, however, keep their steady, plodding pace, as if they are only returning to the familiarity of their stalls.

The path turns sharply and loops under the waterfall. The way behind the great column of water is narrow, forcing us all to go single file into a vast, echoing cavern.

We march onward into the gloom, straining our night vision with the increased darkness. I note movement above, ripples of black and gray, like dark sheets flapping on the cavern's ceiling. It seems to be one thing and countless things at the same time.

"Those are cave leeches," Dagan explains. "Do not be alarmed. They have no taste for Singa blood. That is what makes them the perfect guardians for this way in and out of the Academy."

"If they don't like Singas, why are they slithering down here?" Stick wonders.

Dagan stares at the nearest cavern wall, now teeming with waves of shiny gray skin. "You have keen eyes, cadet," she says. "This is strange. They usually stay above and do not chance to come this close."

The karkadanns have noticed the descending leeches as well. Their heads jerk this way and that, eyes wide, nostrils flaring.

Stick voices what we are all thinking: "Should we be concerned about this?"

"Stay calm," Dagan says. "Keep the karkadanns steady, go forward, and don't make sudden movements. There is no reason for them to attack unless we give them one."

It's hard to tell where one leech ends and another begins. Each one is about half the size of an average Singa, without limbs or any facial features that I can make out. I estimate several hundred assembling on the walls and gliding toward us on the floor. They may not have a taste for Singa blood, but they could smother us to death without much effort.

The leeches form two triangles on either side, like giant arrowheads pointed directly at us and closing in fast. The nearer they come, the more one thing becomes clear: They are not focused on all of us.

They are focused on me only.

The slimy wretches circle around Stick's and Zoya's feet, then latch on to the legs of my karkadann. He rears up and kicks.

"Hack them off!" Dagan says, sliding out of the saddle and drawing her short blade and dagger. Anjali dodges my karkadann's flailing front hooves and drives a blade point into the head of a leech aiming for my leg with its hideous mouth. The skewered creature squeals and twists under her blade. Anjali flings it into the mass of incoming leeches, which scurry away from the corpse of their fallen brother.

Dagan, Zoya, and Stick follow Anjali's lead, stabbing and hurling leeches, while I sit as high as possible atop my jittery karkadann, dagger in hand. With every one we kill, two more take its place. If I fall, it's over. If my four companions stop stabbing and hacking, it would be the end of me, too. As the supply of leeches appears endless, it is only a matter of time before I am served for dinner.

"Make a perimeter of dead leeches around the prince!" Dagan shouts.

I see her plan. The living leeches keep away from the dead ones. If we create a barrier of leech corpses, it might buy us enough time to come up with a better strategy. In less than a minute, we are surrounded by a circle of bleeding carcasses, and the leeches keep their distance.

My karkadann stops bucking but continues to search our surroundings with round, bloodshot eyes. Dagan inspects our perimeter and steps directly into the hungry mass of leeches. She snatches the tail end of the nearest one, lifts it high with one hand, and plunges her blade deep into its wriggling body. After removing the blade and dropping the dead leech, she tosses her blood-soaked weapon a few meters off, and the nearby leeches slither away. Dagan leaps gracefully to her blade, holds it low to the cavern floor, and blazes a trail back to our circle as the leeches scatter.

"Do you see?" Dagan exclaims. "They are repulsed by the smell of their own blood. Lord Leo, as far as I know, you are the first Singa they have shown an interest in. I'm sure Galil will be very curious about that when we return to the castle, but for now, we need to get you out of here."

"Sounds great!" Stick affirms. "How?"

"I think I know," Anjali says warily.

Dagan's whiskers wilt. "Begging your forgiveness, Lord, we're going to cover you in leech blood."

It sounds gross, but it's better than letting them drink *my* blood.

"Anjali, and you two," Dagan says, pointing to Stick and Zoya, and I realize she never bothered to learn their names or numbers. "Kill four leeches and bring them here. Now."

They obey and return with carcasses while I dismount from my karkadann.

"Hold each leech over the prince with the kill wound down," Dagan orders Zoya. "Leo, you'll need to spread the blood through every centimeter of your fur."

Zoya raises the first dead leech. Hot, sticky blood spills onto my head and shoulders. I rub it around, shuddering and trying not to gag. She picks up another and then another, and finally the last, until I'm covered in blood from head to toe.

I want to vomit. Stick and Zoya don't look much better.

"Let's get moving before the blood dries," Dagan says. She hoists me onto the karkadann but stays on foot herself. "Keep your blades ready in case this doesn't work."

We step over the boundary of dead leeches into the heaving mass of living ones. As we walk among them, the creatures slink back to the cavern walls.

"It's working!" Stick cries.

"Shut it and keep moving," Dagan orders.

Fifty meters later, Anjali encounters a metal door carved into the cavern wall.

Dagan hands a key to Zoya. "Pass this to Anjali."

Anjali slips the key into the center of the door and turns it; the door slides open. The smells of plants and earth and other living beings dance in our noses.

When the door is closed, sealing us off from the cavern and the leeches, Stick sniffs the air over my head. "Funny, I can still smell those disgusting creatures!"

It's true. Globs of half-dried blood cling to my fur, leggings, and cloak. I look and smell like death.

"There's a stream up ahead, Lord," Dagan offers. "You can wash yourself there."

The stream is cold, but the leech blood washes away easily enough. I scrub until my hide stings. When

I'm clean and our journey has resumed, I ask, "Any more threats I should know about, General?"

Anjali's ears angle back at my question. She knows I'm not wondering about things like cave leeches, but about bloodsuckers of another kind, such as the one waiting for me at the castle.

"Every journey has its share of perils, Lord," Dagan replies guardedly.

"Kaydan will want to see me as soon as we arrive at the castle, don't you think?" Kaydan, second only to Grandfather, has been on my mind since Dagan made her announcement in the feeding hall.

"You have been missed by many Singas, I'm sure," she says.

Halfway through the Mountain Pass, my head fills with the sound of a rushing wind as fiction bangs against my teeth. There's almost no place worse than this for it to happen. In this corridor, even a whisper bounces around like a rubber ball.

"I have to make water," I announce, keeping my muzzle closed as tight as possible. "Now." I slide off my karkadann and hustle back the way we came before Dagan can argue. She can't be too troubled. She is the one with the key to the doors on either side of the Mountain Pass.

Anjali, wise to what's going on, starts chatting away to Dagan about her time at the Academy to provide some noise cover. The fiction thrashes about in my mouth until my aching jaws give up. I kneel down, head between my knees, and let the words spurt out.

Once there was a prince in a faraway land who decided to remove all the stories and tales from his Pride. Wherever he went, whomever he met, he would demand, "Tell me a story."

Each time, he would take the story out of the storyteller's mouth and put it in a bag tied to his belt. Before long the bag was packed with hundreds of stories. To ensure none of the stories escaped, he locked the bag in a strongbox at the back of his closet.

The words spin into a dim vision of the prince strolling through the streets of his realm, demanding stories from others and stuffing them into his bag, then putting the bulging bag into a storage chest in his closet. It plays out between my feet, tiny because of my hushed voice. My jaw aches with the strain.

The prince grew into a handsome and majestic figure. A bride was chosen from a neighboring land, and when the day of the wedding arrived, the whole castle was busy with preparations.

One of the prince's oldest servants went into the prince's closet to find his wedding clothes and heard whispering voices. Listening carefully, he traced the voices to a strongbox at the back of the closet.

"My friends, listen to me," one voice said. "Today is the day of the prince's wedding. He has imprisoned us in this bag and strongbox for far too long. Stories are meant to be heard, not hidden away as we are! We have suffered greatly and we must punish him for his crime."

"I agree," said a second voice. "Here is what I am going to do. This afternoon, the prince will go to the neighboring realm to fetch his bride. I shall cause the delicious bright-red berries that grow by the road to become poison. He will eat them and die."

"And if the berries don't kill him," offered a third speaker, "I shall turn the cool spring of water by the road into poison. He will drink and die."

A fourth voice spoke up: "If that fails, I will cause the chimney to fall upon him as soon as he reaches his bride's front door."

A fifth voice said: "If all of you are not successful, I will send a poisonous serpent to hide in the prince's bed. When the newlyweds lie down, the serpent will strike and they will both die."

Naturally, the old servant was very concerned. "This is terrible," he said to himself. "I must do whatever I can to protect my master."

That afternoon, as the prince mounted his

*karkadann to meet his bride, the old faithful servant
run out and seized the karkadann's bridle. He asked
to lead the prince to his destination.*

*The prince said, "I do not require a guide, and
you have work to do here."*

*"You may punish me if you like," the servant
declared, "but I insist that I lead you to the home of
your wife-to-be."*

*Surprised and confused by the old servant's
determination, the prince granted his wish. On
the way, they passed ripe, delicious-looking berries
growing by the roadside.*

*"Those berries look wonderful!" the prince
called out to his servant. "Stop and pick some
for me."*

*But the servant would not stop. He said, "Oh,
these berries are too small for Your Majesty. There
are bigger berries up ahead. Be patient and I shall
pick some for you down the road."*

*Farther ahead, they came to a spring of clear,
cool water. A ladle floated on the surface.*

*"Bring me a ladleful of that cool, refreshing
water," the prince commanded his servant, "for I am
parched!"*

*Once again, the servant would not stop.
"When we pass under the shade of those trees up
ahead, your thirst will go away," he said.*

The prince growled, but the servant ignored

him. He only made the karkadann travel more quickly.

Soon they came to the bride's home. Instead of going to the front door by the chimney, the old servant led the karkadann and the prince to the back door.

"Wait!" said the prince. "Why are you taking me to the back door? That door is only for family members and servants."

"Ah yes, my prince," said the servant. "But by going to the back door you will impress your bride's parents with your humility and desire to be counted as their kin."

The wedding ceremony was held on the grounds of his bride's home without any problems, and the newlyweds returned to the prince's castle.

When darkness fell, the couple retired to the prince's lair. The old faithful servant had already positioned himself outside the door, out of sight, with blade in hand. As soon as the prince and his bride went into the room, the servant opened the door and rushed in. The prince and his bride were quite alarmed.

"Master," the servant shouted, waving his blade in the air, "I will explain everything in a moment. For now, get out of my way!"

The prince and his frightened bride stepped aside as the servant pulled the sheets and blankets *from the bed to reveal a terrible hissing serpent. The servant hacked at the serpent, cutting it to pieces with his blade.*

Then he dropped his blade, knelt before the prince, and told him about the bag of stories in the strongbox and their plans to punish the prince for keeping them locked away for so many years.

"Perhaps," the servant concluded, "my lord could offer a story each night to his bride as a wedding gift? After all, stories are meant to be shared." The prince praised his faithful servant and agreed to this plan. Every night he shared one of the stories in the bag with his bride. It brought them much happiness, and the stories were delighted to be free at last.

The vision fades, and my senses return to the dim dampness of the Mountain Pass. In front of me is a leather sack, overstuffed and bulging. The contents stir and echo with strange voices:

"Let me out!"

"Free us!"

"Share us and let us go!"

"We don't belong here!"

Of all the ghostly things conjured up by my disease, this is the creepiest. I'm torn between freeing whatever is trapped in there and abandoning it to the darkness. Down the pass, the glow of torch light illuminates

Anjali, Dagan, Stick, and Zoya. Anjali is still chatter-
ing away. Dagan appears bored and impatient, making it
clear she heard nothing.

"Prince Leo!" Dagan booms. "Are you finished?"

"All done. Coming back now."

The bag stirs and shifts, voices overlapping like an
angry mob. I turn away and dash back to my companions.

. . .

We set foot in the castle courtyard a few hours before
midnight. If not for the stone of grief in my gut and having to face Tamir, I would be thrilled to be home again.

The soldiers on watch snap to attention with the
appearance of Dagan and our quadron.

But where is Kaydan? He would be here if he could.

A screeching bird's call draws my gaze to the top
of the castle's main door. The firewing is perched there:
fully grown, proud and strong, with a bright white head,
gold-yellow talons, and red feathers edged with yellow
adorning his body. He is as tall as an adult Singa. The
sight of him fills me with confidence as a reminder that
I am not alone.

The castle's main door opens. Every soldier we
encounter takes notice of my return. I don't recognize
any of them except Mandar, whose quadron is stationed
just inside the central hall.

"Welcome home, Prince Leo," he says without the
customary bow.

Anjali's eyes burn with rage, as if she might claw Mandar's face and hang him by his own tail.

I keep my eyes on the floor, tracing the familiar jagged crack running the length of the central hall. Hot steam drifts up from the crevice. I've never seen that happen before. I nudge Anjali, who shrugs, equally mystified.

Stick and Zoya gape around the castle. The lofty vaulted ceiling and the ornately carved doors leading to the feeding hall, battle laboratories, and royal court display more artistry and grandeur than they've ever seen. If things were different, I'd give Stick and Zoya a full tour of all the chambers, halls, and secret passageways running up and down the castle's ten floors.

Dagan leads us to the royal courtroom. Galil lingers outside the door. He trails us and slides a piece of paper into Anjali's hand.

I expect to find Tamir sneering at me from the royal throne, but the great chair is empty. The supreme military commander is gathered with a group of senior soldiers in one of the court's alcoves, poring over documents and maps spread out on a table. I'm relieved there is no crown on his head. However, one of Grandfather's royal cloaks is draped over his armored shoulders. It's a statement of authority that also hides the shame of his missing tail.

Dagan announces our arrival. "Lord Regent, I have brought you the prince, as requested."

Tamir looks up and smiles. "Leave us," he commands the soldiers around the table. "And you, Galil." Galil bows and exits with the others.

His obedience sickens me.

Dagan turns to go.

"No, General Dagan," Tamir says, "you will stay with us."

Tamir saunters to the center of the hall, inspecting Zoya and Stick. "Are these your quadron-mates, Leo? I had no idea our latest crop of cadets had such unusual Singa specimens. I suppose with a captain like Anjali you are in good hands?"

"Where is Kaydan?" I ask directly. "What have you done with him?"

"Ah yes," Tamir says knowledgeably. "'Whoever asks the questions controls the conversation.' One of your grandfather's many lessons."

"Where is he?"

Tamir sighs. "This is a sad night for Singara, Leo. We lost our Kahn and one of our most respected generals. General Kaydan lives, but he did not agree with the decision to appoint me as regent and supreme military commander."

"What did he propose instead?" Kaydan wouldn't have put his own name forward as temporary ruler. He's much too humble.

"That doesn't matter now."

"I want to see him."

"Impossible. He is in a cage, and he will remain there until he swears allegiance to me. I don't expect that to happen anytime soon, do you?"

"Why do you think Kaydan won't support you?"

"A clever question, cousin, but the important question right now is whether or not *you* will pledge your support to me as Singara's temporary ruler until you are finished at the Academy. It would be a great consolation to our grieving Pride. If you pledge allegiance to me," Tamir continues, "General Kaydan will live, and you may return to the Academy to continue your training."

"And if not?" Stick probes.

Tamir shoots him a look that would split a boulder.

"Dagan tells me you plan to attack the Maguar," I say, hoping to get Stick out of the line of fire.

"Their aggression cannot go unpunished," Tamir growls. "You saw the breach in the Great Wall. You experienced the devilish beast that attacked the Academy. There's no telling what they are plotting. Unlike your grandfather, I'm not going to wait and find out. My first priority is to keep our realm safe."

"I agree." I can't believe I said that without choking. I agree that protecting the Pride is a ruler's first priority, but going to war will put the safety of many, many soldiers at risk. Perhaps the whole realm. "When do you plan to attack?"

"It will take time to prepare," Tamir says. "I am

building new weapons against which the Maguar will have no defense. Victory is assured."

"Singara is in good hands, then."

"Will you say that in a public statement?"

"I want to see Grandfather's body first."

Tamir pivots and marches to the throne. "Dagan will escort you," he says, easing himself into the royal seat and wincing at the pain in his backside.

"There is power in this chair, cousin," he says, rubbing the arms of the throne. "Power that is now mine to use. And there is a far greater power in the mountain, which your grandfather knew nothing about. The world is about to change, Leo, and if I were you, I would not want to be on the wrong side."

. . .

"That Singa is so mean, he could scare the green off grass," Stick murmurs when we are back in the central hall, trailing Dagan toward the first leaping platform. We pounce and bound our way up to the royal chambers. Along the way, Anjali bumps my arm. She hands me a slip of paper, the one from Galil. I unfold it and read: *Come to me after you see the Kahn's body. You know the way.*

Anjali's expression begs for an explanation. I know the way Galil is thinking of, but it's too much to explain now.

We reach the eighth level, where a company of

soldiers, Tamir's finest, meet us. Dagan brushes past them and rounds the corner into the royal chambers. She turns again, and we make our way down the Hall of Kahns, lined with portraits of my ancestors.

My nose tingles and my eyes brim with tears as we draw closer to the tapestry that marks the entry to Grandfather's private lair. Dagan steps aside and allows me to enter. Anjali attempts to follow, but Dagan blocks her way.

"Only the prince," she says.

"We are a quadron, General," I say. "We stay together."

"My orders are that *you* may pay your last respects. Your quadron will wait—"

Thunk! Suddenly Dagan moans, sways, and crumples to the floor.

Anjali rubs her hand. "She's a hardheaded one."

Stick gasps. "You knocked out a general!"

"Shut it! You think all those soldiers back there are on break? They're waiting for Dagan's orders to take us out."

"Out where?" Stick asks innocently.

"Out as in dead," Zoya explains.

"Dead or locked away and tortured until Leo pledges support to Tamir," Anjali says.

"Which will be never," I add.

"24-2, drag General Dagan through the tapestry into the Kahn's lair," Anjali commands.

Zoya doesn't move.

"That's an order, 24-2! What are you waiting for?"

"I don't want to be a number anymore. I have a name. It's Zoya. And my brother goes by Stick."

Anjali bristles with frustration. "Fine, just do it!"

Zoya lifts her chin and angles her ears forward.

"Zoya, would you please move the general into the Kahn's lair? Now!"

Satisfied, Zoya grabs Dagan by the underarms and pulls her through the tapestry.

The Kahn's lair is lit by a few candles mounted on stands at either side of his bed. Grandfather lies there, dressed in his finest robes. His arms hug my winged chest plate.

I've never seen him so peaceful.

Or so still.

That's a tragedy in itself. Does peace come for a Kahn only at death?

I take Grandfather's hand in mine. His fur is cold; his bones are stiff.

"Grandfather," I murmur, stroking the palm of his wrinkled, leathery hand. "What am I supposed to do?"

"Leo, we need to get out of here before Dagan wakes up or those soldiers start to wonder what's taking so long," Anjali says. "What did Galil mean by 'You know the way'?"

I lean over and kiss Grandfather's forehead. "Goodbye, my Kahn." We huddle for a moment around the bed, Anjali looking anxious and sad, Stick and Zoya struggling to take it all in, their first time in the castle, their first and last audience with the Kahn.

"Leo . . ." Anjali pleads.

I remove my winged chest plate from Grandfather's stiffened arms and slide it on.

"Over here." I lead our quadron to Grandfather's broad oak desk. I pull the bottom right drawer all the way out, reach inside, and tug a small metal lever. Instantly, the section of floor beneath the desk, where Grandfather would put his feet, drops away.

"This passageway leads to Galil's secret reading room and laboratory three floors down. There are metal rungs on one side, forming a ladder."

Anjali seems doubtful. "Who else knows about this?"

"No one except Grandfather, Galil, and me. And now the three of you."

"Not the generals?"

Dagan, across the room, begins to stir.

I shake my head.

Anjali points into the tunnel, urging me to go first.

I put my mouth to her ear. "Me last. Only I know how to close it."

Anjali sends Stick down, followed by Zoya. Then she follows. I replace the desk drawer and drop into the hole. From the darkness, Anjali's eyes glow up at me like gems. With a tiny click, the floor locks into place.

"There are thirty-two rungs," I whisper to Stick. "At the end you will find a wooden panel opposite the ladder."

I descended this ladder countless times as a cub, often with Grandfather right behind me, until he became too old to make the journey. Sometimes, at the end of a long day of studying in the Kahn's lair, reading books on the Science of Nature, the Science of Numbers, the Science of Language, and the Kahn's History, Grandfather would wink at me and say, "Let's go down the ladder, eh?"

I lived to hear those words and catch the mischievous glint in his eye, inviting me to open the hidden door under his desk. In the privacy of Galil's secret reading room, we would explore books of another kind—the forbidden books of ancient times, preserved from the fires of our ancestors, books of sayings and incantations, strange potions, poems, songs, and religious ideas. The oldest books are in a language none of us could decipher except Galil, who worked out the meaning of a word or phrase here and there.

Yet none of these volumes mentions the Maguar. It's as if they never existed. On the other hand, there isn't one word about Singas, either. When I brought up the question to Galil, he said the Ancients did not see a need to mention our two races, one being naturally superior to the other.

Grandfather and I never spoke of visiting this room

with its collection of forbidden books. That's one secret I'm very grateful for tonight.

There's a scuffling sound below.

"I'm at the bottom!" Stick announces.

"Knock on the wood panel like this." I clap my hands eleven times, one-two-three, one-two-three, one-two-three-four-five. Stick repeats the sequence, and the panel opens, hinging inward and drenching the passageway with light. The shadow of a heavyset Singa appears, and a moment later Galil's wide, fleshy face greets us. "Come in, all of you. We have much to discuss. And very little time."

CHAPTER 20

Like the sun,
the truth cannot be hidden for very long.
— *Sayings of the Ancients*

L EATHER-BOUND BOOKS climb the walls of Galil's reading room. We sit on chairs or on stacks of books and try to relax. Galil bustles about in his laboratory, preparing a brew that will give us energy and strength. Stick inspects the swinging bookcase that doubles as the door to the passageway up to Grandfather's lair.

"When I'm done being a soldier, I want to make stuff like this," he says admiringly.

Zoya looks like she could drop her head and sleep for the rest of the week. I'm not far behind. Anjali, ever the soldier, sits alert, perched on the edge of the chair, her mind churning away like there's no tomorrow.

At last Galil returns with a tray of steaming mugs.

"There you go," he says, passing a mug to each of us. "It might not taste like much, but it will do you a world of good."

Zoya regards her drink suspiciously. I tap mine to hers and take a sip.

Galil settles into a cushiony, creaking chair. He rubs his hands together, preparing to say something and not knowing where to start.

"Leo, I'm so sorry about your grandfather," he begins. "I will miss him very, very much."

My nose tingles and I fight back tears. "Did Tamir have anything to do with his death?"

"It is possible, Leo. Tamir is a gifted scientist, and he could have done something to cause or hasten his demise."

Ever since Dagan announced Grandfather's death, I've been wondering if Tamir managed to sneak a bit of poison into his food. Maybe the same poison that killed Storm but was meant for me.

"Your grandfather was quite old and unwell for a long time," Galil continues. "I believe he has been dying of a broken heart for the last thirteen years since your mother . . ." His voice trails off. "You were the only thing keeping him going. You and his love for the Pride."

"Do our laws say anything about the appointment of a regent in a situation like this?" Anjali inquires.

"Fables and fantasy!" Galil grunts. "The law states that when the Singa-Kahn dies, the Kahn's heir takes the throne in his place. That's it! This business about Tamir filling in as ruler until you finish at the Academy is perfect nonsense. But if you can get enough people to agree that the sky is purple, then purple it is!"

"Where is Leo supposed to go?" Stick pleads. "Back to the Academy?"

"For the love of science, no!" Galil exclaims. "None of you are safe anywhere in Singara now, not even here for very long."

I nearly bound out of my chair. "Then where? What's our next move?"

Galil draws in a long, rueful breath. "Leo, I have some things to tell you that will be difficult to hear . . . about your mother."

My mother! Now I'm ready to fall out of my chair.

"Would you prefer that I share them with you in private?"

"You may speak freely in front of my quadron."

"Very well." His shoulders sag. "So many lies, so many lies," he mumbles to himself. "You see, Leo, your grandfather and I have not shared everything with you, only what is recorded in the Kahn's History, which, as you know by now, is not the complete truth."

Would he just get to the point? What about my mother?

"When it was clear that your mother was bearing a cub, pregnant with you, and would not say who the father was, your grandfather was furious, because she was putting the future of the throne in jeopardy. He ordered her to confess or to leave Singara forever."

"And she didn't confess?"

"She did confess. But your grandfather could not accept her answer. He flew into a blind rage and locked her in her den until she gave birth. He never told anyone who your father is. Not even me."

Galil takes a drink from Zoya's mug; she has barely touched it.

"As soon as you were born, he secretly banished her from our realm and told everyone she died giving birth to you. It broke his heart."

As these facts emerge and arrange themselves in my mind, I don't know whether to dance for joy or melt into a puddle of tears. If she did not die giving birth to me, if she was banished, could that mean . . . ?

"Your mother is not dead, Leo. She lives."

"Among the exiles?" Stick asks.

"She was sent over the Great Mountain to the exiles, but that is not where she went. She lives among the Maguar."

Anjali flinches. "Impossible!"

"How do you know all this?" I blurt out, my voice cracking. "How do I know this isn't another bunch of lies?"

With an unsteady hand, Galil produces a half sheet of paper from the folds of his robe and passes it to me. "A few moons ago, a shepherd gave me this note."

I snatch the note and unfold it, tearing it a bit in my haste. In clear, fresh handwriting are these words:

Galil, my teacher and friend,

Before Eliyah turns thirteen, you must send him to me. The shepherd who carries this note will guide him. He lives in the Border Caves. Upon your life, let no one other than Eliyah read this, especially Father.

Alayah be praised,

—Mira

"There is no doubting its authenticity," Galil insists before I can question the origin of the note. "The hand-writing is hers."

"Who is Eliyah?" Stick asks.

"It's me," I say, still staring at my mother's words.

"Another piece of evidence that it is from her hand. Before you were born, she told the Kahn you were to be called Eliyah. It means something in the Maguar tongue."

"Naturally, your grandfather did not approve of a Maguar name, so he called you his little leo instead. At first it was just a nickname, but in time, it stuck, as all names do."

"After he sent her away," I say, surprised by the icy edge in my words. Yet how could I not be angry to learn I've been lied to all this time, and that Grandfather is responsible for separating me from my mother?

"Your grandfather did what he thought was right at the time. That is all we can ask of anyone. Leo, I apologize for not sharing this note with you sooner, as your mother clearly hoped, but out of loyalty to your grandfather I did not. However, I respected her wish and did not share the note with him."

I flip the note over, half expecting to see a map or some directions. "How will I find her?"

"That is uncertain," Galil admits. "You must have faith."

"Faith?"

"Another Maguar word. There is no equivalent in our language. Faith is a special kind of knowing outside of the evidence, sometimes even contrary to the evidence. Your grandfather and I often spoke of it . . . toward the end of his life."

"Faith," I say again, rolling this light and feathery word around on my tongue.

"Wait," Stick cuts in, "you're not actually suggesting we go over the Great Wall into the Maguar realm? We'll be ripped to shreds!"

Galil nods. "That is a distinct possibility."

"The shepherd who gave you this note," I inquire. "Was his name Shanti?"

"I believe it was. Do you know him?"

"We've met." I refold the note and tuck it into a pocket of my cloak. "How did Shanti get this?"

"He didn't say, and I didn't have the chance to ask,"

Galil replies. "By the time I read it, he was gone. Vanished, as if he had dissolved into the air."

"My kind of Singa!" Stick affirms.

"Then we will ask him ourselves," I declare.

Anjali looks up. "Where are the Border Caves?"

"I know," Stick says with an impish grin.

"He knows where everything is," Zoya adds. "And how to steal whatever is there."

Stick shrugs. "Not much to steal among those caves. Just some poor shepherds and their flocks. They live so simply, even I wouldn't rob them."

"Nice to know you have some morals," Anjali says before suddenly becoming suspicious. "Stick, what have you taken since you entered the castle?"

"Only a few things." Stick reaches into his cloak and removes a set of keys. "Like these."

"General Dagan's keys?" Anjali asks, unable to conceal her astonishment.

Galil claps his hands. "Well done! Those will serve you well on your escape." He beams at the four of us. "I dare say this quadron might have what it takes to survive an impossible journey."

"Then we'd better get started," Anjali says before taking a final swig from her mug.

A furious banging sounds at the main door to Galil's lair. "Open up immediately, by order of Regent Tamir!"

CHAPTER 21

Friendship is not made by many years.
It is made by showing up and caring.
— *Sayings of the Ancients*

GALIL RISES AS FAST as his old bones allow. "It seems we have company." He opens the bookcase door concealing the ladder to Grandfather's lair. "You'd better get back in there for the time being."

We obey without question. The door shuts, and we are submerged in darkness. Galil closes the door separating his laboratory from the secret reading room. We strain to listen to the muffled voices of Galil talking with a soldier while other warriors make a terrible racket searching his lair and laboratory.

For us.

Eventually Galil bids the soldiers farewell, pledging to report any sign of the prince and his companions. The main door closes, and Galil reopens the door to the reading room, and then the bookcase door.

"There are soldiers in both directions of the hall," he says as we hop back into the reading room.

Anjali has already come up with a plan, probably one of a dozen she has laid out in her head. "You must have a trash chute somewhere."

Galil brightens. He directs us to a storeroom at the back of his laboratory. The room is a monument of clutter, with barrels and bins, bottles and jars, drawers and shelves, some labeled, some not. How Galil finds anything in here is more mysterious than what each container holds. The square metal cover of the trash chute on the far wall is a welcome contrast to the chaotic surroundings. The arched handle appears to be smiling at us.

"This chute empties into a bin on the first floor of the castle. It will be a bumpy ride and not an easy landing, but it is the most direct route."

"Stick," Anjali says, "if we can get out of the castle using Dagan's keys, can you get us through the city without being seen?"

"Sure. As long as my clumsy sister can keep up and stay hidden."

Zoya snarls. "I just might get clumsy with your face."

Anjali rolls her eyes. "Grow up, you two."

"He started it," Zoya grumbles.

"He started it," Stick repeats mockingly.

Anjali throws Galil a look that says, *See what I have to put up with?*

Galil winks. "All the best to the four of you. May the Laws of Science be favorable."

"Let's hope gravity is one of them," Stick says.

I embrace Galil. "I'll come back."

"You'd better. You are the rightful Singa-Kahn, not that fool-headed cousin of yours. Find your mother before Tamir launches his attack on the Maguar. She will know what to do."

A thought bursts open in my brain, an idea that could be the answer to all my problems. "Isn't my mother the rightful heir to Singara's throne?! Couldn't she—"

Galil's whiskers sag. "Mira has been gone a long, long time, Leo. She would have a lot of explaining to do, and I don't think her answers would be easy to accept."

I suppose he's right. Again.

"Go quickly," Galil urges. "You must get to the Border Caves before dawn. Tamir will never guess that you have gone to the Maguar's realm, but he will search every centimeter of our realm until you are found."

I hesitate, unable to move. "Kaydan," I gasp. "If I leave the castle, Tamir won't need him anymore."

"He would die gladly," the Royal Scientist states solemnly, "knowing you have escaped Tamir's hand."

"Somehow that makes it worse."

"You have a large heart for one so small, Lord. But now is a time for courage, not for looking back."

Stick inserts his head into the trash chute. He plucks an old, cheap-looking gold ring from his cloak and drops it into the shaft. The ring pings and rattles, then fades into silence.

"I hope there's a lot of soft, fluffy trash down there," Stick says.

"I hope you get your ring back," I say.

"It wasn't exactly mine."

"You first, Zoya," Anjali orders.

"Good call, Captain," Stick agrees. "I wouldn't want her landing on me either."

Anjali ignores him. "Find out what we're dealing with down there, Zoya. If you're not too injured, do what you can to catch the rest of us."

The chute doesn't look wide enough, but somehow Zoya squeezes in. Most Singas are adept at landing on their feet no matter which way they fall, but Zoya goes down feet first anyway. She crosses her arms over her torso and begins her descent. We cluster around the chute, listening. For a long stretch, we hear nothing.

"Maybe she got stuck?" Stick wonders.

Anjali pokes her head into the chute and says, "All clear down there?"

"Clear!" comes the unmistakable gruff voice of Zoya.

Anjali nudges me. "You next."

I follow Zoya's example, going down feet first, arms folded over my chest.

"Keep your head up," Stick advises. "I'm sure your skull isn't half as thick as hers."

I let go of the chute's opening and drop into the stuffy darkness. The advice to keep my head up was good, but there is no way to prevent my backside, elbows, and shoulder blades from taking a serious beating. In under ten seconds, the chute vanishes, and I find myself enfolded in Zoya's waiting arms.

"Your Majesty," she says.

"Thanks," I answer, feeling both relieved and awkward.

We're in a huge bin of rotting animal corpses, discarded clothes, broken furniture, and all manner of filth. It's a miracle Zoya landed without being skewered by one of the many sharp objects lying about.

Stick and finally Anjali make the same entrance, with Zoya having a slightly more difficult time catching each of them.

"Phew! The stink down here could gag a maggot!" Stick proclaims.

"I agree," Anjali says, covering her nose. "Let's go."

We pick our way through the rot and heave ourselves over the sides of the bin.

Except Zoya.

"Come on, Zoy!" Stick calls.

"Can't," Zoya says from within the bin. "I think my leg is broken."

"We need to get her out," I beg Anjali.

"Don't bother," Zoya protests. "Just get Leo away from the castle."

"We're not leaving you here," I say. "Give me a lift, Anjali."

"We don't have time," Anjali warns.

"Just help me get back in!" I growl.

Anjali groans, makes a step with her hand, and launches me into the trash bin.

Zoya rests on a tattered carpet, cradling her outstretched leg.

"Amazing you were able to catch all of us with that injury."

She shrugs. "You should leave me. Every moment you sit here is another moment wasted getting away from Tamir."

"She's right, Leo," Anjali says impatiently.

"You didn't leave me when I was trying to get into the Academy," I remind Zoya.

A hint of a smile alights on her lips. "So are *you* going to carry *me*?"

"I won't have to. You're going to climb out by yourself."

"I don't think so. It's broken badly."

I bend to her ear and whisper, "Close your eyes, Zoya. Don't open them until I tell you. Can you do that?"

"Sure." Her eyelids lower as she rests her muzzle on her broad chest.

"Remember, don't open your eyes until I say."

"What's going on in there?" Stick asks.

Ignoring Stick, I speak the name of the old sage and healer: "Vishna."

Instantly, Vishna appears at my side. Without glancing at me, the strange elder squats down and lays her hands on Zoya's damaged leg. She mutters something in the Old Language. Zoya's ears angle forward, but true to her word, her eyes remain shut. Vishna removes her hands, looks at me, and nods.

I mouth the words *Thank you*. Vishna bows and fades from sight.

I lay a hand on Zoya's shoulder. "You can open your eyes now."

Zoya stares at her leg. "What did you do to me?"

"I didn't do anything."

"The pain is gone!" She flexes her leg, beaming with astonishment.

I take her arm. "Let me help you up."

Zoya rises in the squishy filth.

"How does it feel?"

"Stiff, but I can walk."

"Then let's get out of here."

Zoya hauls her bulk over the side of the bin and I follow.

Stick shakes his head. "Not like you to fake an injury."

Zoya scowls but says nothing.

"Let's get going," Anjali urges. "Tamir must be searching every part of the castle. Then he'll widen the search to the city and all of Singara."

Anjali steers us to a large door that slides up on a track mounted to the ceiling. She locates the lock at the center and holds out her hand to Stick. "Dagan's keys, please."

Stick rummages around in his cloak, growing increasingly distressed. "They were right here a minute ago. Maybe they fell out in the chute?"

"What kind of a thief doesn't keep track of his stolen loot?" Anjali demands. "I know you have them."

Stick's muzzle breaks into a playful grin. "Oh, now I remember where I put them." His hand glides into Anjali's cloak and extracts the keys from her pocket.

I'm astounded.

Anjali isn't.

She snatches the keys from Stick. "Do that again and I will break you in half! Do you understand?!"

Stick's only response is to look extremely pleased with himself.

Huffing mad, Anjali sorts through the keys and fits one into the lock. The lock clicks, and the bottom of the door bounces up a centimeter or two. She gestures for Zoya to help.

"Let's hope there isn't anyone on the other side," Anjali says as they pull the door up. A gust of night air beats back the offensive odors of the trash room. We are all so relieved to breathe easier, we don't see the Singa staring at us, mouth agape.

"What are you doing in there?" he asks.

The trash worker is dressed in common laborers' clothes: deerskin leggings, a heavy apron tied around his neck and waist, foot coverings, and gloves. He's about thirty-five, which is middle-aged for Singas, and doesn't look too harmful, as long as he doesn't call out for help. Anjali's hand is on her dagger, ready to cut him down if he raises his voice.

The worker's eyes land on me. "Lord Prince!" he exclaims, falling to one knee. "You have returned! Accept my humble condolences on the death of your grandfather, our good Kahn."

Anjali relaxes. "Kind sir, the prince's life is in danger. We must leave the city without being seen. Can you help us?"

"I am at your command," the worker replies, holding his head low.

"Rise, loyal servant of Singara," I say, surprising everyone with my royal tone. "Allow us to put our lives in your hands."

The worker climbs to his feet, quaking. "It is a great

honor, Sire. As it happens, I am about to take a load of trash from the castle to the old quarry for disposal. We do it under the cover of night when everyone is asleep, as a courtesy to the Pride, because of the smell, you see."

Anjali is uninterested in these details. "We have no time to lose."

"Of course. Forgive me. Come this way."

He escorts us to a team of karkadanns harnessed to an empty cart waiting beside another bin of waste. A tarp rests on the cart's flatbed.

"If you climb under the tarp, I will cover you with garbage. It won't be a pleasant ride and will be far, far beneath you, my prince, but no one will bother to investigate."

"Not at all," I say, trying to keep up my royal tone. "Your kindness will not be forgotten."

The worker glows at that, and even Stick looks impressed.

"You only need to take us two kilometers beyond the city wall," Anjali says.

Our new friend agrees and lifts the tarp at the back of the cart. "Lie down, flat as you can."

We arrange ourselves like logs on the cart's bed, and I find myself wedged between Zoya and Anjali. The worker tenderly covers us with the tarp as though tucking four cubs into bed.

"Looks like we won't need your stealth talents after all," Zoya says.

"It's not too late to let me guide us out of the city," Stick offers.

"You might be able to sneak us out," Anjali says. "The hard part is getting off the castle grounds with every available soldier looking for us. This is our best option."

"I'm going to cover you with garbage now," the worker says. "With my sincere apologies."

"Go ahead," Anjali assures him.

The worker dumps piles of filth onto the tarp. At first it's just the smell that irritates, but soon the weight of the stuff presses down, like a giant hand crushing walnuts. Zoya rolls onto her stomach, draping an arm over my shoulders to shield me from the mounting load. I don't know how she can possibly hold this position for the entire ride, but I'm grateful.

The air grows thick and unbreathable.

"Stick!" Anjali calls. "Dig out an airhole from your side and I'll do the same from mine."

There is a good deal of scraping and sloshing on either side, until a steady stream of cool, delicious air wafts over us.

The worker climbs onto the driver's bench, and the cart lurches forward, powered by the karkadanns.

My eyes get heavy. Thoughts swirl into a blurry mosaic of memories, words, and longings. This time, I do not dream in stories or visions of the past or future. This time, there is only blue sky.

I stretch out my arms.

And soar.

. . .

Anjali nudges me. "Time to go."

I look to my right and find Zoya and Stick at the end of the cart, holding up the tarp. I crawl out, stifling a yawn. Anjali is right behind me.

Stick sweeps some filth off my shoulders. "I slept too. It's the only way to travel when covered by garbage."

Over the open field, stars sparkle and flash in an unending blanket of light, so many that it seems wasteful. Or maybe the stars are only pinpricks in the fabric separating this world from a brighter place beyond.

"We are in your debt, sir," Anjali says to the trash worker.

He bows. "The honor is mine. Where will you go now?"

"We will stay hidden for a time" is all that Anjali says.

Our friend lowers himself to one knee. "Strength and prosperity to our Kahn."

At first I'm not sure who he's talking about. Grandfather is dead, after all. Then my companions take similar positions around me and offer the customary response.

"And to all who serve him."

CHAPTER 22

The quieter you become, the more you can hear.
— *Sayings of the Ancients*

ARE YOU SURE you know where you're going?" Anjali growls.

"Did I question your judgment when we were buried in garbage?" Stick fires back.

"Yes, you did," Zoya says. "You only stopped complaining after you fell asleep."

We've been walking for nearly two hours with only the stars and a claw-shaped moon to guide us. The ground is a level plain, dressed with tall grass that tickles our knees.

"The Border Caves are just ahead," Stick says confidently.

Anjali is skeptical. "Funny, I don't hear any bleating goats."

Stick stops suddenly, becoming still as a statue. "But did you hear *that*?" His ears tilt forward.

"Hear what?" Anjali's ears swivel, searching the night air.

"Something's coming closer." Stick's words are dripping with fright.

"I don't hear anything," Anjali says, unconcerned.

Just then, someone springs up from the tall grass and Stick is knocked off his feet. Anjali cries out and wobbles as if she's been struck in the back of her head. Zoya folds herself over me as a shield when her legs are swept upward, and she too falls to the ground with a great thud.

Anjali's blades flash and whistle at a hooded figure bending and twirling like a streamer in the wind. Stick and Zoya draw their blades as Anjali yowls and falls to her knees.

"Anjali!" Stick cries.

"Stand down!" Anjali croaks. Two blades rest on either side of her neck. Empty-handed, Anjali's arms are stretched out in surrender, which means the weapons at her neck are her own blades now in the hands of our triumphant opponent.

I never imagined Anjali could be defeated so easily.

"Do what she says." The stranger's voice is relaxed and unhurried. "Sheathe your weapons."

"Do it!" Anjali orders.

Stick and Zoya return blades to their scabbards. Zoya takes a protective half step in front of me.

"I'm curious," the stranger says, sounding more like a concerned parent than a menace. "What is a young quadron doing this far from the city so late at night?"

"We are on an official mission to protect the throne," Stick says proudly. And stupidly.

"Shut it!" Anjali barks.

"Really, I once protected the Kahn. It is a noble thing."

There is something familiar about this Singa. The voice. The way he stands so tall despite his age.

I peer out from behind Zoya's arm. "Shanti?"

"*This* is the old shepherd you were talking about?" Stick blurts out. "The one we're looking for?"

"Your Majesty!" Shanti says, throwing back his hood. "I am glad to see you again."

"He fought with Grandfather in the Great War. He was Kaydan's captain."

Stick leans closer. "That means he's on our side, right?"

"Please return those blades to my captain," I say.

"As you wish, Lord."

Shanti lifts the blades from Anjali's neck. He twirls them in the air and yields the weapons with the handles facing Anjali and the blades pointed at him. Anjali reclaims her blades, leaps up, and snarls defiantly into Shanti's face.

Shanti smiles. "It's too bad we don't have time for some training, Captain. I could teach you a thing or two for your next encounter with an old shepherd."

He picks up a long metal pole with a slight bend at one end. He defeated Anjali with that?

"For now, you'd better come with me."

He ambles off, singing one of his strange tunes peppered with words from the Old Language.

Anjali watches him warily. "You trust him?"

"He helped me before. He's the one who delivered the note from my mother to Galil. We have to go with him."

"He's going in the right direction, at least," Stick adds. "The Border Caves are only a few hundred meters ahead."

"All right, then," Anjali grumbles. "Let's fall in."

Shanti strolls through a field, over a gurgling stream, and finally to a lightly wooded area where the sounds and smells of live goats and sheep fill the air and call to our stomachs. Firelight pulses in three different places. The flames illuminate six Singa figures and the entrances to several yawning caves.

"The Border Caves," Stick says knowledgeably. "You think all those shepherds can fight as well as Shanti?"

"Maybe," I say. "But I don't think we have anything to worry about."

Shanti escorts us to one of the fires and speaks to two shepherds gathered there. They contemplate us with gentle eyes and move on. Shanti invites us to sit on the log benches encircling the fire and passes a plate of meat. As we eat, Shanti hums and purrs another tune.

When his song fades away and we have had our fill

of food, I dig out my mother's note from my cloak and hold it up to Shanti. "How did you come by this?"

The old shepherd stares into the flickering flames. Light dances about his face and makes his graying mane shimmer in golds, oranges, and deep browns. And there is something else woven into the threads of his mane.

Feathers. Firewing feathers.

"First let me tell you a story," he says, as if he were only offering to fetch another log for the fire instead of engaging in criminal activity.

Before Shanti can breathe another word, Stick springs to his feet, draws his short blade, and points it at Shanti's muzzle.

"He's a Spinner!" he sputters. "By order of the Kahn, you are under arrest! Hold your tongue before we cut it right out of your diseased and lawbreaking head!"

Shepherds from the neighboring fires bound over to us, but Shanti waves them off.

Anjali rises and puts a reassuring hand on Stick's shoulder. "Relax, Stick. Since when did you become so concerned about lawbreakers? Come on. Sit down. It's all right."

Stick stares at her as if she's just asked him to pull his brain out through his nose.

Anjali switches tactics. "Look," she whispers, "we can't take them all on. We might as well listen, right? Deep down, haven't you always wanted to know what fiction is?"

"But stories are not true, not real. They're just evil, dangerous lies!" he says, reciting what we have been taught since the day we were born. "They infect and pollute the mind, take us away from the facts. A fiction is a dereliction—"

"It's okay, Stick," I say as soothingly as I can. "Have a seat. Please."

Stick still isn't sure about this, but he lowers himself to the log, laying the blade protectively over his knees.

"Why don't you let me hold that for you?" Anjali says, sliding the weapon away.

Shanti clears his throat. I'm so jittery with anticipation, I might pop right out of my fur. I've never met another Spinner, let alone received a story from one. Anjali's eyes are round with expectation, and even Zoya sports an expression of interest.

"In the days when the world was still freshly made," Shanti begins, "long, long before anyone heard of Singas and Maguar, there were people: two-legged creatures, but much different from us. They were called humanas.

"For thousands of years the humanas walked the earth. They built great cities and created many wonderful inventions. But the humanas were a selfish breed. They had little regard for others or for the earth that was their home."

The smoke from the fire swirls into moving images of his words: the strange, hairless, two-legged beings, the cities and inventions, the suffering earth. We listen and watch, spellbound. Stick swats, flabbergasted, at the vision with extended claws. His hands glide through the smoky images, which immediately reassemble themselves.

Shanti continues. "And they were violent. Greed, bloodshed, and war were common. In time, all the spilled blood flowed like rivers and formed one big pool. Drawn to the scent of salty blood, the great and horrible sea demon, Hasatamara, rose up with a mighty wave and flooded the land to claim it for himself."

The smoky image of Hasatamara is almost too horrible to behold. Even the disbelieving Stick shudders and cowers.

"The waters grew higher and higher," Shanti continues, "until everything was submerged except the highest mountain on earth, what we know as the Great Mountain. The humanas tried to climb the mountain to save themselves, but it was of no use. The water swept easily around the base of the mount. Everyone died.

"But Alayah, blessed be the name, punished the sea demon Hasatamara and sealed him into the heart of the mountain. Imprisoned in solid rock and layers of metal, Hasatamara was trapped, close enough to the ocean to hear its waves, but unable to join his spirit with the water."

We're all relieved when the demon is bound up in the Great Mountain.

"The Great Mountain is a prison for a demon?" Zoya queries.

"It is," Shanti says. "To this day, Hasatamara is still at the heart of the Great Mountain, waiting to return."

"Can he get out?" Anjali asks.

"Demons have a way of returning when there is enough anger and violence in the hearts of creatures. Violence gives them strength. Hasatamara nearly had the chance to escape twenty-five years ago."

"The earthquake," I exclaim. "During the Great War. The crack in the castle floor!"

"When evil and violence were all over the land and blood soaked the earth," Shanti says gravely, "Hasatamara almost returned. And because much of the metal from the mountain that imprisons him has been removed for weaponry and the Border Zone Fence, it will be much easier for him to escape if a new war is kindled."

I recall my dream that took me along the crack in the castle and deep into the Great Mountain. There I found Tamir, at a wall of metal-like skin. The wall appeared to be a piece of an incomprehensibly massive creature. Was that terrible creature—

Stick jumps in. "You said all the original beings, the humanas, died. If that's true, how did we get here?"

"Almost all died. Two humanas survived. One young female and one young male."

The hazy visions return as Shanti resumes his story.

"When the water swept around the mountain as the humanas fled in vain for safety, Alayah sent his messenger, the Great Firewing, to rescue these younglings. The Great Firewing let them grab hold of his feet and flew to his nest at the top of a tall tree standing alone on the mountain's peak. This was the only spot on earth not covered by water.

"The Great Firewing protected the young humanas, brought them fish to eat, and made them clothing from his own feathers.

"When the waters subsided, the Great Firewing put the younglings on the dry earth. When their feet touched the ground, they found they had been changed into a new species: stronger and keener than the humanas before them. He told them to become a great Pride. And we did.

"So we owe our existence to the Great Firewing," Shanti concludes. "That is something to be proud of, because the Great Firewing is the messenger of Alayah. In those early days, there were no Singas or Maguar, just one species, one Pride, one nation of leos who are sometimes referred to as the Ancients."

Shanti closes his eyes and hums another tune. The lazy lilt of his voice sends his images into the night sky in a long, curling gray plume.

This serene moment doesn't last long.

"That is ridiculous!" Stick exclaims without

warning. "Our ancestors were great four-legged cats who evolved over millions of years into upright, two-legged, intelligent creatures like us. Everyone knows that. The Maguar are just an older, dumber version who have yet to become extinct!"

"If Tamir has his way and his war," I say, "they just might."

"If that happens," Shanti cautions, "the demon, Hasatamara, is sure to break free and destroy everything. The only way to vanquish Hasatamara, the true enemy, is not with war but by bringing the Singa and Maguar back together, as one Pride of leos, as we were meant to be. The time is coming for one or the other."

"Please tell me you guys don't believe this," Stick pleads. "Demons, gods, floods, a giant firewing? Why are we allowing ourselves to be infected by this garbage?"

"Shut it, Stick!" Anjali snarls.

Stick does, covering his ears, looking like he might explode.

We enjoy another silent moment before I repeat the question that has been burning a hole in my heart since we met Shanti on the grassy plain.

"Shanti, how did you come by this note from my mother?"

Shanti leans closer. Orange firelight spreads across his wrinkled face. "She was here a few moons ago."

My heart might have just stopped. My mother

was here? Right here? Feet touching this very ground. Breathing the same air. So recently?

"How?" I whisper.

"She was the one who punched a hole through the Great Wall!" Stick pipes up.

Shanti dismisses the idea with a wave of his hand. "No. She would never do that. Why go to so much trouble when she can come right through this cave?" he says, gesturing with his tail to the gaping entrance behind him.

CHAPTER 23

The one who keeps secrets is not as wise
as the one with no secrets to keep.
— *Sayings of the Ancients*

ANJALI IS FUMING. "This cave goes under the Great Wall to the realm of the Maguar?"

The old shepherd nods.

"With respect, sir," Anjali continues, and I can tell the next thing she says won't have a lot of respect in it. "Did it occur to you to report this to the military?"

"There is no reason to worry," Shanti replies. "The Maguar want nothing to do with us or our lands. They look upon the Great Mountain and see only a prison for a terrible demon, a place to avoid at all costs."

"Then the Great Wall is unnecessary," I say.

"Not entirely. The wall defines our realm and keeps a certain peace. Your grandfather was right about that."

"But there is no need for war?"

"That is a fact."

"How many Singas and Maguar know about this cave?" Anjali demands.

"As far as Singas are concerned, very few. Just some

lowly shepherds and now you. As for the Maguar, I haven't the slightest idea."

Anjali does not find that encouraging. "What's to stop us from taking this information back to Singara?"

"We both know you will not be going back to the city for a while. Your story continues through there," he says, pointing to the cave.

"How will I find my mother on the other side?"

"I don't know," Shanti confesses.

Stick is exasperated. "So we just go through this cave, end up in the Maguar realm, and start asking around for Mira? Is that our plan?"

"The fact that she did not leave directions suggests she will not be hard to find. I imagine most, if not all, Maguar will know of a Singa named Mira who has made a home among them for the last thirteen years."

It makes sense, but the idea of wandering through the land of our enemies makes my blood run cold.

Shanti stands and stretches. "The sun will be up in a few hours. I suggest getting some sleep and leaving at first light. I have enough bedding for you all." He strolls off to one of the caves.

Stick rubs his head. "I think we should go back to Singara and try to work things out with Tamir."

Anjali nearly gags. "Not on your life."

"Look, Leo," Stick protests. "I know you want to meet your mother, but going through that cave is lunacy."

"My mother survived," I say. "Maybe we can too."

"It's dangerous. I'll grant you that, Stick," Anjali agrees. "Still, the Maguar's realm is the one place Tamir won't dream of looking for Leo."

Shanti returns with an armload of goat and deer hides and tosses several to each of us. My companions quickly drift away. Even Anjali sleeps. Finally, Shanti joins them.

Falling asleep has always come easily to me. Not now. Tonight, I am wide awake.

Everything Shanti said about the demon and the flood, the Great Firewing saving the last female humana on earth, a time when there were no Singa or Maguar, just one Pride—it all bustles about in my brain and leaves no room for sleep. Most of all, I'm dizzy with hope about meeting my mother.

If the Maguar don't cut us to ribbons first.

Zoya's nose whistles as she sleeps, just like in our bunkhouse. Eventually, the fire dwindles to a few persistent embers, while the horizon glows with the approaching dawn. Trilling birds, including one squawking raven, announce the birth of a new day.

Shanti is the first to awaken. He sits up and takes in the sights and smells of the morning. Then he speaks in a voice too soft to hear, as though he's talking to the birds. The old shepherd is odd enough to do something like that.

"Who were you talking to?"

"It was the prayer of thanks to Alayah for the return of the sun," he says. "Did you sleep, Lord?"

I shake my head.

"Your mind is a jumble of thoughts. Hopes and fears."

A layer of golden sunlight outlines his mane and shoulders. He appears completely at peace with himself and the world.

I envy him.

"When did you discover that you are a Spinner?" I ask, shocked to hear myself speak freely about the disease we share.

Shanti looks away. "I was a cub, five years old, when the first fiction arrived. I was helping my mother in the kitchen, and the story poured out of me before I knew what was happening. It was a simple tale about a golden fish who saves his family, even though they despised him. I had no idea where it came from."

I recall the first time the fiction affliction struck me. Like Shanti, I was only a cub and it terrified me. It was a story about a cub who traps and kills a giant serpent threatening to eat all the cubs in her village. When it was over, the little warrior she-cub appeared like a ghost before me, the first of many. I screamed and she fled.

"I didn't get very far," Shanti goes on, snapping me back to the present. "As my mother realized what I was doing and saw the images rising up from the dust on the ground, she became frightened and slapped me, knocking me down, warning me that I'd bring the family to ruin." Shanti draws in a sorrowful breath. "Of course, I couldn't prevent the stories from coming, much as I wanted to. Whenever one would drop into my mouth, I would run away to some private place. I thought I was being careful, but one day my mother heard me for the second time and saw the wispy images. I will never forget the way she looked at me: ashamed, disgusted, fearful.

"The next day my older brother died in a clash with the Maguar while guarding our borders." The old shepherd dips his head. "My mother blamed my disease and never spoke to me again.

"So I trained to become the best soldier I could be," Shanti continues, "to earn back my mother's love and to avenge my brother's death. No matter how much I tried to be like everyone else, I could not change what I was, what I am. The stories kept coming and coming. A stream that would not stop. I grew to despise them. And myself."

Shanti's stare becomes as piercing as an arrowhead. "Know this, Leo. It is hard to be a Spinner. It is much worse to hate yourself for it. We have been raised to view ourselves as afflicted instead of gifted, but that is just another lie we Singas tell."

My stomach tips over as the terrible truth is laid bare between us.

I do hate myself.

Or at least the part of myself I've tried to keep hidden all my life.

If I can't stop the sickness, and the strange creatures that come with it, if I can't close the door on them forever, how can I become like this old shepherd, so wise and at peace?

I don't really expect an answer, but one arrives anyway, in an unwanted package. The familiar feeling begins: the nausea, a rushing wind in my head, my heart beating like a drum.

Not now.

Please not now.

Just leave me alone!

A little lump of fiction tumbles onto my tongue in a mad rush to escape. I shut my mouth, grinding my teeth as a barricade. The fiction rattles around like an angry caged slaycon, growing larger by the second.

My eyes bulge; my face twists and contorts.

At that moment the bag of stories, the one belonging to the prince who would not share his collection of fictions, appears on the ground between the old shepherd and me. The contents of the bag shift under the membrane of leather in nightmarish fashion. Voices from inside cry out:

"Free us!"

"Let us out!"

"We don't belong here!"

Shanti doesn't see the bag, but he knows what's happening.

"Let it out," he says.

I look at my sleeping companions and shake my head. Anjali knows, but Stick and Zoya are ignorant of my disease. The story vision is jarring enough, but who can predict what strange things will appear afterward? I can't afford to lose my companions right before our journey to the Maguar's realm. I scan the area, looking for a place to run and hide.

Shanti reads my mind and skittish movements. "You don't need to run from others or from yourself anymore, Leo."

The voices in the bag grow louder and more demanding. Meanwhile, the fiction balloons up in my mouth and threatens to split my skull. I fall to my knees, cradling my aching head.

"Let. It. Out!" Shanti repeats, his voice stinging my ears and rousing my friends.

The fiction has grown so large, my tongue and gums are burning under the pressure.

Long ago in a distant land . . .

The words squeeze through my lips. I slam my

teeth together and wrap my hands tight around my muzzle. The pain is unbearable.

The bag of voices is screaming now: "Free us!"

No wonder they were locked in a box.

"*Say it!*" Shanti roars. He might as well have slapped me on the back, because my head lurches forward. My jaws part. And there is nothing I can do but surrender to what comes next. I close my eyes and give in to the outpouring of sickness.

Long ago in a distant land there was a youngling who hated himself. He thought poorly not only of himself, but of everyone, making him perfectly miserable to be around. Tired of his self-loathing and lonely life, he decided to seek the help of a wise man who lived just outside the village.

The words produce a vision over the space where the fire once burned, expanding with every word, until we are all immersed in the scene. Unlike Shanti's dull, smoky images, mine are vivid and detailed, bursting with color, light, and life. In my afflicted story stupor, I see Stick stagger back in fear and wonder. His eyes jump from elements of the vision to me and back to the vision.

Much as I want to, I can't stop.

"Give me a potion," the youngling demanded, "that will make me love myself."

"It is possible to make such a potion," the sage replied. "But the ingredients are not easily found. You must bring me a whisker from the chin of Nagarjuna, the draycon who lives in the cave at the top of the mountain."

The youngling went away in despair. "I am too small, too stupid, and too cowardly to pluck a whisker from the chin of that draycon," he lamented. "I will be killed before I get within ten meters of the monster."

And yet he was determined. "I have so little to lose, I might as well try," he told himself. The next morning the youngling climbed the mountain carrying a large bowl filled with meat.

As he approached the top, he could see the head of the draycon Nagarjuna lying just outside the cave, watching him. The youngling stopped some distance away, put the bowl of meat on the ground, and ran home. The draycon slithered out of his lair and gobbled up the meat, grateful for a free meal without having the trouble of killing it himself.

Every day the youngling repeated this offering, getting closer and closer to the draycon. Every time, the youngling fled while Nagarjuna devoured the meat with delight. One day, after many weeks of this ritual, the youngling put down the bowl of meat but did not run. He watched in fearful fascination as the great beast crept forward. While Nagarjuna slurped down the meat, the youngling snipped a small whisker from the chin of the beast, who hardly seemed to notice. As the draycon continued to eat, he slunk away and then ran to the home of the sage.

"I have brought you a whisker from the chin of Nagarjuna, the draycon who lives in the cave on top of the mountain!" he exclaimed triumphantly. The sage took the whisker and held it up to the light.

"This is indeed a whisker from the chin of Nagarjuna, the draycon who lives in the cave on the mountain." Then he dropped the whisker into the fire.

"What have you done!" the youngling cried. "That whisker was for the potion to cure me of my self-hatred. Do you have any idea how long it took and how hard it was to get that whisker? You are a stupid, worthless sage!"

"How could you hate someone as clever and brave as yourself?" the wise man replied. "You have shown great patience and courage in attaining that whisker. Is learning to love yourself really more difficult than that?"

The youngling went home and slowly, with great patience and courage, began to love himself.

When the story is over and the vision fades, I am breathless and gasping for air, as if I've just run up and down that mountain ten times myself.

Shanti is jubilant. "A wonderful story, Lord Leo, and just the one you needed! That is the sign of a great teller: the right story at the right time."

Zoya sits up from where she slept, half covered in goatskin bedding, the ends of her mouth turned slightly upward.

That last detail is a good sign.

Her brother is another matter. "So you're a Spinner too?"

Exactly the reaction I feared.

"You got a problem with that?" Anjali snaps.

Stick is indignant. "Well, yeah! The prince and future Singa-Kahn is a diseased Spinner, a criminal, a deviant—you *don't* have a problem with that?"

Anjali draws her long blade. "Show some respect for the throne or I'll—"

"He's the one who needs your blade." Stick thrusts a finger at me. "On his tongue!"

"You are under arrest for high treason!" Anjali snarls.

"How can I be under arrest by someone who is protecting an outlaw? I should be arresting you!" Stick counters.

I can't take this anymore. "Both of you, stop! We're

all outlaws now. There's no point in arresting each other."

"The prince speaks truly," a new, commanding voice breaks in. "You are all under arrest."

CHAPTER 24

If you want to go quickly, go alone.
If you want to go far, go together.
— *Sayings of the Ancients*

SOLDIERS SLIDE OUT of the morning mist from every direction. Most have arrows notched on the strings of their bows. At first there are five, then ten. Soon sixteen warriors, a full company, encircle us.

"Put down your weapons, and upon my honor as a soldier, no one will be harmed!" The commander of this company is familiar to me. It's Mandar, and this time he has the upper hand. His confident, buoyant tone suggests he is enjoying the reversal immensely. His armor colors boast of a promotion.

"I see Tamir has rewarded you for your loyalty, Company Commander," Anjali scoffs.

Shanti raises his staff, preparing for battle.

"You won't be needing that, shepherd. We are only here to escort the prince home. We come in peace."

Anjali growls. "If you come in peace, Mandar, why all the arrows and blades?"

"A precaution, Captain, to ensure you don't run off again." Mandar gloats.

A thunderous yet muted roar echoes from deep within the nearest cave, followed by a series of booming footsteps. My quadron exchanges nervous glances. Shanti winks at me. Mandar and his soldiers take no notice, proving that they did not hear or witness the story.

Mandar gestures to a group of warriors. "Take their weapons. Bind their hands but not their feet, unless they prefer to be dragged back to the castle."

Two quadrons advance, ropes in hand.

A second roar blasts, louder and closer.

Stick's ears go flat with dread. "What *is* that?"

I know exactly what it is. A creature that big could only be Nagarjuna, the draycon from the story.

"Whatever it is, I don't like the sound of it," Anjali states.

"*Damar ha shem*," Shanti says to me.

I've heard those words before, in Grandfather's account of the Great War. "What?"

"*Damar ha shem*. It means 'Say the name' in the Old Language. Say the name, Leo," he repeats, as if he's encouraging a little cub to take his first steps. "This is what you were born to do."

The draycon continues his noisy approach. In a moment the creature will appear, but only to the five of us who heard the story. To make the beast visible and real to everyone, to bring him fully into this world, I only have to *damar ha shem*, or say his name.

That, or I let these goons take us back to Tamir.

"Nagarjuna!"

The cave shakes with an earsplitting roar. The warriors freeze.

"What the devil was that?" Mandar cries.

"Just a draycon I keep in the cave," Shanti says. "He doesn't take kindly to strangers."

"There are no draycons inside the Great Wall!" Mandar insists, shuddering.

"That's true," Shanti agrees. "Except for this one. His name is Nagarjuna, and he does not sound happy. If I were you, I would leave as soon as possible."

Mandar's troops instinctively take a step back, ready to follow the shepherd's advice and turn tail.

"Hold your ground!" Mandar commands. "We have our orders, draycon or no draycon!"

"As you wish," Shanti says.

Stick and Zoya put a blade to each hand and stand behind Anjali. We all gape into the throat of the cave.

Out of the darkness, a huge horned reptilian head with bright green eyes appears, suspended on a serpentine neck. The scaly skin of his body flashes red, then copper, then brown, like a fish in sunlit water. Hot breath pumps from nostrils larger than a full-grown Singa.

"That's one ugly creature," Stick moans.

"He is magnificent," Shanti proclaims in awe. "The likes of whom I have not seen since the Great War."

The draycon's entire body is in view now. Only the end of a long spiked tail lingers in the cave.

"Prepare to attack!" Mandar orders. "Fire arrows!"

Bows twang and arrows whistle through the air at Nagarjuna's head and body, but no arrowhead is strong enough to penetrate his armorlike hide. The draycon roars again, and the warriors recoil.

"Run for the cave behind the draycon," Shanti orders my quadron. "Stay close to Lord Leo. The beast will not harm his master."

Before we can challenge this insane plan, Shanti seizes my arm and charges straight for Nagarjuna, through his legs, and into the cave beyond. The draycon lowers his great head and observes me thoughtfully.

Shanti clues me in. "He is yours to command, Leo. Give him an order!"

The company of soldiers shoulder their bows and organize an assault with their blades. My mind struggles to form a sentence in the face of this terrible creature and the advancing soldiers.

"Um . . . could you please . . . make those soldiers leave this place?"

Nagarjuna roars in reply, and my heart withers. Stick holds his ears and scrunches up his face. "Can you order him to not do that again? My head is about to burst!"

"That command was well phrased, Lord Leo," Shanti affirms. "For the soldiers to leave this place, they must do so alive. The draycon now knows not to kill."

Let's hope so. This beast could wipe us all out in seconds if he had a mind to.

Nagarjuna rises up on his hind legs, towering over everyone and everything. He leaps at the soldiers and knocks five of them off their feet with one swat of his tail. Mandar and the remaining soldiers stage a brave attack from multiple directions. A few manage to score blows to the draycon's legs and tail, but hardly enough to matter. The draycon releases a deafening roar in the face of Mandar, who immediately passes out.

"Take your commander and leave while you can!" Shanti advises the remaining soldiers. The draycon scoops up two soldiers in his front claws and pitches them over the trees. That's all the convincing the last warriors need. They collect Mandar and drag away their fallen comrades. Nagarjuna howls triumphantly, which hastens the soldiers' retreat. When the last of them have disappeared, the draycon swivels his head and locks his raging eyes on us.

Only Shanti is fearless in the face of the monster's attention. "Give chase!" he directs the other shepherds, who have watched the battle from the shelter of their own caves. "Make sure those soldiers stay far away from here." Immediately, the shepherds take up discarded weapons and pursue the retreating warriors.

Nagarjuna lowers himself to the ground before me. His dreadful head and thorny face are only a few meters from my feet. Instead of attacking, the beast whimpers like a pup.

"He wants to be rewarded," Shanti says, "for his service to you."

"With a snack?" Stick asks. "Give him Zoya. She's biggest!"

"No," Shanti says in a faraway voice. "He wants to go back home. He wants you to open the door to the Haven, Leo."

"I don't know what that means."

"Leo," Shanti says over the warm gusts wafting from the beast's nostrils. "This might be the right moment to tell you what a Spinner actually is. Spinners are gateways to and from another world. The fictions are gifts from Alayah, sent through Spinners, gifts of wisdom and truth. For a few very powerful Spinners, beings from the stories are pulled into our world to protect and serve the one who brought them here. Only the Spinner who summoned them can send them back. To my knowledge no such Spinner has ever been born among the Singa."

"I don't understand."

The draycon groans to remind us of his presence. In fact, he is impossible to ignore.

Shanti points at the draycon. "The only way this stranded creature can get back to the Haven, his home, is the way he came, through the teller. You!" He pokes a finger into my chest. "You, Prince Leo, are the door between our world and the Haven. Such a precious gift comes very, very rarely."

"Is it a gift?" I question. "Or a curse?"

Shanti sighs. "The only curse is that you have been taught to see yourself as diseased. You are nothing of the kind."

I want him to be right, but I don't know what to believe anymore.

"I can prove it to you," he adds. "How many Jin do you remember?"

"Jin?"

"The visitors who have come through your stories! How many names can you recall?"

"Three, maybe four?"

"Say every name you can."

"What? Now? Here?"

"Start with one name. Pick any one of them. Say it!"

The name of the hunter comes to mind. "Oreyon."

"Bravo, Lord!" Oreyon appears next to the draycon and leans against the beast's meaty foreleg, as casually as he might rest against a tree. "I thought you might have forgotten about me."

"I tried."

Stick is shocked. "Where did he come from?"

"*Ha!*" Shanti is giddy at the appearance of the hunter. "What other names do you remember?"

"Wait," Stick mutters. "The wolf at the Academy. Was that you?"

"Rukan!" I say, and the giant black wolf materializes behind Nagarjuna's shoulder, dipping his head respectfully.

"Your Majesty," he says in greeting.

Anjali growls and draws her long blade. Rukan bares his bladelike teeth and growls in return.

Shanti chuckles and slides between them. "Return your blade to its sheath, Captain. We are not in danger. Indeed, we have never been safer than we are right now. Keep going, Leo!"

I take a deep breath. "Kensho! Vishna!" The wise prince and the old healer pop into view.

Then my mind goes blank. Shanti and I hold each other in a silent, anxious gaze.

"I can't remember any more."

"There are many, many more, Lord," Vishna says, stepping toward me. "Let me help you."

Vishna wraps my head in her arms and presses me to her chest. Her body is as warm and fragrant as spring. She hums and mutters some words in the Old Language. When she's done, a blast of memory crashes over my tongue. Names gush out of my mouth, like a story desperate to get free.

"Mohanu! Shankara! Gulati! Vijayah! Iyengar!" I pronounce.

I am scarcely aware of the creatures and figures bursting into view, all smiling broadly and bowing. The names keep coming and coming, dozens of them, then hundreds. All of them characters I pushed away because they reminded me of what I am.

"Sajagi! Sophia! Shudra! Doji! Pitri! Madhavah! Ameelah!"

A great and growing multitude of beings surrounds us. If Shanti and Vishna are right, these creatures have been with me ever since their particular stories pulled them into our world. Some of them have been with me for years. All waiting for me to call them into service and then to be sent home, back to the Haven.

"Ishvarah! Kumar! Dalah! Valmiki! Tarah! Gokhalah! Balini!"

Stick, Zoya, and Anjali examine the swelling army of creatures with fear and fascination. I can't imagine what's going through their heads as they discover just how strange I really am.

"Sahni! Shudrah! Negimah! Ishvar! Barman!"

The last name escapes my mouth and I nearly collapse.

Anjali holds me steady. "You okay?"

Stick gawks at the gathered crowd of witnesses. "This is unbelievable."

"Kind of creepy having all these strange eyes on you," Anjali whispers.

"All my life," I say.

Oreyon edges forward and speaks for the whole assembly. "If it pleases you, Lord, may we return home?"

The ears of every being tilt forward, eager to hear my reply.

My answer comes quicker than I expect. "Yes."

The gathering sighs with relief and delight. Oreyon claps his hands. "He is *willing!* Alayah be praised!"

A fluttering sensation swirls in my torso. Something cracks open and expands within me. Anjali stares at my torso, horrified. "What's happening to you?"

I look down. Where I would normally find my chest and stomach, there is a patch of blue sky and that glorious light spinning over an infinite sea. Countless winged beings soar and swirl around the light, singing with joy. The whole scene is not much wider or longer than the space between my shoulders and legs. It's as if my torso has become a window to the Haven. Or, as Shanti says, a door.

I know what I have to do. For the first time in my bizarre little life, everything is clear. Meanwhile, Anjali draws closer, transfixed by the vision of the Haven. Her hand reaches for the light turning in my chest.

"No, Anjali," I warn her. "Stand clear."

"Get over here, all of you," Shanti calls from the mouth of the cave. "Give Leo room."

I step forward.

"Come," I invite our otherworldly guests. "I understand now. Come."

Oreyon approaches first. He bows and walks directly into me, disappearing in a flash of light.

It kind of tickles.

The same happens for Kensho, the prince who sought wisdom; Vishna, the healer; and Rukan, the great wolf. No matter what their size, the characters walk into me one by one without breaking stride and depart from this world with a burst of light.

Once the first group has made its exit, the rest charge forward, jubilantly returning to the Haven. Each creature departs with a flash as it dives into me. They are coming so fast now, I can no longer make out the faces barreling forward. Soon I even lose track of myself, swallowed up in the light.

Nagarjuna advances last of all. His fearsome face has softened. He waddles forward, hunkered to the ground, as if preparing to squeeze through a low door.

Which is what I am.

I hold out my hand. "No. Not yet." The opening in my torso closes. Anjali wilts as the draycon growls and scrapes the earth with his foreclaws.

"Leo, what are you doing?" Stick whines. "Get rid of that thing before he gets rid of us!"

"No," I repeat firmly, both to the draycon and to Stick. "Nagarjuna will stay here!"

The draycon rears up on his hind legs and hovers over us.

"You will stay here and guard these caves against all intruders, but you will not harm any of the shepherds who live here!" I command the towering monster, wondering if he can even hear me from up there.

Nagarjuna slams his forelegs to the ground. It takes every ounce of courage I can muster not to cower in fear. The draycon's head is centimeters from my own. He releases a deafening roar and every bone in my body quakes with dread.

Then it happens: An urgent desire to make this beast obey bubbles up from my gut. Anger climbs the length of my spine, blowing out of my mouth in a thundering volcano of sound!

I'm as surprised by my own roar as by the draycon's reaction. Nagarjuna shudders, steps back, and dips his head.

I repeat my instructions. "You will return to the Haven one day, my friend. For now, I need you to guard these caves against all intruders. But you will not harm or disturb the shepherds who stay here."

The beast groans with frustration and, I hope, acceptance.

"Well done, Lord," Shanti says admiringly. "Well done."

Stick is still protecting his ears. "Is it over? I think I'm losing my mind in addition to my hearing."

A flash of light sweeps the ground, followed by the rustle of wings.

What now?

The draycon has taken notice as well. He searches the sky before lowering himself farther, whimpering and whining.

A big bright bird flaps to the ground, its mighty wings stirring up the dust at our feet. It is the same firewing who has appeared to me before. He is much larger now, twice the height of a Singa, and wrapped in flames, outshining the sun.

"The Great Firewing!" Shanti marvels as the majestic bird touches down. "Kneel, all of you! Bow your heads!"

I sink to one knee and lower my eyes. In the presence of such a powerful and blazing creature, there is nothing else to do. The Great Firewing rests his beak on my head. His glowing neck feathers wrap around my face until I am enveloped in flames that caress instead of burn. His scent is sweet as honey and strong as blood.

For the first time since my trip to the Haven, and for the second time in my life, I am completely at peace. I want to stay with him, melt into him. There are many things I want to ask, so much I want to say, but all I can manage is "Daviyah."

"*Eliyah.*" Daviyah's strange, soothing voice rings in my head and warms my bones. It is a voice that is many voices, overlapping and speaking as one. *"I am proud of you. Alayah is pleased with you."*

"Have you come to take me with you?"

"No, Eliyah. Your story has only just begun."

My heart sinks. I feel like Nagarjuna, stuck here to complete some assignment when I'd rather be elsewhere.

"What am I supposed to do?"

"Follow the path before you. Find out who you are."

Daviyah lifts his fiery head and lowers his beak. Our eyes meet.

"I am with you always, Eliyah."

And then he vanishes, just like all the others but without passing through me. Deflated, I face my quadron and Shanti.

Anjali and Zoya stare at me, slack-jawed and starry-eyed. Shanti is radiant. Stick avoids my eyes altogether. He groans and shakes his head. Despite everything he's seen over the past ten minutes, he's still struggling to fit it into his Singa upbringing.

Anjali struggles to put some words together. "Th . . . th . . . that . . . was amazing."

"Are you going to be okay with this, Stick?" I ask.

Stick studies the ground. "There has to be a logical explanation. Maybe Shanti gave us some weird potion while we slept and we hallucinated everything."

Zoya scowls. "Don't be stupid."

"Logic has its place. Science is good," I affirm. "But

maybe today is a day for . . . what was that word Galil taught us?"

"Faith," Anjali says.

"Faith," I repeat, enjoying the sound of it. "A different kind of knowing, outside of the evidence."

"Faith is for the birds," Stick mumbles.

"Like firewings?" Zoya says with an uncharacteristically large smile.

"We should go," Anjali says, snapping us all back to the mission before us. "Time to leave Singara and find Leo's mother. Great idea to have this draycon guard the cave, Leo. Once Tamir gets a report from Mandar and his company, he will send legions of soldiers here in no time."

Tamir. The Maguar. Mother. I had nearly forgotten.

Anjali brushes past me and peers into the dark void of the cave. "How far is the Maguar's realm?"

"It's about a kilometer until you get under the Great Wall, and about a kilometer back up to the surface," Shanti says. "The way is marked with painted handprints."

"Stick, are you with us or not?" Anjali asks pointedly.

I search Stick's face for some sign that he might be coming around and find none. "Please, Stick. We need you."

"Stick?" Anjali repeats, touching the hilt of her blade.

"We're a quadron," he grumbles mechanically. "We stay together."

"Good, because otherwise I'd have to kill you," Anjali says. "You know too much."

Stick can't tell if she's serious. He looks at me, and I shrug.

"Get your weapons, quadron," Anjali commands. "We're moving out."

"No weapons," Shanti says. "You must leave those here."

Anjali almost chokes. "What?"

"If the Maguar see you with weapons," Shanti explains, "and believe me, the Maguar will see you long before you see them, they will kill you on sight. If the Maguar find you without weapons, they might allow you to live long enough to explain what you are doing on their lands."

Anjali unstraps her blades, signaling for us to do the same.

"And your armor, Captain," Shanti adds. "I will keep it all safe until you return."

Return.

It's a comfort to know we might come back to our homeland.

Shanti lights a torch and gives it to Anjali. "Stay on the trail," he cautions. "If you explore another path along the way, you might not find your way back."

"Any leeches down there?" Stick asks, throwing

me his signature smirk before striding into the inky, unknown regions of the cave. Zoya rolls her eyes and follows.

I grin.

The old Stick is back.

"Only a million or so spiders, rats, bats, and countless insects," Shanti calls after him, "but no leeches."

I approach Shanti. I want to take him along, but he has barely moved from his place near the mouth of the cave. He has no intention of going with us. Before we part, there is something I need to confess.

"Shanti, the place where the Jin come from and returned to, the Haven, I've been there."

Shanti nods. "We are all players in a story told by Alayah, who is the Great Narrator. You may be small by Singa standards, but you have a very large part to play."

"How does the story end?"

"That is difficult to say because every ending is a new beginning in disguise."

I hand him my winged chest plate, offering a deep bow. "Thank you, dear friend."

Shanti cradles my chest plate as if it is a delicate living thing and bows. "I served the Kahn once. It is an honor to do so again."

My heart lurches.

Even after the brain-bending events of the morning, this simple reference to Grandfather brings a sudden weight to my shoulders. The memory of his death, the fact that I am supposed to be claiming the throne instead of marching into the land of our enemies to find my not-dead-after-all mother, whom Grandfather lied about all these years, is almost more than I can bear.

Yet there is Anjali, the ever constant Anjali, standing tall and strong, waiting for me in a circle of torch light. Absent her weapons and armor, she appears younger and not so fierce. Maybe this is the way she looked on the day of her slaycon hunt three years ago, just like any other young Singa waiting to be tested.

And we will be tested.

This time together.

And this time I am not afraid.

ACKNOWLEDGMENTS

I WOULD LIKE TO THANK my amazing family and first readers Ann, Halladay, Camden, David and Peg, whose steadfast support made this book possible.

I'm deeply grateful for my outstanding agent, Joy Tutela of the David Black Literary Agency, who often understands my books and characters better than I do. Thank you to Julia Richardson and Mary Wilcox who acquired the manuscript for Houghton Mifflin Harcourt for Young Readers. The entire team at HMH has been a joy to work with, including my editor Lily Kessinger.

Special thanks to Julie Goldstein, Lisa Perucki, Kim Persons for sharing drafts of this book with their students at Breakthrough Magnet School. Thanks also to April Clark for allowing me to read an early draft to her students at Webster Hill Elementary School. These students and their enthusiasm for the story encouraged me to keep writing.

The expert advice of fellow authors Susan Aller, Stacy DeKeyser, Susan Schoenberger and storyteller Jane Torrey was generous and invaluable. Thanks to author Tim Hollister for introducing me to Joy Tutela.

And to the two dozen or so people (young and not so) who reviewed early drafts forced upon them by the author: thank you for carving out time to read and to offer constructive feedback. I'm glad we're still friends.

Praise be to God from whom all blessings flow.

FOLKTALE SOURCES

THE STORIES TOLD BY LEO are based on folktales from many cultures and traditions.

THE FIREWINGS is related to a Buddhist story about a flock of quail who escape a hunter's net. I based my version on "The Quails' Song" found in *Doorways to the Soul*, edited by Elisa Davy Pearmain, (Resource Publications, 2007).

OREYON THE HUNTER is a retelling of an Indian folktale.

THE TORN CLOAK is an adapted wisdom tale from the first Christian monastics also known as the "Desert Fathers."

THE WISDOM SEEKING PRINCE is adapted from an ancient Indian story.

THE SAGE BY THE RIVER is inspired by a tale told in Antony DeMello's book *One Minute Wisdom* (Doubleday, 1985) also retold in *Doorways to the Soul*.

RUKAN THE WOLF is based on a Tibetan story.

THE STORY-HOARDING PRINCE is a retelling of a Korean folktale.

THE DRAYCON'S WHISKER is adapted from an Ethiopian tale.

Join Leo as the adventure continues in the second
Pride Wars book, coming Spring 2019!